THE DAY HE WENT AWAY

by
Jennifer Millikin

JNM, LLC
Scottsdale, AZ

jennifermillikinwrites@gmail.com
Cover design by Sarah Hansen at Okay Creations
Editing by Robin Patchen of Robin's Red Pen
ISBN: 978-0-9967845-3-5

To Tyler Prewitt.
Thank you for everything you've given me.

1

KATE

His hands are on my hips. He squeezes, fingers digging into my skin, and I like it. I try to open my eyes but they won't obey. I don't know who's making me feel this way, but I know I'm not scared. His five o'clock shadow gently scrapes my cheek as his face drags across mine. Just before his lips touch mine, his scent fills my nose.

I know who it is.

The scent of his skin is seared into my soul.

My best friend.

My Ethan.

THE CREAK of metal brings me back to reality, and I shake off the images.

I swivel my chair and cross my ankles, pretending to listen to Belinda as she introduces her new client and the concepts she's working on.

The conference room at work is not the place to relive that dream. The earth-shattering, mind-bending, rule breaking dream. *My Ethan dream.*

His hands. On me. Touching me in a whole new way.

"Kate, where are you with your new client?"

I look into the expectant eyes of my boss, Lynn, and the bright red lipstick that never seems to leave her lips.

I clear my throat, buying myself a few seconds. *Rookie move.*

"Kate and I are still in the planning phase of the Rodgers account." Sarah, seated on my right, speaks up.

Ethan's fingers digging into my skin...

Focus.

Lynn looks at Sarah and regards her with cool eyes. She flicks her eyes back to me. "But you're taking the lead on Rodgers, right, Kate?"

I nod. "For the remainder of the morning I'll concentrate on getting all the information as complete as possible and the releases perfected. I'm taking a half day today, and I'll be out until the twenty-seventh. Sarah will run with everything I've created. And I'll be available for any questions or to help in any way, of course."

Lynn sighs. Just a tiny, barely perceptible sigh, and I hope Sarah didn't pick up on it. Sarah is capable of completing tasks without me. Besides, I'm going to make it foolproof. Everything will be so perfect that Sarah will have to *work* to make a mistake.

Lynn sets her sights on someone on the other side of the long, dark wood table, and I relax. My mind wanders back to Ethan's lips...hands...

A totally different hand taps my knee.

Sarah's giving me her irritated look.

"Thanks for saving me," I mouth.

She scribbles on her notepad and slides it to me. *Are you okay? That wasn't like you.*

I give her a thumbs up and turn my attention to Lynn. I can't be caught daydreaming again. Totally unacceptable.

But that dream... For weeks I haven't been able to get it out of my head. But I have to. Ethan will be here this afternoon.

There's work to be done before I can head to the airport. Everything needs to be handled before I can take time off from Simone PR.

Ten days. With Ethan Shepherd.

My best friend.

And also the person who has been on my mind while I'm asleep.

How many times am I going to relive the dream when I'm awake?

I'm trying to pay attention to what Lynn's saying, I really am, but... *His scratchy face on my skin...* I'm a goner. Might as well give in and let myself enjoy the daydream.

"Kate, seriously?"

Sarah stares down at me, hands on her hips. I look around. The room is empty. My cheeks warm.

"I'm sorry, my mind is elsewhere today."

"That's clear. Want to tell me where?"

I bite my lip. I've hardly dared to tell myself where my mind has been. There's no way I'm telling anybody else.

I rise from my seat and lead the way out of the now empty conference room. Sarah is on my heels.

"We have some work to do. Let's get to it." I throw the directive behind me.

I'm Kate Masters, and I'm back in control.

***

IT'S FUNNY HOW, when I think I'm in control, something happens to remind me how wrong I am. Not haha funny, but funny like *of course you have no control over Ethan's flight home.* If I'd checked my phone before I ran out of work, I would've known his plane is late. But I was busy, pushing it to the final second before jumping from my seat and thundering to the elevator. *There had been so much to accomplish before I left.*

At work Sarah kept reminding me of the time. And asking why I'd been a space cadet in the morning meeting.

I know something's up. Does it have to do with Ethan?

No, why would anything be up with Ethan?

Because you're taking a lot of time off work to spend with him, and you've been weird for weeks. And extra weird today.

I took time off to spend with him last summer when he was home.

But you weren't absent minded and forgetful and—

Weird?

Yes.

Everything is cool. Promise. I just need to get through all this work before I can leave.

Now I'm sitting in front of terminal four security at the airport with forty-five minutes to spare.

Forty-five minutes to think.

About Ethan.

About how Ethan and I have been best friends since we were five. *Two decades.*

And about my dream. And what it means.

I've never dreamed of Ethan before. Not like that, anyway.

Ethan has always been... Well, Ethan.

But now he's not.

Now he's *Ethan.*

And that terrifies me. It shakes the foundation of my life. I've spent a lot of time building the solid, stable floor I stand on. Having feelings for Ethan is like taking a sledgehammer to one of the wooden planks. I need Ethan the way I need air and water to live. Ethan's unyielding, loyal friendship is my safe haven. He's the only person I don't try to be perfect for. Everyone else... They expect it. Perfection. And I don't do disappointment.

But these feelings... They've consumed me. Infiltrated my heart and swallowed me whole.

And they're already affecting my behavior. Last night he called from the airport in Germany, and I turned into a thirteen-year-old with a crush, stammering and sweating. When he asked what was wrong, I assured him I was great, just preoccupied with work. He believed me. *I think.*

What if I told him everything?

I know what would happen.

I sigh and glance at the time on my phone. Twenty more minutes until he arrives. I look up, survey the weaving security line, watch the TSA employees with their stiff shoulders, and look again at the stream of people exiting the concourses, fresh from their flight's arrival. My fingers tap my knees. I need a change of scenery. These gray walls are driving me crazy. *Or maybe it's me and all this overthinking.*

I rise from the seat I've been planted in too long. The blood rushes into my left foot, and it tingles. I wobble, but make it to the restroom without an embarrassing scene.

Instead of walking toward a stall, I go to the mirror. Ethan has seen me thousands of times—at my absolute best and complete worst. Still, I fuss with my hair and check my makeup. *Brown hair still brown, lower lip still bigger than upper lip, one ear still a millimeter higher than the other. Makeup in place.* I look down at my red shirt, happy I remembered clothes to change into. I didn't want to greet Ethan in my sensible blouse and gray slacks. *It's possible I chose this color for a reason...*

After all our years together, physical appearance falls low on the yardstick by which we measure one another. We'd made mud pies together, scraped our knees on the harsh asphalt of the street we grew up on, and spent days cooped up together while we battled chicken pox. Our pain, happiness, heartbreaks, and successes are wrapped up within each other, intertwined in a way only time can accomplish.

My fingers curl around the edge of the sink, knuckles growing whiter. *If I let these feelings take control, things might not end well.*

Our friendship is strong, but feelings like this make us fragile.

The strength of our relationship has been the one thing I could always count on. While I was busy achieving, accomplishing, *mastering*, Ethan was by my side. He's the only person who didn't need me to achieve, accomplish, or master in order to love me.

Something implicit exists between us, an unspoken declaration, and it states that nothing will ever divide us. I felt it the day I watched a moving truck pull up to the empty house across the street. A little boy bounded out and somersaulted his way across the front yard, and my five-year-old self *knew*. Twenty years together hasn't changed it.

I look into the mirror and watch the emotions ripple over my face. Excitement, fear, apprehension. Fear dominates.

But there isn't anything concrete to be scared of. I can't reach out and take hold of what has my heart racing.

My fear is a shadow, pursuing me soundlessly. *If you tell him you have feelings for him, you'll lose. Would you really risk Ethan? He's your biggest fan, your other half, your... soulmate.* I shake my head. I can't think like that.

"Get it together, Masters." Saying my last name out loud makes me feel better. Like I'm in control. *Kate will Master it... Master of Everything.* I loved those nicknames at first, but now they're a reminder of the impossibly high expectations people had for me. Or maybe I just had them for myself. With a last name like Masters, what else could I become but an over-achieving perfectionist? Of course, the last name didn't rub off on my little brother. I picture him tucking his wild, shoulder length hair behind his ears, and shake my head. *Running an organic beet farm... The opposite of everything my dad wanted for him.* I've given Noah the grief my dad would have, if he were alive. Honestly, it's probably time to let my little brother own his career choice, as exasperating as it is.

Running off to Noah's modest farm in Oregon doesn't sound too bad right now. I'd love to escape my mind for a while.

Stop being unrealistic. I need to deal with these feelings. I need to be practical, pragmatic, level-headed, and logical.

Telling Ethan about my dream would be foolish. Telling him about how I can't stop thinking of him would be irrational. What I need to do is forget about it.

Because I know how he would respond if I came clean.

My dependable, loyal, compassionate Ethan. He's been in love with me for ten years. And he's never been shy about telling me.

Once a year, on our shared birthday, he asks if I've changed my mind yet.

His caramel eyes radiate with hope after the question leaves his lips. *And I always tell him no.*

But now... My God, what am I doing?

I can't.

Absolutely, unequivocally, without a doubt.

I need to do less dreaming and more forgetting.

The fear in my seizing stomach tells me I'm making the right choice. If I give in to my feelings and Ethan and I fail at a relationship, I'll lose him forever.

I cannot tolerate a life without Ethan. So my mouth will stay shut.

His visit home will be like all the others. We'll have order, structure, and solid plans. I like those things, I *need* those things. And Ethan understands that about me. He's always been that for me. Nobody knows me like Ethan.

I just want *us,* the Kate and Ethan I'm used to. Ease embodies our time together, like an old, comfy sweatshirt, worn from time and use, but continuing to serve its purpose. *We're sweatshirts.*

If I tell him...well, we won't be sweatshirts anymore. We'll be crisp and stiff, new clothes from a new store.

And I can't have that. I need my best friend.

***

THE BRIGHT LIGHTS of the airport blind me when I walk out of the women's room. I blink a few times. It's louder now. Lots of people, enthusiastic greetings. I stand on the periphery and scan the area.

There he is, walking down the long, wide hallway, away

from the concourse. *Ethan!* My insides go topsy-turvy, my heart hammers like it wants to leap out of me and run to him. *Calm down. He's still the same person you've known since before you could ride a bike.*

Ethan strides past security and slows, peering around and above the people who are in the midst of their own reunions.

His jet black hair shines in the light overhead. For a brief moment, I'm struck by how different he looks. It's not the classic military hair cut or the tan fatigues he's wearing that make him look so different. It's his face, his shoulders, his chest, even his neck, that have changed. He looks so *big*, so strong.

Something even more alarming than Ethan's changed appearance is snaking its way through me. The warmth spreads, starting in my heart and running out to the tips of my fingers and all the way down to my toes. My skin feels alive.

Desire. That's what this feeling is. My brain tells my body to stop, but my body isn't listening.

Ethan hasn't seen me yet. *Petite girl problems.* His warm brown eyes continue to scan the throng of people. I'm halfway to him when his eyes meet mine. His face lights up.

My feet accelerate. Deftly I dodge elbows and purses as I make my way toward him. I smile, but he just stares at me, transfixed, like my face isn't the same face he's known for most of his life. Finally, he smiles back, but his eyes continue to stare at me, absorbing me in a way that puts a blush on my cheeks.

Ethan finally comes to life, dropping the bag from his shoulder and taking a few steps forward.

I don't even stop to think about what I'm doing. The talk I had with myself in the bathroom flies out the window. This is *Ethan*, my best friend, and I've missed him so much, it's become a physical ache.

As soon as we're close enough I launch myself at him. My legs wrap around his waist and he catches me, arms encircling my back, holding me up. I let my face fall into his neck, feeling comforted by what I find there. I inhale deeply, breathe him in, and his familiar scent tattoos my heart.

I'm in love with him.

I can lie to myself as much as I want when I'm alone. But right now, with my nose pressed to his skin, my heart knows my truth.

His hand falls down my back, rises, falls again. My shoulders shudder and bow. My insides twist and arc, a convolution of confused excitement.

I break first, jumping down and backing away from the circle of Ethan's arms. Heat fills my cheeks as I peek up at him.

His eyes bore into mine. He squints, like he's trying to wrap his mind around what just happened. I should apologize for leaping into his arms like a gazelle. My lack of control is mortifying.

Ethan grins his beautiful, happy smile and lifts his left hand up to my face, his thumb tracing its way along my jawbone. *He's never touched me like this.*

I lean into it, forgetting myself again. I can't help it. *This must be how he felt all these years.* Why did it take me so long?

His hand is touching me. *Ethan.* And now my stomach is starting to feel funny, and it's *Ethan* making me feel this way.

I want to grab him and kiss him right there, in the middle of this mass of people, but I don't.

I take a step back, forcing his hand to drop. His eyebrows draw together as though he's trying to solve a difficult math problem. *Well, haven't you been a difficult problem for years? And now you're acting like this.*

I'm not ready to tell him. I want to say the words, but they aren't there. Adrenaline courses through me, and I hate how it makes me feel. I want my control back.

Ethan's staring at me, waiting for me to explain my behavior.

"Are you hungry?" It's a lame question. I wish I could do better.

His eyes narrow like he's evaluating. Whatever he's thinking of, he makes a choice. "I'll grab my bag, and we can go." He turns, walking to his backpack lying on the ground a few feet away.

Oh, thank God. He's letting it go.

He hefts it to his shoulder. "I know it's the middle of the afternoon, but I'm hungry. Starving, actually. Airplane food." He wrinkles his nose. "I ate in Philly on my layover, but that was almost six hours ago. I had a Philly cheese steak. It sucked. Don't you think it should have been better, considering where I was? Maybe ordering one at an airport wasn't the best idea. And the snacks they handed out on the flight were crap."

Yes, this is definitely my best friend. Live, in the flesh, and acting like himself. His chatter is infectious. I find myself smiling as I picture him working his way through the bad cheese steak while he waited for his next flight.

"Okay, so no cheese steaks, peanuts, or pretzels. Where would you like to go?"

"You won't believe this, but I want a burger. A good old drive-thru burger."

It's my turn to wrinkle my nose. "That's gross, but I won't deny you. Your wish is my command. After all, you do spend your days protecting me."

As usual, one word of the war, and Ethan withdraws instantly. I shouldn't have said anything. I know better. But I'm so grateful to him for giving up his civilian life for me... for everybody.

I let his withdrawal pass without comment.

In baggage claim, he grabs his green duffel like it weighs nothing, then nods to the door. "Take me anywhere. Surprise me."

We reach my car, and there's that familiar stab of disappointment when I see it. *Dad wasn't even alive when I bought this car, and still I chose something that would've made him happy. Even if it didn't make me happy.* I can still hear him expounding the virtues of Hondas. *Reliable, safe, trustworthy.*

Ethan grins. "Good old Helen the Honda. Gotta love her."

I give him a side-eye and he laughs.

"Can I drive?" His eyebrows raise with hope.

"No way."

He gives me a dirty look and tosses his bag in the back seat. *My God, those muscles. Since when?* I climb into my car and blink a few times, trying to clear my head. This is Ethan. I'm looking at *Ethan* like he's a piece of meat. Or a treat. Yes, a treat. A gorgeous, raven-haired, caramel-eyed delectable man. *One who can dig his fingers into my skin and run his stubble across my face and—*

"Kate, what's with you?"

I feel the flush in my cheeks. There's no way Ethan will miss it.

"Nothing. Why?"

Ethan's eyes narrow. "I asked you where we're going. Twice. And you're blushing."

I don't answer. I just point the car towards downtown Phoenix and drive.

2

ETHAN

THERE IS A BOY
And he loves a girl
She doesn't love him back
He doesn't care
One day she will love him
Until then, he waits.

I WAS fifteen when I wrote that poem. Scrawled it onto a ripped piece of flimsy, white computer paper. The tape holding the ripped paper to the inside of my desk drawer is just beginning to lose its stickiness. Every time I go home on leave, I open the drawer and make sure it's still there. Seeing it resets my focus and reminds me that waiting for Kate is a marathon, and the prize will be worth it.

I'm afraid to think it. Even daring to hope might kill the hope altogether. And I've loved her for so long.

But her reaction to me... She's never done that before. Smiles, hugs, happiness when she sees me, that's all normal.

But this time she was breathless, even nervous. Her beautiful brown eyes were dilated.

It's hard to concentrate on anything right now. I've allowed Kate to distract me with the promise of food. It works, a least a little. I'm starving. I've been eating like a horse since I started lifting weights. I have my best Army friend to thank for my gym-rat status. *Nick Hunter, expert marksman, skilled medic, and bench press extraordinaire.* And future Arizona resident. I've convinced him that Phoenix is more than tumbleweeds and cactus. He'll exit the Army and be here in three months. Seven months earlier than me.

Kate's lucky I love her so much. Otherwise her comment about my driving would have upset me. Yeah, I have a few black marks on my record. But that was a long time ago. I was still a boy back when I did dumb stuff like drive into Kate's front yard. I'm a man now.

Army strong.

Four years of my life, dedicated to the safety and protection of this great nation and its people. I'm seventy-five percent of the way through my time. Just this one last deployment, and then I'm done. Forever. And if I get my way, I'll spend the rest of my life with my Katie girl.

She's driving now, so I take the opportunity to watch her navigate her car onto the freeway. Long brown hair, shining as the sun streaks into her car. Full, rosy cheeks. Straight nose. Plump, pink lips. No lipstick on those lips. That's just her natural lip color. And that red tank top... I love her in red.

I don't have to look at her to know all those details. Every inch of her exquisite face is seared into my memory.

I've loved her forever. I'll never stop. *And the way she touched me at the airport. The way she stared into my eyes.* A thrill runs through me. I feel like an idiot, a lovesick fool. *Yep, I'm definitely both those things.*

It's hard, but I tear my eyes away from her and look out across my hometown. Sprawling Phoenix, suburbia as far as the eye can see. Mountains shoot up randomly through the city, houses built around them and on them. Palm trees sway, the never ending sunshine permeates the window and warms my chest. I couldn't have asked for a better season to visit. Avoiding summer here was crucial. It's bad enough that where I'm going next will be a hot desert made hotter by my uniform and gear. Dealing with a Phoenix summer on my R&R and then being deployed to the Middle East would have been a double whammy.

I stare at the mountain on our right. It's big, but the mountains of Afghanistan are bigger. None of them resemble a camel lying down, though.

"Camelback hasn't moved." Kate's voice is close to me as she turns in her seat and motions out my window.

Bump bump bump. My teeth clatter as Kate's car drifts over the lines. *And I'm the questionable driver?*

"Pay attention to the road, Kate. I'd prefer not to die in your car." I love teasing her. Someone needs to, to keep her from being so serious. Her little brother's not around to do it.

Kate's hands go back to the wheel at exactly ten and two. Her body is at attention, but it's too stiff.

The excitement starts up, but I squash it.

It's not Kate's fault. She won't do anything unless it has been well thought out. If list-writing were an Olympic event, Kate would be a gold medalist. The girl has drawn up a t-chart before deciding to date someone. I watched her do it, and it should have discouraged me.

I will not hope. I know Kate too well. She won't risk our friendship, even for love.

But that greeting. It wasn't just *nothing*. She's different. I want to blurt out how uneasy I feel, to make Kate tell me what the hell is going on here.

I'm half a second from hitting my breaking point and demanding answers when Kate pulls into the only empty spot in front of a brick house.

"Let's go, hungry man."

I peer out at the house. The sign on the white wooden front door makes me pause. *Kate's outdone herself this time.*

We climb from the car. "Really?" I ask.

Her sigh is loud. "Whiners eat outside."

"I gathered that from the sign." I eye the big block letters written on a piece of poster board.

She pushes past me and bounds up the three stairs, impatient as always. Sometimes it's annoying, but I secretly like that about her. Kate knows how to get stuff done.

She turns back to me. Her legs are tanned and toned in those white shorts. And that red tank top... *Damn.* She's poised at the top of the stairs, watching me.

"Hungry here." I try to look exasperated, but mostly I'm embarrassed because she's just caught me admiring her body. I'm usually much stealthier than that. Must be all the time we've spent apart. I'll have to hone my skills while I'm here.

From where she's standing at the top of the stairs, she's only a little bit taller than I. And she's smirking. *She's being playful.*

No, she's not.

Holy shit.

She's flirting. Kate Masters is flirting with me.

I watch the spark fade from her eyes. Practical, rule

following Kate has taken over. Whatever's going on inside her, she has control over it again.

Disappointed, I watch her turn and grab the door handle.

"Come on, if you're so starving. And seriously, don't whine. Because I refuse to eat in the sun."

I follow her into the brick house, halted immediately by the line that reaches back to where we've just entered.

Long picnic tables fill what I assume used to be the living room. Little wooden tables dot the room to our right. The walls are stuffed with memorabilia and newspaper articles from Arizona sports teams. *I'm about to go to Afghanistan for ten months. I really don't want to eat crappy food while I'm here. I should've asked Kate to take me back to her place and cook for me. I've been craving her chicken noodle soup.*

I lean into Kate. "Are you sure about this place?" My voice is low. I doubt they're serious about that whining stuff, but you never know.

"Well"—Kate cocks her head to the side—"I heard from a friend of a friend that this place is decent. And it finally passed its last health inspection, so we're in the clear there!" She wipes her brow, ramping up the drama.

I look down at her, my eyes narrowed. *A mistake.*

The citrus and vanilla scent of her perfume rises off her skin, swirling into my nose and making her joke a distant memory.

Her freckles captivate me. They run across the bridge of her nose and fall off either side, steadily decreasing until they fade out completely. She thinks they're a flaw, but she's wrong. Those freckles are a beacon of hope.

Somewhere in there, childhood Kate still exists. The Kate who lay in the grass, devouring books and writing her own stories. That was before she believed being Master of

Everything was the only way to make her dad proud. Her freckles are more than just a facial feature. And they're incredibly cute.

The longer I stare at her, the more I lose my grasp on reality. Kate doesn't put any distance between us like she normally would.

I want her.

Her face grows soft. Below her chin, her chest rises and falls, faster and faster. I'm not breathing at all.

We stand like that for what feels like a full minute, communicating without speaking. It's something only couples who've been together for a long time can achieve.

But we *have* been a twosome for a long time. I know her on the most basic, barest level. I can pick out her mood just by looking into her eyes. Her favorite color is green, even though she tells everyone it's pink. The tiny scar above her left eyebrow is a remnant from the night of our thirteenth birthday when she snuck out of her parents' house. I cleaned her wound by the light of a street lamp. *My Katie girl.*

A throat clearing and shuffle of feet behind us breaks into our starry-eyed gazing. I look back and meet the eyes of an old man. He smiles apologetically and points in front of us.

I look and see there's enough space for three people to stand between us and the next person in line.

"Oops," Kate murmurs, her face sheepish. "I'm sorry." She says to the man. "We weren't paying attention." She hurries forward to close the space.

That's my Kate. Never one to step out of line.

I nod my apology to the man and follow her. Her pupils are dilated, and her cheeks are a shade of pink I've only ever seen on her face. Her gaze looks away, flicks back to me, and looks away again.

There's a tap on my shoulder. It's the old man again. He's smiling kindly, hand outstretched.

"Thank you for your service, young man. You're a blessing to this great nation."

My throat tightens. I didn't join the Army to receive recognition. I wanted to serve my country and protect my loved ones. *And to make Dad proud.*

The old man keeps smiling while these thoughts fly through my head. I shake his hand and thank him for his kind words.

We're up next, and Kate squeezes my arm as she orders for herself and me.

"No fries, please." Kate adds at the end, puffing out her cheeks at me. I roll my eyes.

"How do you know what I want?" I ask.

Her gaze pierces me, travels right down into my soul and shakes it.

"I know you by heart." Her voice is soft.

On quick feet she walks away to find a table, while I wait for our order and try to understand what just happened.

I know you by heart, too, Kate. And something is happening inside you. Kate doesn't say things like that. She's careful with her words. Especially when it comes to me. She knows I love her. She's known it for ten years, and she's done everything she can think to do not to lead me on.

I haven't been led on. Not once. I'm the one leading this mission. The mission to win Kate's heart. And I think I'm close to the end.

She's been fighting against the idea of *us* for a long time. Whatever is happening inside her must be terrifying her. As much as every fiber of my being is screaming to push through her barrier, I give her a break, because she needs it.

I pick up our order and take it to the table she has chosen. The food is a good distraction. The taste of grease, ketchup, pickles, fried potatoes, it sends my eyes upward with my first bite. "Mmmm... This is exactly what I've been missing. Well, this and you, of course."

Kate laughs and takes a bite of her own lettuce wrapped burger.

I swallow and clear my throat. Kate isn't going to like what I have to tell her, but it's better to get it out of the way early. "I told Trent we would see him tomorrow." My words come out on top of each other, making it sound like one long word.

Kate stops chewing and stares at me. She absolutely hates Trent. And the feeling is mutual.

To be fair, I see her point about him. He's rude and narcissistic. He also happens to be my college roommate and a hell of a lot of fun. I don't spend much time with him when I come home, because they despise each other.

"Kate, he's my friend. Just come with me. I'm only going to see him once while I'm here."

Kate folds her arms in front of her. She's pissed. "I can't figure out why he's still your friend. You two are polar opposites." She snatches a fry out of my basket. Her nostrils flare. A sure sign her temper is beginning to boil. Few people know that perfect, people-pleasing Kate Masters has a temper, and I just happen to be one of them.

"So are you and Harper," I say calmly. It's a safe comparison. And it's one hundred percent true.

Kate's roommate and closest friend —aside from me— is outgoing and loves attention. She and Kate are nothing alike.

"Harper's my roommate. Not an old friend I hang onto for reasons that escape everyone besides me."

"Messy. Disorganized. Spontaneous."

Kate's lip curls. "What are you doing?"

"Naming some of Harper's characteristics that make you opposites."

Kate groans.

She's accepting defeat. I actually won.

She takes another fry from me. "Please tell me Zane will be there. I need a buffer."

Zane Smith. My other childhood friend. The guy who offered his silent support of all my unrequited feelings for Kate over the years. I know she wishes Zane would have gone to ASU with us, instead of heading down to Tucson to attend U of A. In Kate's eyes, there would be no Trent if Zane hadn't stepped off the path we were all on.

"I invited him. He's busy, but he said he'd make time." The poor guy sounded stressed when I talked to him a few days ago. He's in his second year of law school. Sometimes I forget how smart Zane is. His brawn, paired with his quiet nature, mask his intelligence.

Kate looks relieved. She bites into her lettuce-burger thing and glances out the large front window. A flush fills her cheeks, and I have no idea why. Usually I know what she's feeling, but right now, it's like there's another person inside my best friend, doing things and feeling things I'm not able to see.

"What is it?"

"Nothing," she mumbles, and shoves in another bite of food.

I know what she's doing. Except it doesn't work with me. I don't care if she talks with a full bite of food.

"Katie girl..." I sing her nickname. It's the name only I'm

allowed to use. She goes by Kate, because it sounds strong and grown up. According to her, anyway. I still like Katie, and I'd call her that even if she didn't want me to. Probably.

She swallows and smiles just a little too sweetly at me. "It's nothing. So, I talked to my mom yesterday. She told me your mom's so excited to see you she's practically coming out of her skin."

Once again, I know what she's doing. And, once again, I'll let her slide. Because that's what I always do.

I start telling her about last week when I talked to my mom, and Kate looks so relieved I almost feel bad for her. If I were a betting man, I'd wager there's a battle raging inside Kate right now. And if I were a hopeless, stupid romantic, which I must be, considering I've loved her for this long, I'd say this battle is about me.

3

KATE

HE KNOWS SOMETHING IS GOING ON.

It's those questioning looks he keeps giving me.

Good luck figuring me out.

I can't even figure myself out right now.

Can't you?

It's not difficult. You love Ethan. Ethan loves you. Done.

That answer is too easy. This is a real life problem with real life outcomes. The biggest by far being the risk to me and Ethan.

I need to be more careful. I can't act like I've been acting since the airport.

Going to Ethan's parents' house will make it easier. No opportunities to touch him and get lost in his eyes.

If our parents could see our airport reunion, we'd be on the receiving end of some serious questions. It's no secret that our parents are huge fans of an Ethan-and-Kate union. Especially his mother. Whom I love dearly. And who wants me to love her son just as dearly. *I already do.*

My hand comes off the wheel to fidget with the neck of my dress. Stopping at my apartment to change was a good idea. I want to look nice. That red tank top was too casual for dinner at Ethan's parents' house.

My lips twist as I spare a quick glance at myself. "I wish Harper had been home when I was getting dressed." *Her style is lightyears better than mine.*

"I'm pretty happy she wasn't there."

"Ethan!"

"Sorry, sorry. She's just not my favorite person."

"I know, but be nice. Besides, I really needed her today. After the lunch we had, I should be wearing maternity pants. Not this cute dress."

"You ate five fries."

"I tanked your whole basket when you were busy dropping the Trent bomb on me."

"You really hate him, don't you?"

I tap the steering wheel and toss an admonishing look his way. "I have good reason to."

One day. Trent knew me for just *one day* before he decided I was leading Ethan on. And apparently I remind him of a foster mother he had who repeatedly acted like she would adopt him and never did. After that experience, Trent had been shuffled between foster parents before he was finally adopted. According to him, I'm just like the woman who gave a little boy false hope.

"You know, he had a really rough start in life. Try to give him a break." Ethan boomerangs the admonishing look.

A loud, short stream of air comes from my nose. "He could give me a break too. I'm not his foster mother. We all have our issues, maybe some more than others. We're adults now. He can't keep using his childhood as a reason to be a jerk."

He tugs my ponytail. "Not everybody can be perfect like you. Kate Masters. Straight-A student. Valedictorian. Serious rule follower. Weird ability to accomplish any task. *Kate will Master it.*" He sing-songs the last sentence.

I smile, but it feels wrong on my face. *I'm ready to leave that phrase in the dust.* Being perfect is exhausting.

I turn onto the street we grew up on. Instantly I'm comforted by the big, green lawns and old, leafy trees.

"Look at Mrs. Witherby." Ethan points at the old woman standing in her front yard with a garden hose. "She looks...old."

I glance at the cloud of white hair puffing out over her head. "She is old. She was old when we were little."

"I know, but... Wow." He waves at her as we drive past.

She waves back, but she looks confused.

"It's been less than a year since I've been here, but it feels like longer. Everything is green in this neighborhood. A world away from where I'm headed." I glance over to see a pensive look on his face.

In his parent's driveway, I put the car in park. I reach for his hand and give it a squeeze. *This is something I would have done before I knew I loved him. This is okay.*

"I'm sorry you feel upset." *And I wish you didn't have to go.*

He shakes his head. "I'm fine."

He watches me, not moving his hand. I don't move my hand, but I definitely should.

"Ethan..." I stop. I don't know what I was about to say. I have no words. Just a swirling feeling. Growing and stretching, consuming me from the inside.

He leans over, just an inch. *One inch closer to me.* His eyes drill into mine, like he's willing me to *just say it.*

My mouth opens, closes. Opens, closes. A muscle in my thigh starts twitching.

"Ethan!"

A woman's voice breaks up the moment. My brain is thankful. My heart is despondent.

Ethan jumps from the car and rushes to his mom and dad. I follow slowly, giving them time for a reunion before I join.

"Mom, Dad. Good to see you." His voice is thick.

Evie finally lets go of Ethan and reaches for me.

"Kate, I haven't seen you at your mom's house. Where have you been?"

"Oh, here and there." The truth is that I've been avoiding my mom. She has a keen sense of knowing when something is up with me.

"Sounds like there's a new man in your life." She grins back at me, but it's fleeting. Her next look is to Ethan, and it's worried.

Ethan rocks back on his heels and purses his lips, shrugging. "If that's the case, Kate's not divulging any info to me. But she has been a little off today. Maybe there's trouble in paradise."

I cross my arms. "I'm in paradise by myself, thank you very much." *No I'm not. I'm in hell. A mental and emotional hell of my own making.*

"Ethan Shepherd, you come hug me this instant." My mother's voice sounds from the end of the front yard.

Ethan laughs and jogs to her. "Linda, long time no see."

Yes, everyone loves Ethan. Including me.

"Hi, Mr. Shepherd." I smile at Ethan's father. It's hard to know exactly how to act around him. He was my high school principal, not just my best friend's dad.

"How many times do I have to tell you to call me by my first name?" He laughs at my discomfort. "I haven't been your principal in a long time."

"Hi, James. How are you?"

"Great now that my boy is home for ten days." His chest puffs up with pride as he watches Ethan and my mom walk to us. "Or are you going to steal him away like you usually do?"

I balk. Steal? Is that what I do?

James elbows me lightly. "I'm joking. Ethan is perfectly happy spending the majority of his time with you."

I nod, attempting a smile. The Trent conversation on the drive over has made me sensitive.

"Katherine Rae Masters, you missed dinner on Sunday." My mom comes up behind me and swats my butt.

Ethan's laughter breaks through the group. "Did you just spank her?"

I step into my mom's open arms. "Sorry, Mom. I wasn't feeling well. I left you a message."

The corners of her lips turn down. "You weren't feeling well a few weeks ago when you canceled on me for a shopping day. Are you pregnant?"

"Mom!" My face flames.

Ethan looks like he wants to vomit.

James smirks and Evie howls.

"What?" My mom raises her hands. "You're an adult."

I frown. "New subject. Now."

Ethan steps in. "Let's move this party inside."

Evie squeals an unintelligible sound. "Oh! Dinner. I better check on it." She darts in front of us and into the house.

I let my mom and James go in front. Ethan grabs my hand and pulls me back a few inches. His lips go to my ear, and my whole body shudders.

"Are you pregnant?" He breathes the question, his words nearly inaudible. The barely hidden current of horror sounds much louder than his words.

I scowl at him. "No."

For a second he looks chagrined. "Well, I just had to ask. Your mom said you were sick. Twice."

"And somehow that means I have a baby growing inside me?"

My words put a softening in his eyes, giving them a dream-like quality. "No. Sorry." He steps aside and opens the door for me.

I see the banner right away. Two feet tall and at least ten feet long, the behemoth extends from the fireplace across the entire length of the wall. *Welcome Home Ethan.* Scrawled in big block letters with American flags drawn on either end.

I watch Ethan see it. He smiles, nods his head slowly, swallows the lump in his throat, and walks to his mom.

"Thank you." He hugs her.

She pulls back and takes his face into her hands. Her eyes are shiny. "We are so happy to have you home. Safe and sound."

James claps Ethan on the back. Ethan, eye-to-eye with his dad, looks at him and nods in that manly, respectful way that men sometimes do.

Is that what Ethan is now? A man? He's always been Ethan, the best friend. But right now... I sneak a peek at his profile. *He looks like a man.* He certainly felt like a man in my dream.

I want to run, hide, understand what's happening and plan my reaction. My best friend, the boy from all my child-hood memories, is now a *man.* I need time to absorb this realization.

"Kate, want to help me in the kitchen? I need your skills." Evie's gaze is expectant.

I clear my throat, pushing away my thoughts. "Sure." I

have to pass Ethan to get to Evie. When I do, I take great care not to touch him. Not even a brush of arms.

The kitchen is a disaster. It looks like she used every pot and pan she owns to make dinner. I walk to the stove and look down at the contents of a pan.

"Umm... This is burned."

She winces. "I thought it might be but I wanted your expert opinion."

I can't contain my laughter. "So what's the plan?"

"Pizza?"

"Order-in?"

"Well, I'm certainly not making it." She points at the stove and wrinkles her nose.

"Who's cleaning this kitchen?" I ask, looking at the piles of used cooking utensils and dirty countertops.

"The guys." She laughs the words.

Evie orders pizza while she pulls down a bottle of wine and three glasses from a cabinet. I go to the fridge and remove two beers for Ethan and James, then follow Evie to the living room.

"Mom, I'm kind of glad you burned dinner." Ethan is reclining on the sofa in the living room when Evie announces the impending pizza delivery. "I haven't had good pizza since I went to Italy."

"When were you in Italy?" My mom asks.

"A few months ago. We can go off-post when we're between deployments. My friend Nick and I got on a train and left Germany for the weekend." The corners of his mouth turn up, like he's remembering something funny.

"Ethan, is Nick still planning to move here?" Evie pours the third glass of wine and hands it to me.

I murmur a thank you, my eyes on Ethan as he drinks from his beer bottle, his Adam's apple moving. That tiny action, and suddenly my knees feel like they weigh less. I may or may not be panting. I can't tell. I'm a mess.

"Yep." Ethan watches me, curiosity raging in his eyes. "Lucky bastard gets out seven months earlier than I do. I told him you all will help him adjust and get his life together. Right, Katie?"

"Of course." I agreed to the task months ago.

"You guys are going to love him." Ethan's voice is excited. "He's a solid guy. He's been through a lot."

"Is he anything like Trent?" I ask.

Ethan laughs. "More like Zane. Nothing like Trent."

I let out a loud breath. "Thank God. I like Nick already."

Evie laughs and high fives me. She tolerates Trent for Ethan's sake.

We talk and laugh until the pizza arrives. Ethan eats like he hasn't seen food in days and swears he doesn't have room for any more, but when Evie walks out with a store bought dessert she had in the fridge, he changes his tune.

After dessert, we continue to visit until Ethan reminds us that his body clock is out of whack, and he's about to pass out on the floor.

"You can take your old room. It's ready for you." Evie looks hopeful.

Ethan looks at me. "Sleepover? Like old times?" His eyebrows are raised.

My insides turn to jelly. The pizza and cannoli in my stomach threaten to re-enter the world. "Sure," I manage to mumble.

Evie claps her hands together. "I'll make up the trundle." She starts for the stairs, but turns back suddenly. "Wait a minute. Is it safe to let you two sleep in the same room without adult supervision?"

A flush ignites on my cheeks.

Ethan rolls his eyes. "Mom? You know Kate and I are just friends. And even if we weren't just friends, we're—"

"Adults. I know, I know." Evie throws up her arms. "Forgot for a second. I'm just happy to have you here, that's all. Have sex, I don't care."

"Mom!" Ethan yells.

"Evie!" I yell.

She laughs and runs to the stairs. "I'm getting out of here."

By the time my mom leaves, I'm dangerously close to fainting. I don't know if I've taken more than ten breaths since I agreed to stay the night.

Evie and James say good night to us and go to their bedroom on the first floor.

I look at Ethan.

Ethan looks at me.

"So..." I draw out the word.

"Ready for bed?" He has that softness to his eyes again. It makes me want to melt into a puddle right there at the bottom of the stairs. I gulp and nod.

We climb the stairs together, arms bumping, and I want to reach out and curl my fingers through his.

Once we're in his bedroom, he hands me a t-shirt from his dresser. "Are you okay to sleep in this?"

I take the oversize white T-shirt. "Turn around."

He obeys. Unzipping my dress is a struggle, but there's no way I'm asking him for help. Finally, I get it down far enough that I can slide the dress down my body and step out.

I slip his T-shirt over my head, silently inhaling the scent. Of course it's freshly laundered and smells of fabric softener. I wish it smelled of him. It's a good thing I'm petite. As it is, the bottom of his shirt only reaches mid-thigh.

"Okay." I sit down on the trundle, legs carefully folded beneath me so the shirt covers as much as it can.

Ethan isn't shy about changing into his pajamas in front of me. With one hand he reaches over his shoulder and grabs a fistful of fabric, then pulls the shirt over his hand in a single graceful motion.

Oh my god, that was sexy.

Ethan is sexy.

My brain is trying to wrap itself around the fact I'm thinking this of Ethan, of all people. My libido is acting independent of my brain. It's a racehorse out in front of the rest of my reason, screaming for more.

Ethan unbuttons the top button of his jeans. I look away, but it's too late. The image, seared into my brain, is already doing things to me.

Heart galloping.

Pulse racing.

Blood boiling in the very best way.

I need to go to sleep. Immediately. The rustle of his jeans as they're removed from his body makes me want to give up all my secrets.

My head hits the pillow as fast as I can. My body faces away from the man behind me taking off his pants.

I'm in love with you. Now can we please pick up where my dream left off?

I shake my head. *Go to bed. Close your eyes and forget about it.*

Ethan's voice is suddenly right next to me. His lips move against my ear. "Take my bed. I'm not letting you sleep on the trundle. We both know it's not comfortable."

"I'm fine." I need to be in this exact spot, curled up with my face pointing away from him. This is safe.

He sighs. I feel the mattress roll under his shifting weight. Two arms slip under me, and then I'm airborne.

I stay silent, unmoving. Gently I'm laid back down, this time on Ethan's bed.

"Goodnight, Kate." There's a long pause between those two words, and when he says my name it sounds like there are so many more words hiding behind it.

"Goodnight, Ethan."

Just like him, I could say so much more.

But I don't.

4

ETHAN

My eyes open. I sit up and peek over the side of my bed, careful not to make noise.

She's still there.

Kate's mouth is parted halfway, her deep, even breaths passing through her pink lips.

My eyes travel down, away from her face. Her restlessness during the night has moved the blanket to the foot of the bed. Now she only has the sheet, and it's tangled in her legs. My white T-shirt has bunched at her waist. The twisted sheet exposes one half of her bottom curves. My heart beats faster. I roll my eyes at my excitement. *It's like she's wearing bikini bottoms.* No big deal.

But it is a big deal. I saw what happened inside her last night. As if her skin were translucent, I saw everything that went on in her head. And her body. She was at war with herself.

She's attracted to me.

But does she love me?

I would never do anything casual with Kate. Talk about

ruining things between us. We've come too far to ever be bed buddies.

I want her love. I want her every morning and every night. I want to marry her and have babies with her and be by her side until we're old and wrinkled. I want her in the spaces between seconds, when the clock tells a boring story of time filled with nothingness.

I want her in moments of nothingness.

Does she want me the same way?

I get up as quietly as I can and leave my bedroom. My desire and my love for Kate overwhelms me. It takes me away from my senses and makes me want to see if her attraction to me is more.

And I know Kate. She has to come to me. On her own time. So now I just have to wait.

Thanks to Kate, I'm an expert in waiting.

***

I GOT OUT OF MY PARENTS' house with a lot of hugs from my mom and a promise to come back later today. We've stopped at Kate's so she can shower and change. And then we're going somewhere Kate has no desire to go.

I feel for Kate. Really, I do. I don't like spending time around her roommate either.

Truth be told, I think my friendship with Trent has run its course. He's the same person he was in college, but now he has money and a good job. Kate tells me I'm loyal to a fault, and I'm starting to think she's right about the *fault* part.

"Ready." Kate walks into the living room. She's changed into pink shorts and a white shirt. Personally I liked when she was wearing *my* old white shirt. *I learned that last night... and this morning.*

Kate walks ahead of me. She pretends to drag her feet, and I laugh.

She looks over her shoulder and grins. "Remind me to force you to spend time with Harper sometime in the next week."

"Deal." I reach past her for the door handle.

Our drive to Trent's house is short, but I use the ten minutes to ask Kate about something that has been on my mind.

"When was the last time you wrote something?"

Kate turns confused eyes to me. "I wrote a grocery list on my phone this morning." Her eyes have gone back to the road, so she doesn't see me roll mine.

"When was the last time you wrote for pleasure?"

"At work, the day you arrived."

I shake my head. "Still not what I meant. When was the last time you wrote a story?"

"I write non-fiction stories all the time. They're called press releases." She spares a quick, weary glance at me.

This is painful. "Okay, let's try this again, and I'll be very specific. When was the last time you wrote a story for pleasure while you were not at work?"

She gives a short, disbelieving chuckle and says, "Years."

"Why?"

"I don't have time for that stuff anymore. I can't waste my time on anything that doesn't have a direct impact on my career."

Achieve, succeed. So Kate. So her father.

"You used to love writing stories." My reminder is as gentle as it can be. Kate and art don't mix. She doesn't do abstract thought. But she used to.

She opens her mouth, but I stop her with a raised hand. "*A Gust of Wind and He Was Gone. The Princess and her Unruly Dragon. Ethan and Kate: Apocalypse Partners. Where the Red Roses Grow.*" The titles tick off on the fingers of my raised hand. "Need I continue? I can."

"I can't believe you remember all those stories." Her voice is soft.

"I remember a lot more than those four. You read them to me every time you got a chance." I shift in my seat to look at her, so I can see how she takes what I'm about to say. "I know why you stopped writing. But what about now? Your dad... He's been gone for five years. And don't you think the Master of Everything has achieved it all? Can you go back to your true passion? Rekindle the flame?"

Kate's lips push together until they turn white in the center. She stares at the road.

This is about so much more than just Kate returning to writing. Defeating the beliefs of what would make her father proudest is Kate's battle.

She's still quiet.

"Katie?"

No response.

A few minutes later, she pulls up at Trent's house. Zane's car is parked in the driveway, and I feel a twinge of guilt for not arriving before him. Zane likes Trent enough, but I know he wouldn't go out of his way to be his friend. They don't hang out unless I'm around.

We step from her car, and she looks at me over the roof.

"Thank you for being my best friend. You're the very best friend in the history of best friends."

"Is that your way of saying '*Thanks, but no thanks*'?"

Her head shakes. "It isn't something I can think about

right now." She throws an uneasy glance back at Trent's house.

I drop it. Besides, I did what I wanted to do. I planted a seed.

Kate looks up at me when we get to the front door. I grab her hand and wink. "Everything will be fine. We'll just be here for a little while."

I drop her hand and hit the door twice with two knuckles, then open it without waiting for Trent to let us in.

"Dude!" Trent's voice booms as he comes toward us. Zane's head bobs behind him. "What have they been feeding you over there?" He grabs my bicep and squeezes. "I bet the ladies love that."

I glance at Kate. Her lip is curled.

"Kate!" Zane comes from behind Trent. He grabs her shoulders and pulls her in for a hug, like he doesn't remember she's tiny and he's huge. Her face smashes into his chest, then he releases her.

Kate steps back and wiggles her nose, but she's smiling. "Nice to see you too, Zane."

One side of my mouth turns up as I watch them, but falls when I look at Trent. He looks sullen.

Zane extends his hand and I take it, pulling him to me for a hug at the same time.

"Good to see you, man." Zane's voice is emotional. His huge heart is another thing hidden by his brawn. He lets me go after a couple solid slaps on my back.

"I hope we're not interrupting your plans." Trent doesn't look the tiniest bit sincere as he says it.

"No way." Another grab and squeeze of Kate's hand to reassure her, just like before we walked in the house.

Trent turns and starts for the kitchen. "Ethan, come help

me grab drinks. Kate, make yourself comfortable in the living room."

She follows Zane while I go with Trent.

"What's going on with you and Masters these days?" Trent throws a thumb back to where Kate is.

"What do you mean?" I take the two beers Trent's holding out. He turns back to the fridge and grabs one more.

"It's been a long time. I was just checking to see if you're still wasting your time on her."

My eyes narrow. "Kate's off-limits. Don't talk about her." My voice is rough, precise. Like my sergeant when he's smoking someone for not making it to formation on time.

Trent doesn't say anything else. Which is good for him, because I'm at the end of my rope, and we just walked in the door.

Kate's right. It's time for Trent to stop using his past as a crutch.

We walk back out to the living room, where Zane's asking Kate a question.

"So, Masters, what have you been doing with yourself? I haven't seen you since the last time Ethan was here."

She shrugs. "Same old, same old. I'm still in PR at Simone. How about you?"

Zane grimaces. "Studying my ass off. I added a science and technology focus, which will be good when I'm done. But right now it means more work."

Kate smiles sympathetically. "Are you at least going to Idaho for the summer?"

He nods, taking the beer I'm holding out for him. "My grandma would be upset if I didn't. It's tradition."

"I wish I had a place to escape to every summer," Trent says as he tosses a bottle of water to Kate.

"Thanks!" She says with fake cheerfulness.

"Sure thing!" He responds in the same tone.

I settle myself on the couch next to Kate. She winds her right arm through my left. I look at her, remembering how she looked this morning before she woke up. Her long, toned legs, those adorable pink panties with the white ruffled trim.

"How's Harper doing?" Trent leans back into his chair and crosses an ankle over a knee.

It's a small miracle Harper isn't interested in Trent, even though he's made it clear how interested he is in her. If they dated Kate would have to spend more time around him than she's already forced to. Bad enough she has to spend time with Harper.

She musters a polite smile. "Great. She loves her job. It's pretty much all she does. Well, that and party. But the two go hand in hand. Being a party planner has its perks, according to her."

Trent nods and shifts his attention to me.

"Ethan, tell me about life over there." I'm happy he's moved his attention off Kate. She'd rather go to the dentist than make conversation with Trent.

"It's whatever." I shrug. "I'm headed to Afghanistan after I leave here. Just trading one desert for another."

"What do you do every day?" Trent prods.

I shrug again. "I've been in Germany, getting ready for deployment. It leaves a lot of downtime, so I've been at the gym."

Trent grins. "I know someone who's going to like your buff arms."

Oh shit. My leg that's touching Kate tenses. She turns to me, but I can't bring myself to look at her. I don't want to see the look on her face right now. *This is going to ruin everything. Whatever Kate was starting to feel for me, this will end it.*

"Who's going to like Ethan's arms?" I hear the struggle in Kate's voice as she tries to sound calm. Zane clears his throat.

Trent waves a hand in the air. "I've been seeing this girl, and we thought it would be fun to set Ethan up with her friend. Everything is ready for tomorrow night."

Tomorrow night? Shit. I forgot. The blind date. It's been so long since I agreed to go.

Trent glances from Kate to me. "Amaya says her friend loves military guys." His eyebrows wiggle suggestively.

Without a doubt, Trent is trying to provoke Kate. I want to tell him off, but I'm frozen. All I can think of is Kate and how she's feeling inside. And how I'm going to make this situation right. And if I can. And if I even need to. *You've seen how she's been acting. You definitely need to.*

If I'm right and she's starting to change her mind about us, then right now, Kate feels humiliated. And it's made worse by the fact that she has to experience this in front of Trent, who clearly enjoys watching her react. He brought up this date on purpose. It's classic, meddling Trent.

Trent got what he wanted. Kate's angry. But he's also going to get a little something extra. From me.

Kate stands up from the couch and snatches her purse from the floor in one swift motion.

"I need to go." She turns flashing eyes on me. "Maybe Amaya's friend can take you to your parents' house."

She makes it three steps when I finally regain the ability to speak. "It's not what you think."

She whips around, glaring down at me where I perch on the edge of the couch. Her eyes aren't flashing anymore.

"I need to go," she repeats, her face morose.

"Calm down, Kate." Trent's voice is caustic. Toxic. "You

know he loves you. He's loved you since before he could write his own name."

Kate's temper is something to be reckoned with, and very few people get to see it. She keeps it under wraps, because Kate Masters is perfect, and having a temper isn't acceptable for a perfect person.

She stomps to him and points a finger in his face. "You are your own self-sustaining group of high school mean girls. You gossip, you lie, and you orchestrate fights. Here's a tip: Real men don't behave that way."

She pivots and hurries out of Trent's house. I stay seated, giving Kate the space she needs. Zane's concerned eyes meet mine and his lips twist.

It's quiet until Trent breaks the silence. "Masters can really be dramatic when she wants to be. Typical girl."

"You did that on purpose." I say quietly, standing up from the couch.

Trent has the nerve to look affronted. It's the fundamental issue with the guy. He's a victim, no matter what he's done to contribute to the problem. Somehow, he'll always manage to be the victim.

"I need to go after her." I pinch the bridge of my nose and picture Kate's face before she ran out.

Zane stands. "I'll take you."

"Just let her go." Trent crosses his arms. "She's made it clear she only wants you when someone else does."

"That's not for you to decide."

When I stride out of Trent's house, it feels like an ending. Sometimes, people have to be cut off. *Trim the fat,* as Nick would say.

Zane points his car in the direction of Kate's apartment.

He doesn't make small talk, but at a red light he taps my chest with the back of his hand, his head moving up and down in one slow nod. *Is he approving of me going after Kate? Or saying goodbye to Trent?* I don't ask. I don't want to talk.

My elbow rests against the car door and I toy with my lip as I recall Kate's reaction.

Her devastated face macerates my insides.

I have to make this right.

I can't lose her now. Not when she's so close.

***

ZANE DROPPED me off with a wave, and now I'm pacing the walkway in front of Kate's apartment complex. I stop to send up a silent prayer of thanks that Harper's car is gone. I don't need her here for this.

I take deep breaths, building up my nerve. I'm going to have to demand answers from Kate. I deserve to hear the reason why she's getting jealous and running from houses, leaving me stranded. I have nine precious days left on my leave before I head to Afghanistan, and I can't spend them at odds with her.

Each step, each stair, takes me closer and closer to Kate. To her truth. Quite possibly the truth I've been waiting ten years to hear.

My mouth is dry. My fingers find my wrist and check my pulse. *Racing.*

What am I going to do when she opens the door? How is this going to go?

I reach her door. I stand there, but I can't knock. I stare at the glass in the peephole and wipe my hands on the front of my shorts. This might be it. This might be the moment I've dreamed of, over and over, for years.

You can do this. I shift onto my left foot, then bounce to my right. Left, right. Left, right. Left, right.

My limbs feel warm now. Not so stiff. My head clears as the adrenaline pumps.

> *There is a boy*
> *And he loves a girl*
> *She doesn't love him back*
> *He doesn't care*
> *One day she will love him*
> *Until then, he waits.*

Not anymore.
I want answers.
I lift my hand and knock.

5

KATE

Someone is banging on my door.

Ethan. Please be Ethan.

I see a blue shirt when I peer through the peephole. *He came after me.* I should have known he would. He's Ethan. He'll always come for me.

I take a deep breath, prepared to say what I've been practicing since I stopped crying.

I open the door, mouth open, ready to speak, but I don't get to.

Ethan barrels in as soon as the door is open wide enough, knocking me off balance.

"Hey," I sputter, grabbing the door handle to catch myself.

Ethan's eyes are bright. He doesn't mention anything about nearly knocking me over.

I shut my front door and watch Ethan as he moves from foot to foot, agitated.

"You have no right to be angry with me." His eyes are intense, pulled together. His voice is loud and deep.

Where is my mild-mannered, even-keeled best friend?

"Why do you care if I take someone on a date? *You* don't want to date me. You've made that clear." Ethan's hands run across his closely cropped hair. "I've been waiting for you for years. Literally. I've been in love with you for ten years. How much longer am I supposed to wait?" Ethan's voice is louder now. He watches me. I'm so shocked and confused by this angry Ethan, I can't speak.

"I...I..." I hate when I stammer. Thoughts bounce around my head, but nothing comes together to form a coherent sentence.

Say something.

But I can't. My mouth, my brain, my body, everything is failing me. I'm supposed to keep my mouth shut about my feelings and give Ethan my blessing. That was the brilliant plan I came up with on my drive home from Trent's. Tell Ethan to move on, once and for all. Then I can ensure he'll stay my best friend forever. No risk, no loss.

And no reward either.

I close my eyes and take a deep breath. "You should take out Amaya's friend. I overreacted." I hate every word slithering out of my lying mouth. "I was being overprotective. I'm sorry." When I look into Ethan's eyes, I see disappointment, but I continue. "You're my best friend, but you don't belong to me. You can date whomever you please." *Knife, heart, twist. Ouch.*

Ethan reaches for me. I let him pull me in. When his forehead touches mine, it takes everything in me not to lean in just a little more and press my lips to his. Our first kiss.

Let him go.

My eyes burn. Tears are seconds away.

Ethan's eyes close. I follow. This is too much to bear.

"There's a problem, Katie." The heat of his whisper is on my face. "I gave my heart away a long, long time ago. To a girl with brown hair and freckles. And she's never given it back."

My heart...I *feel* the most vital organ in my body.

Pulsing.

Throbbing.

Galloping.

Suddenly a memory crashes down on me. We were eighteen, and it was our birthday. My high school boyfriend broke up with me the day before and I was devastated. Ethan left an envelope at my front door. I opened it, expecting a birthday card. It was a piece of white paper, folded in half, the inside blank except for his writing. *I would give anything for what he threw away,* he'd scrawled in his terrible, chicken scratch handwriting. When Ethan came over later for cake he pretended like nothing happened. So did I.

He would give anything for me...

What am I doing?

This man is my best friend. He knows my ugliest parts and he would still give anything for me.

My breath comes in shaky gasps as my love for him flows over me.

It's him. It's always been him.

My limbs feel hollow. The warmth of his skin radiates off him, pouring onto me. I gulp in a breath and open my mouth. "The girl with brown hair and freckles... She isn't going to give your heart back." *These words... I love every one of them.*

The pressure of his forehead disappears. I open my eyes and see he's moved only inches away. Emotion rides across his face. But all of it good. So, so good.

"Katie, I need you to be very clear. What are you saying?" His deep voice rumbles in his chest.

My heart pounds so furiously it may leap from me. Little notes of giddy laughter escape my throat.

"I'm sorry I made you wait so long." I pull back another inch, so I can look into his eyes when I say it. "I love you. I'm in love with you."

The smile on his face is brighter than a sunrise. His head dips toward me, slowly closing the distance between our faces. His lips press against mine, and there's trembling, and I don't know if it's him or me or if we're creating an earthquake together.

The flavor of love is on his lips, and it tastes so *good*. Real emotion, pouring out of him and into me, filling every space and crevasse, satisfying my soul. *I'm kissing my best friend.*

My Ethan.

I love him.

Ethan touches my neck, and I feel it quiver as he strokes the space beneath my ear, down to my collarbone. *I really like that.*

My lips push against his with urgency. I press myself into him, needing to be closer. I'm no longer thinking about the fact that this is my best friend. Without that title, Ethan is just a man, and I'm a woman who's in desperate need of him.

Ethan pulls away first. "Wow." He breathes the word.

A flush spreads across my cheeks.

His eyes roam over my face, and I know what he's seeing. My freckles, my flushed cheeks. Lightly he taps my freckles with his fingertips, like he's touching the keys of a piano. "Now I definitely know it's you." This only makes me blush more.

I nod. "It's still me in here." I'm so astonished I can barely manage a whisper.

This time Ethan bypasses my face and brings his lips to

my ear. "You were worth the wait." He pulls back to look at me.

"I'm so sorry. I've always loved you. And now I'm *in* love with you." I say it again, and it feels even more true.

Ethan shakes his head. "Hearing these words from you, it's an actual dream come true. I wish I'd known a long time ago the trick was to make you jealous." He tries to cover up his laugh with his hand.

My eyes bulge. "That's not what happened."

Ethan drops his teasing smile. "I'm sorry about Amaya's friend."

Ugh, Amaya's friend. I don't want to hear about her. I'm too high to come back down right now. My heart is still somewhere in the sky, soaring through clouds.

"I never meant to upset you. I mean it, Kate. Trent was trying to put a double-date together a while ago. At that point it sounded like fun, and I was starting to fear you would never come around." He stares at me, eyes pleading.

"I know." Shame washes over me. What more can I say? I'm only beginning to understand what I've put him through in the last decade.

"I told Trent we could do it when I was home on my next leave, and then I forgot about it." Ethan turns my hand over, tracing designs with one finger. "I'm really sorry. Please know that I never, ever meant to hurt you." His voice sounds so strong and confident. "It's always been you," he adds, staring down at our mix of hands.

I reach up, lifting his face with two fingers beneath his chin. "Ethan, I overreacted." I grin sheepishly. "I've been told I have a temper."

Ethan smiles, but he still looks upset.

I step closer, my heart racing and my mind still reeling.

"Want to kiss and make up?" *I can't believe I'm saying those words to Ethan.*

He grins, excitement on his face. "Like you wouldn't believe."

Ethan's body pushes into me, and my back bumps into the wall beside the front door. This kiss is not like our first.

Gone is the timid sweetness. His hands are on my hips, fingers digging into my skin just like my dream, and I'm touching his face, his neck, his ears. Exploring. Discovering the secrets his hands and lips have been hiding from me all these years.

And I never want to stop.

***

ETHAN'S FALLEN asleep on the couch. Jet lag is getting the best of him. And an hour of kissing is getting the best of me. A yawn widens my mouth. I stretch my arms over my head.

A midday, mid-week nap feels so decadent. Normally I'm knee-deep in writing pitches and putting out proverbial fires. But not today. Today I'm going to indulge in a nap. With Ethan. *My best friend. And my...*

What? What is he?

I bite my lip. We better figure that out before he leaves.

Ethan's face is serene, a small part in his lips. I want to cover his lips with my own, but I hold back. I never get the chance to see Ethan like this. If it weren't for the military haircut, he'd look like a young boy again.

His eyelashes flutter, then his eyes open fully. He blinks at me, a look of confusion flitting across his face. He grabs my hand.

"What's wrong?"

"I came out here to ask if you wanted to ditch this uncomfortable couch and take a nap with me. But instead I stared at you."

"Voyeur."

"Guilty as charged."

Ethan stands, the blanket falling to the couch below him. It's hard to tear my eyes away from his chest. And his stomach. And his shoulders.

"Enjoying the view?" He smirks.

I cross my arms. "Don't make me regret coming to get you."

"Just be happy I don't sleep in my underwear. Or in nothing at all."

"Come on." I groan the words and lead him to my room. The sun-blocking blinds are closed, and it's pitch black even though it's the afternoon. I pause in the light from the open door. "You get that side." I point to the side closest to the window.

"I know what side you sleep on." He goes to my bed and lies down.

I shut the door and climb in beside him, nerves nipping at my stomach. *He's still Ethan.* Once I'm horizontal, he scoots closer, his knees molding to my knees, his top arm wrapping around my waist. His face nuzzles my hair.

"You smell incredible," he murmurs.

"Thanks." My voice is small.

"Are you nervous?"

"No."

"Are you biting the inside of your lip?"

Dammit, I am.

"It's only me, Katie."

"That's just it. It's...you. And me. Me and you."

Ethan's fingers pull through the long strands of my hair. "Everything will be okay. I promise."

"How can you be so sure?" The fear bubbles up, accompanied by its ugly friend, doubt.

"Because ours is a once-in-a-lifetime love." His voice is rich with emotion, saturated with affection. "Nothing can touch that. Nothing. Not your fear. Not even death."

I gasp. "Don't say that. Don't even mention death."

"I'm sorry. I didn't mean to make you think about your dad."

My eyes squeeze shut. It was five years ago, and it's still the worst day of my existence so far. Nobody expected my dad's two a.m. heart attack. He was my hero.

Ethan shifts, I slide onto my back, and he moves over me, supporting his weight with one forearm.

"I'm scared for you, Ethan. You're fighting in a *war*."

"Nothing is going to happen to me. I'll be fine." He dips down to press his lips to mine, just for a moment. Thrills run the length of my body. Here in the dark, I can't see Ethan's face clearly, but I feel the intensity of his gaze.

"I'll always love you, Katie girl." His voice flows down to me, pierces my chest, and infiltrates my heart.

Gently I brush the tip of my nose against his. "I'll always love you. Until our wrinkles have wrinkles."

He closes the gap between our lips, and I taste the sweetness of him. Of my best friend. Of this man who has loved me for a decade.

***

IT'S HOT. Something heavy is on my chest. I open my eyes and find Ethan's arm stretched out on top of me.

With care I extract myself from the cage Ethan has made with his arms. He's still passed out, mouth open and snoring softly.

I make my way out to the kitchen. It's the middle of the afternoon, but it feels like morning. Harper stands at the counter, pouring herself a glass of iced tea. Her back is to me, one foot balanced on the inner thigh of her other leg.

"Hey, Harps. Why are you home from work so early?"

"I have a happy hour meeting with a client," she says without looking at me. "I had to come home to charge my phone and change." Harper changes positions and grabs a straw from the box on the counter. She turns back to glance at me.

I smile. I want to gush to her about Ethan, but I'm not sure how to say it. And I'm not sure she'll be supportive.

Harper doesn't do love. Locked in a fierce competition with her two sisters, Harper goes on date after date, trying to find a wealthy, successful, gorgeous man (that is somehow still, in her words, *"you know, grounded"*) who will make her sisters turn green with envy. Harper doesn't have a specific reason for the competition. Or she doesn't want to divulge. Either way, I watch from the sidelines like it's a spectator sport.

She sips from her straw, blue eyes narrowed. "What's going on?" A little 'v' forms between her brows. I contemplate telling her to stop or she'll need Botox, but Harper won't take it as a joke. She'll make an appointment.

I bite my lip, trying to decide how to answer. I need to tread lightly.

"Harper, hey." Ethan strolls into the kitchen. No shirt. Again. His black hair is cut too short to be messy. *I want his longer hair back.*

"Long time no see," he tells her, stopping at my side.

Harper, a person who's never short on words, is stunned. She walks to him slowly, the 'v' in between her eyebrows now an uppercase.

"It's good to see you. A lot of you." She hugs him. A few seconds go by. *Time to let go, Harper.*

Ethan extracts himself from her embrace. His cheeks are pink. *Finally, someone besides me is blushing.*

"I left my shirt in the living room. I'll go grab it."

Ethan hurries out, and Harper grabs my arm. Her nails dig in.

"Start talking," she hisses. "And don't tell me you were just sleeping. Your door was closed."

I shoot her a dirty look. Ethan walks back in and stands next to me, resting his hand on my hip. When I look at him, I see twinkling in his eyes. I didn't know that was possible, but I swear I see it. My heartbeats pick up speed.

"So, Ethan, Kate's unable to talk right now because her nether regions are pulsating wildly." She levels her gaze at him, ignoring the shock and horror on my face. "Fill me in on how you came to sleep in her bed. And why your arm is around her right now. It appears she's been holding out on me."

Red. Beet red. Tomato red. Lobster red. A fire burns on my face. *How could Harper say that?* Ethan and I didn't have sex. Not that the thought didn't cross my mind. We're in love, he was in my bed, and it's not like we're strangers. *Still...* He didn't make a move, and neither did I.

Ethan, calm and unruffled like always, focuses on the last part of Harper's statement. "Kate and I have realized we're in love."

Harper's eyebrows lift, her expression dubious. She snaps her fingers. "Just like that?"

Again, Ethan is unruffled by Harper's less than excited response. "I've loved her for ten years."

Harper sips her drink. "We all know that."

"Harper!" My temper flares.

She sips again and shrugs. "You guys are crazy. Good luck."

She walks from the room without a backwards glance.

Ethan shakes his head. "It's possible she's worse than Trent."

I stare at her bedroom door. "Sometimes I want to shake some sensitivity into her." I settle for filling two glasses with ice and helping myself to Harper's pitcher of tea.

"I have another way you can blow off some steam." Ethan takes his glass and chugs until only ice cubes are left.

Is he talking about what I think he's talking about? Because I haven't shaved my legs in two days. And...and... and I need more time to plan.

"Camelback, Kate. Let's hike Camelback." He tilts his head to the side. "What did you think I was talking about?" His lips press together, and his mouth turns up at the ends.

"Nothing," I lie.

Ethan smirks.

"What?" I demand.

"For the record, I know you're lying."

I lift my nose in the air and stick out my lower lip. "No, you don't."

"I know you by heart."

Yes, you do.

Ethan sets our glasses on the counter and pulls me into his arms. "Don't let what she said get to you, okay?" His voice is a whisper in my ear.

"She said we're crazy. What if she's right?"

I feel his head shake. "Go get dressed for hiking. I have something to show you."

***

AN HOUR later we're on the mountain. It's only March, but the sun is warm in the cloudless sky.

Ethan laughs when I set the wide brimmed hat on my head.

"Don't make fun of me. I don't want skin cancer. Or premature wrinkles." I double check my little backpack.

"Did you remember the kitchen sink?"

"You'll be happy I packed this thing when you get hungry at the top. You better be nice or I won't share my energy bar with you."

Ethan bows with a flourish. "My dearest Kate, please excuse my bad behavior. I sincerely hope you choose to share your gluten free, dairy free, taste free bar with me."

"Shut up." I start for the trailhead.

Ethan falls into step beside me and grabs my hand. "How many times have we hiked Camelback?"

"I don't know. At least thirty. Why?"

"Because we've been on this mountain at least thirty times, and I've never been able to do this." He grabs me, bends me over backward, and kisses me.

I cling to him for two reasons. One, I don't want to fall. Two, I'm desperate to keep kissing him.

When he lifts me back to upright, I'm panting.

Ethan's lips quirk. "Already out of breath? I think you're going to have trouble on this mountain."

I snatch my hat that fell when he bent me over, shove it

on my head, and start walking. "My mouth was just attacked."

Ethan walks behind me. "Don't let the Saguaro that's fallen onto the path attack you. Ouch."

I look ahead and see the mammoth cactus draped across the path. It looks sorrowful, lying on the ground where it once stood so tall and proud.

"Ethan?" I step over the fallen cactus. "Why don't you like to talk about the Army?" I wait for him to shut down like he always does. I know I'm asking a loaded question.

He takes off his baseball cap and wipes his forehead with the sleeve of his T-shirt. Buying time, probably. He sighs.

"It's not that I don't like it. It's just that people act so indebted to me. I appreciate the recognition, but the attention gets uncomfortable."

"I guess I can understand that." My response is drawn out as I consider his words. "I'm not a huge fan of attention either."

We continue our climb, a peaceful quiet falling over us. This is one of a thousand reasons why I love Ethan. Our comfortable silences are as rich as a conversation.

Finally we make it to the top. I look west. The little plots of farmland captivate me. Green squares in a city full of red-tile roof homes and outdoor shopping malls. They stayed put while progress crept up and overtook the area around them. I admire the fortitude.

"Kate, I want you to turn in a circle and look at all the homes, schools, businesses, cars on freeways, and planes in the air."

I'd love to know why I'm doing this before I agree, but I do as I'm told.

Ethan stands behind me, his arms coming over my

shoulders. He holds me with one arm across my clavicle, the other makes a sweeping motion.

"How many people live in the Phoenix metro area?"

"Seven million." There is no hesitation in my response. It's part of my job to stay current on local demographics.

"You know that self-obsessed, inconsiderate twit who just called us crazy?"

My head jerks to the side as I gape at Ethan. I nod slowly.

"She's just one of the seven million people who live here. And I don't give a shit about her opinion."

He spins me around and takes the hat off my head. His eyes burn into mine, his face more serious than I've ever seen it.

"We are not crazy," he says. "Our paths were always going to join. We are meant to be together. Why do you think I waited for you? Not because I'm stupid, or stubborn, or loyal. Because I knew you were the one. And there was no way I was going to let your denial change my mind. And I won't let Harper's negativity get to you." Ethan presses his hand over my heart. "Follow your heart, not your head."

Tears roll down my face as I listen to my best friend. His passion, his energy, his love. All for me.

Ethan wipes my tears. "Why are you crying?"

"I've never seen you like this. I thought I knew everything about you, but... You're so passionate." My whole body is alight with wonder for this new person in front of me.

"It's you, Kate. You bring it out in me."

I sniff. "I wish you didn't have to go back."

Ethan sighs, the sound heavy. He lays his cheek on top of my head. "Me too."

I eye the two day old stubble on his neck, already missing him even though he's right here. A plane flies into my field of vision, drawing my attention to the city below us. "Thank you for bringing me up here." I watch the plane drop lower in preparation for landing. "I needed the perspective."

He kisses my hair. My Ethan. He's right. Harper's is one infinitesimal, unimportant opinion. She's my roommate. And my friend. But she's not my Ethan.

We aren't crazy. We're right. And nothing is going to stop us now.

6

ETHAN

She did it. Kate Masters is finally in love with me. For Kate to do something that doesn't make perfect sense to her is a feat. But she did it. *That's how much she loves me.*

I'd never say this out loud, but I think I finally understand the meaning of a singing heart. My chest feels full, like my heart is belting out a deep, joyful melody. My dream has come true.

Before my longest, most heartfelt wish was granted, Kate attempted to let me go. She's practical to a fault. Trying so hard to do what she thought would be best for me. *No way.* I didn't wait a decade just to accept defeat so easily. I'm a fighter.

I watched, held my breath, as Kate's mouth formed the words I've been waiting forever to hear. *I'm sorry I made you wait so long. I love you. I'm in love with you.*

Kissing her. *Holy shit.* Now that was literally a dream come true. I've lost count of all the dreams she's starred in. And today I learned the real thing is better. Way better.

We're on our way to my parents' house now. Kate's been

quiet the whole drive. The air is charged with a palpable nervousness.

"Your parents are going to be happy when they find out about us, right?" Kate bites her lip as she gets off the freeway.

I can't figure out why she's nervous. My parents have known her since she was five, and my mom considers her the daughter she never had.

At this point all I can do is roll my eyes at her. "That's a really dumb question."

She smacks my arm.

I laugh, hands held up. "Okay, okay. Yes, they're going to be happy."

She nods, mollified.

I can't wait for my mom's reaction. She's going to do cartwheels when she finds out Kate and I have finally found our way to each other.

Kate puts the car in park in my parents' driveway and takes a deep breath. "How should we tell them? Should we sit them down?"

"A sit-down is for bad news." I move through scenarios in my mind. "Maybe I could kiss you in front of them and let them react."

"Your mother would have a coronary. So would mine."

"Is your mom coming over?"

"When isn't she over?"

"Good point. Let's just go in there and let it happen naturally."

Kate looks dubious.

"You don't need to control the flow of information on this one night, okay?" My eyebrows rise, waiting for her agreement.

"Okay." Her laugh is forced, but at least she's trying. "But just this one time. Don't start thinking you're going to win every disagreement now that we're more than friends."

We start for the front door, pausing once we reach the welcome mat. I rub her shoulders with my hands and look into her eyes. "Are we more than friends?"

Alarm widens her eyes. "Yes. I think being in love with each other changes the status of our friendship."

I smirk at her dryness. "How much more than friends are we at this point?"

"Well... I..." She looks flustered.

My hands move up to her face, my thumbs stroke her cheekbones. "I'm not just your best friend anymore. And I'm so much more than your boyfriend. I'm your forever."

Kate nods, eyes closed. "Yes," she breathes.

My chest is pressed against hers, and through our clothes, I feel her heartbeats. My lips are on hers, and my insides erupt in triumph. *I'm kissing the girl I've been in love with for almost half my life.* Unbelievable.

Kate trembles, sighs my name into my own mouth, and all I want to do is take her somewhere and keep learning more about my best friend. *My forever.*

The front door flies open, and my mother stands there, gaping at us with shocked eyes and a hand clutched to her chest. My dad is next to her, smiling.

"Seriously?" Her voice is a happy squeal.

Kate attempts to step away from me, but I tighten my grip. I'm not letting her go. Kate's red face looks up at me, deer in the headlights, but I'm smiling.

My mom makes a whooping sound, performs a goofy dance, and pokes my dad in the ribs with her elbow. "I told you, James." Her voice is proud and satisfied.

Dad grins. "Congratulations, you two." He gives me a look that says he knows this is a victory for me.

I smile back. "Thanks, Dad."

Mom opens her mouth, but her eyes fall on something behind us and instead lifts her arm, waving. I turn with Kate, keeping our embrace.

Kate's mom has just crossed the street and is walking through my front yard. Her mouth hangs open, palms up, and she's shaking her head.

"Ethan, my daughter is in your arms." She looks at Kate and then back to me. "Who wants to tell me why you two look like more than friends?"

"It's because they are!" My mom shouts from behind us. She bypasses me and Kate and hurries forward, hooking her elbow through Linda's arm.

"See, Linda?" She stage-whispers to Kate's mom. "I've been telling you for years that it would happen."

Linda eyes Kate, her lips pursed in a smile. "Yeah, but my daughter can be stubborn."

Kate groans. "Hi, Mom."

Linda grabs Kate's hands, pulling her from me. She smiles at Kate, tears shining in her eyes. "Your dad would approve."

Kate nods, and my heart hammers in my chest. I watch Kate's face, waiting for the telltale signs that her heart is hurting. I see her gulp, her eyes squint. But she straightens her shoulders and smiles. *My strong Kate.* If I had to guess, I'd bet she's telling herself there's no reason to be upset.

My mom pokes my shoulder with her pink fingernail. "I told you, too, didn't I? When you were nineteen and telling me how you felt. I told you to wait for her, that she was worth it, and one day she'd realize she's in love with you."

Kate's face is crimson in an instant.

"All right, all right," I say. "Let's give Kate a break."

"Aww, look at you, defending her already." My mom

smiles her sweetest smile. "Wait a minute." Her face gets serious. "Kate, did this happen when you stayed last night? Did my invitation make this happen?" She clasps her hands at her chest, her shoulders squeezing together.

I shake my head. "Mom, no. Come on."

"Well, I just wanted to take credit, if that's what happened."

My dad laughs and kisses her cheek. "Give them a break, Evie. Ethan, do you want us to close this door again? It looked like you two were enjoying yourselves."

I cough once. "No, we're good. Thanks for the...uh... offer." Even I'm starting to get embarrassed.

"Come inside." Mom motions us in. "This time I didn't burn dinner. But that's only because I made a salad."

We settle into our evening, and I feel good. I'll try not to think about how, now that I've finally won Kate's heart, there's a clock counting down the minutes until I have to leave her.

***

"Don't stop now, old man." I pass the ball to my dad. He's bent over and breathing heavily.

"Who are you calling *old man*? I can still beat you." He runs forward into a layup and sinks the shot.

"Game," I yell across the court. "Nice work, Dad."

"Thanks. I'll just wait over here for your high five." He rests his hands on bent knees, dragging in heavy breaths.

I chuckle, jog over to him, and extend my hand. "Wouldn't want to leave the princess waiting."

He straightens and shakes my hand. "Grab two beers for the king and his loyal subject. Let's talk."

I run inside to the kitchen. Kate's voice floats in from the dining room, where she sits with our moms.

"I don't know what happened. Honestly. Suddenly I was just in love with him."

Now this is an interesting conversation. Kate hasn't told me how it happened. As much as I want to stick around to eavesdrop, my dad's waiting for me. Two bottles in hand, I go back outside.

"Cheers," he says.

We tap our bottles together.

He looks up at the sky, where the pink and purple sunset grows darker. "How are you feeling about going to Afghanistan?"

Not great, especially now that Kate's finally in love with me. But I can't say that. He's an ex-Marine, and a damn proud one. I want him to know I share his love for our country. I just also happen to love Kate a hell of a lot too.

"Hoo-rah." I use my military voice.

He touches the bottom of his bottle to mine. I tip it up and finish, the beer flowing smoothly down my throat. *This deployment better end smoothly too.*

***

HARPER ISN'T HOME TONIGHT—THANK God—and Kate doesn't expect her back for a long time.

We're lying on the couch in the living room, Kate's head on my chest. My body clock is adjusted enough that I'm not drooping like I was last night.

"Let's plan the rest of my leave." I look out the window as I speak. Kate's apartment is on the second floor and has a sliver of a mountain in her view. "Now that I know how head-over-heels in love with me you are, I think my visit is going to be a little different."

She reaches forward and kisses the tip of my nose. How my heart stays in my chest, I really don't know. I'm so high on life, so high on Kate, my heart feels like it could shoot straight out of me and catapult into the stars.

I'm brought right back down to earth when I hear the front door open. Harper stomps into the living room and peers down at us over the back of the couch with a look of disgust.

"If I ask you guys to come out with me tonight, are you going to act all lovey-dovey like this?"

Kate looks at Harper, nonplussed. "Depends. Where are you considering asking us to go?"

"A party a friend of mine planned. But if you're going to embarrass me with your canoodling, then you're not allowed to attend."

As though we're dying to go.

Kate pushes herself up on one hand and glances at me, unsure. "How late will we have to stay?"

Harper snorts. "What does that matter? You're off work until Ethan leaves."

Kate blushes. "It was just a question."

Harper, not shockingly, doesn't notice Kate's blush.

"You won't spontaneously combust if you stay up late." Harper grins at Kate. "Promise." She makes a monkey face at Kate, and it works. Kate giggles, and the sound is adorable.

Harper's expression goes back to normal. "I'll take your lack of a no as a yes."

Kate turns to me. "Are you okay with going out tonight? It's already kind of late." She bites her lip. *What else is going through her mind?* I'd give anything to be a mind reader, just for five seconds.

I shrug, about to speak, but Harper cuts me off.

"You guys are already an old, boring couple. I have to go get ready before I catch the couple disease."

She walks to her room, and I've never been happier to see a door close.

I roll my eyes. "She hasn't changed a bit."

"She's good for me. She makes me less serious."

"I like your serious side." Kate's seriousness is what contributes to her unfaltering loyalty. "I also like your funny side. And your sweet side. And your backside."

Kate laughs and snuggles into me. She smells perfect. Like my Katie girl.

"You're crazy," she says.

"Crazy about you."

"Ugh," she groans. "What a line."

"Did it work?"

"Of course."

"What's my prize?"

"A bouncy ball from one of those toy machines?"

"I have a much better prize in mind."

Kate's blush is back and in full force. I brush my fingertips across her cheeks.

"Why are you blushing?"

She shakes her head. *She won't tell me because she can't say the words.* I'm starting to get an idea about why she's acting like this. It happens every time she talks about being physical with me, even just kissing. Like Harper's comment yesterday about Kate's pulsating nether regions. Kate was redder than I've ever seen her. She wasn't just embarrassed...

The puzzle pieces fall into place. *Kate wants to have sex with me.*

My pulse picks up, and my breath comes faster. I want to make love to Kate. For years I've dreamed about it. But the moment has to be perfect. Not forced at all. As long as I've waited for her, there's no way I'm rushing the first time I get to experience her body.

Summoning all my strength, I shut down my urge to pick her up and carry her to the bedroom right now. "You're my prize."

She smiles that beautiful smile, and the little scar on her forehead shifts. She lifts her head from my chest, her perfect pink lips, moist and waiting. My best friend. My forever. My Katie girl.

7

KATE

TIME PASSED TOO QUICKLY. ONE DAY ETHAN WAS JUST arriving, and the next he was preparing to leave. Suddenly his inevitable departure was no longer a gray cloud in the distance that we tried to ignore. We'd done so much during his time here, our attempt at turning ten days into more.

Our days were taken up with visiting Ethan's parents, which invariably meant my mom too. It wasn't too soon after we arrived at the Shepherds' house that my mom would walk in, fresh from a short stroll across the street. I feared Ethan's parent's might feel frustrated at their lack of alone time with their son, but they seemed to have a "more the merrier" kind of attitude. We spent our mornings swimming and our afternoons napping. It felt like childhood again.

The nights were reserved for me and Ethan. If his parents objected, they didn't show it. Every day we left their house after Ethan showered and changed for the night, and they seemed happy as they waved goodbye.

After a stop at my apartment, where I showered and

changed too, we were off to do whatever Ethan declared was his heart's desire.

One evening we went for drinks with old friends from high school. It wasn't unusual for them to see us show up together, of course, but they all wore a shocked expression when Ethan leaned over to kiss me. Everyone except Zane, that is. He winked at me and smiled. And then we ordered another round of drinks, because they all wanted to toast to the fact that Ethan had finally won my heart.

Another night we drove way north of the city, so far up the interstate we were long past even the sparsest section of suburban sprawl. Ethan followed a dirt road that looked like it would keep winding into the mountains if we stayed on it. On a blanket laid over the hood of my car, we sat beneath a night sky black as ink and scattered with the breathtaking twinkling of millions of stars. With our backs leaning against the windshield we talked for hours, about everything and nothing. Creosote perfumed the air with its resinous scent. Ethan leaned over me, and when his lips touched mine, all I could smell was him.

Today is my ninth and final full day with Ethan. The euphoria of the last nine days has given way to a sense of dread tinged with melancholy.

Tomorrow Ethan will leave. He'll fly out in the morning on a flight bound for JFK. From there he'll make the long trek back to Germany, and then on to Afghanistan, to the danger and duty that awaits him. And I'll be here, clinging to my belief that somehow he'll be safe from harm. But the truth is, I'm terrified.

I don't mention my fear to Ethan. He doesn't like talking about leaving, and I don't want that negativity hovering over our last night together. Besides, his personal safety isn't the only thing weighing heavily on my mind tonight.

If Ethan's thinking along the same lines as me, he's not letting on. And I'm way too embarrassed to actually say the words out loud.

Ethan's freshly washed after his shower, and my hair is still ratty from the chlorine of his parents' pool. We're in the living room at their house when Evie walks in.

"What's on the agenda for you kids tonight?" She smiles at us as she settles herself into a chair.

"I don't really know, Mom." Ethan finds my hand and squeezes it. "We might just be lying low."

Evie's lips purse as she regards him with a pensive expression. She sighs and leans slightly forward. "Your dad and I were thinking it would be fun to go out to dinner, all of us. Including your mom, of course, Kate," she adds. "But if you don't want to—"

"Sounds fun to me." I'm quick to agree. I've been feeling guilty about monopolizing Ethan's time.

"Great." Evie jumps from her chair. "I'll call your mom." She walks into the kitchen, opens the back door, and I hear her yell to her husband. "James, the kids want to go to dinner."

Warmth floods over me. I love being a part of "the kids." First, because Ethan's an only child, and it's sweet that she includes me in a category that only Ethan rightfully occupies, and second, because we're both twenty-five, and she's been calling us that for twenty years.

"Are you okay with this?" Ethan looks at me with concern.

"Why wouldn't I be?" I ask.

Ethan looks uncomfortable. "I wasn't sure if you had anything planned for tonight. I just wanted to make sure my mom wasn't stepping on your toes."

Is his mind in the same place as mine? *Most* guys would

have put the moves on me by now. But there's nothing typical about Ethan, so I have no idea what he's thinking.

"My toes are still intact." I point down and wiggle them in my sandals. "Your mom and dad probably feel like they haven't seen you at all this leave, thanks to me. I should have said I had something to take care of so you three could have some alone time." I don't really mean it, but it sounds nice.

"Nah." Ethan waves away my suggestion. "We're a package deal."

Package deal. Oh, my heart.

"I love that. And I love you." I lean over to kiss him.

"Oh, my!" I catch sight of myself in the mirror behind Ethan's head. "I'm going to try and make myself presentable. Tell your mom I'll be ready soon." I grab my purse and head up the stairs to Ethan's old bathroom.

***

HERE WE ARE. Back at my apartment. *Oh boy.* Dinner was... interesting. We were both distracted. Evie mislabeled it as sadness that we had to say goodbye tomorrow, and I wasn't about to correct her.

My stomach is a ball of nerves, and I'm betting Ethan's is too.

I head for the bathroom as soon as we walk through the front door. The chlorine from the pool earlier is making my skin and scalp itch.

I take my time in the shower, letting the hot water work over the tension I'm carrying in my shoulders and back. Slowly the knots begin to unfold as my mind mulls over our situation.

On one hand, it might seem like we're rushing things if

we sleep together tonight. The rational side of me knows we have the rest of our lives to do that, and we don't have to rush things because Ethan's going to be gone for the next ten months. I want things between us to be perfect, and maybe having sex so soon in our relationship isn't a good idea.

On the other hand, why stop ourselves? I like the idea of throwing caution to the wind and doing what *feels* good. So much of my life has been spent doing what I thought was right. I could have lost Ethan because I thought I was following the rules of friendship. Telling Ethan I love him was the bravest and most indulgent thing I've ever done.

Harper's not coming home tonight. She's planning to stay at her friend's house. I know she made plans on purpose, to let me and Ethan have some alone time. Which I suppose tells me exactly what she thinks should happen between Ethan and me tonight.

Quit overthinking this. I take a deep breath, my mind made up.

Now the question is, how are we supposed to get from this point to *that* point? The fluttering in my stomach starts back up again.

We could talk about it...but that might really detract from the romance of it all. And I want our first time to be special. Okay, so no talking about what's going on.

Maybe I can let Ethan know in a non-verbal way. That way I save both of us the extreme embarrassment of turning this into something I will no doubt overanalyze and remove all the excitement from.

I finish my shower, dry off, and head for the top drawer of my dresser. I'm hunting for something satin and lace. The fabric feels so unfamiliar against my skin that I know it as soon as my hand brushes against it.

I lift it into the air, inspecting it. It's bright yellow, which will complement the deep tan I've acquired from all my time by the pool this week, and it reaches to just above mid-thigh. The neckline is sweetheart, and the irony has me grinning wickedly. It's a bit of an oxymoron, as *sweetheart* is not the word I'd use to describe the way the lingerie makes me feel. *Sexy, brazen, tempting.*

Is it really me feeling those things?

Off go the tags, and I pull it over my head. Silently I thank Harper, who was the one to insist a woman needs to own items such as this, even if they're buying it for no one in particular. After a year in the back of a drawer, it's finally seeing the light of day.

I look in the mirror, and my stomach instantly bundles back up into a tight ball of nerves. My confidence wavers. Who is this person wearing this lingerie? For Ethan, of all people.

His knock interrupts my freak out.

"Yeah?" My voice sounds strained.

"You okay? You've been in there for a long time. I just wanted to make sure you didn't slip and hit your head or something." Ethan sounds nervous.

"I'm good. I'll be out in a sec." I press my ear up against the bedroom door, listening for his retreat.

Once I know he's gone, I take a deep breath. Then I take two more.

I shove all my reservations out of my head and open the door. Showtime.

Ethan's on the couch, his back to me. A few steps carry me away from the safety of my door. He hasn't turned around yet. I clear my throat.

Ethan's head swivels. His eyes grow wide, his mouth falls open.

"What do you think?" I round the couch and stand in front of him. I've never been so daring in my whole life, and I'm striving to keep my bravado from cracking.

"Um... Yeah." Ethan coughs. "You look...wow." He coughs again.

"We didn't talk about it, you know, but I just thought..." My voice trails off. Apparently neither of us possesses the ability to finish a sentence.

Ethan nods. He finally looks into my eyes. "I can't believe how beautiful you are."

We stare at each other, silent, absorbing this moment.

Ethan reaches for the blanket sitting balled up on the couch beside him and throws it off to the side. His eyes sweep to the now empty spot beside him.

"Is that an invitation to sit?" I tease. My voice is husky.

Again, Ethan glances back down to the empty spot, a small grin on his face.

My first instinct is to hop onto the sofa next to him, but I need to be mindful of my current outfit. Instead, I lower myself down next to him, tuck my legs underneath me and face him so we're eye to eye.

Ethan reaches for my face as soon as I'm settled next to him. His fingers run through my wet hair, and he places light kisses on my forehead, my eyelids, my nose, my cheeks. He skips over my mouth, his lips landing on the hollow of my throat. I tip my head back, exposing the delicate length of skin. Ethan's hand comes to rest at the back of my head, supporting it while his other hand traces a design from my ear down to my collarbone and across to my shoulder.

I hear myself sigh in satisfaction. Instinctively the blood begins to pool in my cheeks. It's a natural reaction to not only what I'm doing, but to *whom* I'm doing it with.

Ethan's head lifts from my neck, and he pulls back, his eyes thirsty and drinking me in.

"That blush makes you look even more beautiful." He leans forward and I feel his smile against my lips. His kiss is long and deep, and leaves me wanting so much more.

I pull back, reach for the bottom of his shirt, then lift it past his torso and over his shoulders.

My hands skim over his chest, coming to rest at his shoulders. So big and broad. Automatically, I feel safe in the arms of my best friend. *My Ethan.* I pour myself into kissing him, my body pressed up against his.

Ethan hands aren't moving beneath my collarbone, and though I'm no expert at this, I do know that at some point they have to. Maybe he's just really nervous.

I pull away again. Our eyes locked, I drag my arm through one flimsy strap. Ethan's hand shoots out to stop me as I'm pulling my arm through the second strap.

"I'm sorry, was I ruining your plan?" I smile at him. Quickly my grin turns south. Ethan looks uncomfortable.

"What's wrong?"

He bites his lip, and not in a sexy way. Worry etches lines in his forehead.

Embarrassment fills me. Obviously I made a mistake in being so forward. I look down at myself, mortified. I wish I were covered up by more than the scanty yellow lace and satin.

Ethan's head drops into his hands. "Arrrrgh," he groans, the sound full of frustration. "This is so stupid." He shakes his head as it lies in his palms.

"What's stupid, Ethan?" I'm trying to be patient, but it's hard. I really want something to wrap around myself. I could easily go to my room and get my robe, or use the blanket that Ethan tossed somewhere, but that requires me to get up, showcasing the skimpy outfit even more. I'll just have to stay put for now.

"I want to do this with you, Kate. I really do. I promise. Which is why I'm an idiot." Ethan's voice is angry, an anger I know is directed internally. Finally, he lifts his head from his hands and looks at me warily. "You look so beautiful. No guy would turn you down."

"No guy but you." I say it under my breath, but I mean for Ethan to hear me.

It's immature, but my feelings are hurt. If I'd known Ethan was going to run off stage in the middle of the play, I certainly wouldn't have gone to such great lengths. *I'm wearing freaking lingerie!* I look down at myself. This little number would have remained mostly forgotten in the back of my drawer, but I thought he and I were on the same page. Tears sting my eyes.

"Kate, why are you crying?" Ethan looks genuinely perplexed.

"Why ask, Ethan? Isn't it obvious?" I point down at what is now clearly a ridiculous and embarrassing outfit. "Being rejected sucks. And it sucks even more when you're not only rejected by your boyfriend, but rejected by him while you're wearing an outfit that should make him do the opposite!" Another tear rolls down my face.

"Katie, now you're the idiot." Ethan looks at me with exasperation.

"Name calling isn't making this mortifying situation any better." I sniff. I need a tissue. At least that's in arms length of me. I pull a few from the box on the coffee table. Briefly I consider fashioning a cover and making my escape to my bedroom, where I can grab some clothes and have this conversation without being practically naked.

"Of course I want to do this with you!" Ethan's voice rises. He goes back to looking frustrated and worried.

My hands come out in front of me, palms up, asking the question, *"What's the problem, then?"*

"The issue is that I'm not sure it's the best thing for us yet. I've been going over it in my head all night. Believe me, I want to. Look at you," Ethan's eyes rake over me. I cross my arms over my chest.

"I would prefer you not look at me right now."

Ethan smiles apologetically. "I'm sorry, Kate. I didn't mean to make you feel rejected. It's really not you, I promise. It's me."

"It's not you, it's me." I echo sarcastically.

"Katie..." Ethan looks at me pleadingly.

I melt. "Fine, I believe you. It's you. You're the crazy one."

"Yes, I am. I've been fantasizing about you for years. Believe me, the next steps have been mapped out in my head for a very long time. And I want to take those next steps, I promise, but for some reason, I just can't." He pinches the bridge of his nose. "It's hard to explain. Mostly I don't want to rush anything. I want everything to be perfect for us, and it seems needless to hurry something like this. Am I making sense?" Ethan's intense gaze implores me.

"I suppose you make sense." *I had the same reservations.* "It would have been nice if you had told me what you were thinking. *Before* I embarrassed myself with this dumb outfit." I gesture with disgust at my racy article of clothing.

He shakes his head emphatically. "I love what you're wearing, Kate. Please don't be embarrassed. Actually"—he smiles, fingering the strap still lying lifelessly against my arm—"I hope there's a lot more where this came from."

I swat his hand away, trying hard not to think about how good those hands and lips were making me feel a few minutes ago. It's even more difficult not to think about how much better it could have gotten. Roughly I yank the strap back up over my shoulder.

"Well, keep hoping. This is the one piece of lingerie I own." I'm pouting now, and the embarrassment creeps back. My cheeks grow hot again.

"Maybe we can fix that." His looks optimistic with his eyebrows raised and his top teeth digging into his lower lip.

"Why? So we can *not* have sex again in the future? Ethan, maybe you're unaware of the point of this"—I gesture down to the yellow fabric—"but it implies a certain ending." I lift my eyebrows suggestively, then trade the look for a serious face. "And this isn't it."

He laughs in response. "Kate, I love you. I know you're embarrassed. And you hate being embarrassed. It's okay. I'm really sorry I made you feel self-conscious. Now, listen to me." He grabs my shoulders, his grip gentle. "You are beyond sexy and beautiful, especially with that on, and I very much want to make love to you. I've already explained why I can't, so I won't say it again. But in the future, when I'm done with the Army and we don't have to feel like we're rushing anything, we'll finish what we started tonight. And you will have a drawer full of this stuff." Ethan gathers a handful of the lace barely covering my thighs. "I promise, I like it. A lot."

"Fine." I sniff theatrically. He laughs at me.

I climb off the couch and turn for my room. His hand catches mine.

"Where are you going?"

"To change." I tug my hand, but he's not letting go.

"Can't you keep that on?" He looks hopeful.

"Um, no."

"Please? I like torture." Ethan raises one eyebrow, emphasizing his appeal.

Hmm... My pride is still wounded from the rejection Ethan assures me isn't really a rejection. I grin, feeling wicked. This is going to be fun.

"You like torture?" I ask innocently, cocking my head to the side.

Ethan's head bobs in confirmation. I smile sweetly at him.

"Well, in that case..." I stop pulling against his hand that's holding me back. I place my free hand on his chest and push him back against the couch. Ethan's eyes widen, and he drops my other hand.

"Wha...?"

"Shhh, it's okay. You like torture. You said so yourself." I bat my eyelashes coquettishly. Placing my hands on Ethan's shoulders I sink down on his lap, so that my legs hug either side of his body. Ethan's still shirtless, so I run my fingertips over his perfect chest and down his abs. I circle back up his arms to his shoulders, pressing into him gently, and place my lips right next to his ear. Softly I sigh.

Ethan groans. The sound is frustrated, but it's a little something else, too. I take this as encouragement, moving my lips from his ear to his mouth. Lightly I run my tongue across the length of his lower lip, taking it in my mouth and giving it a tiny little bite. Ethan groans again. This time the sound is a whole lot less frustrated and a whole lot more of the something else I heard before. I pull back, satisfied Ethan has suffered enough.

He looks at my amused smile. I know I look satisfied. And I don't care. Ethan leans his head back on the couch and closes his eyes.

"Go change, Kate. Please, put on something that covers

you head to toe. Otherwise..." His unfinished sentence hangs in the air.

I would like for Ethan to complete his sentence, preferably using a physical demonstration. My plan had been to torture him a little, let him get just a small taste of what he was postponing to an undetermined later date, but it wasn't easy on me either. Only my desire to respect Ethan's feelings is keeping me from suggesting he finish his sentence.

I climb off Ethan's lap. "One muumuu, coming up."

He doesn't respond.

I glance back over my shoulder before walking into my bedroom. Ethan's head is still laid back on the couch, eyes closed.

8

ETHAN

"Fooood," Kate grumbles through a sleepy haze. "Coffee."

"Yes, both of those things are in your near future if you get up. We're supposed to meet my parents in twenty minutes." Gently I tug her arm.

I know she's going to remember last night the moment she's fully awake. I don't want her to feel embarrassed, but I know she will. I hated the rejection in her eyes, but it had to happen. Our first time together needs to be more special than she can ever imagine it.

Stopping her was probably the hardest thing I've ever done. Her skin was soft, and so much of it was visible. That yellow lingerie she had on was mind-blowing. It doesn't matter that I've seen her in a bikini at least a hundred times. What she wore last night was for my eyes only.

I see the faint pink in Kate's cheeks, but I ignore it. She doesn't want to re-hash last night, and neither do I. It took every ounce of self-control for me to sleep next to her and not go back on my words. If we start talking about it again this morning, who knows what'll happen? My patience and restraint stores are almost depleted.

Kate's stomach growls, and it's exactly what I need to hear to kick me out of her warm bed. I swing my legs over the side, yawning hugely as I stand.

"You have to hurry," I remind her again.

I look down at the bed where Kate's stretching and making these adorable mewling sounds.

"We overslept." I bend to kiss the top of her head. "I'm going to change. I'll see you out there in a minute, okay?"

She nods and throws back the covers. I leave to give her privacy and grab clothes from the bag that's in her living room.

It's probably good we overslept. It means less time for moping. I'm leaving today, and the less I think about it the better.

While Kate gets ready I send a message to my mom telling her we're running behind. Then I look around to make sure I have everything. And I do. I've left nothing behind. Except my white T-shirt. And my heart.

***

BREAKFAST with my parents is good, but sad too. By the time our order arrives my mom's crying. She sits across from me, attempting to wipe her eyes surreptitiously. Nobody's fooled.

"Mom, it's only ten more months. And then it's all over." I know my words fall on deaf ears.

"I know, I know. Can't a mom be emotional over her son? Her only child?" She tries to smile, but another tear slips out.

I hand her a new napkin. She balls up her used one and adds it to the small but quickly growing mound on the table in front of her.

"Let's talk about you two." She changes the subject.

I take the bait. "What about us?"

"When's the wedding?" She grins, a little of her usual spunkiness showing through.

My dad pretends to choke on his orange juice. "Come on, Evelyn, try to give the kids some space to be crazy about each other before they go making it binding by law." He winks at Mom.

I like hearing him use her full first name. He's the only person who ever does.

Dad turns to me. "Sorry, son, I tried to stop her. She wouldn't listen to me." He lifts his hands up in defeat.

"It's okay. She's a steamroller."

My arm goes around Kate, pulling her in closer.

"The answer is, there isn't a wedding. Yet." I'm speaking to my mom but looking down at Kate.

Kate's eyes grow wide. "Yet?" She squeaks out the word.

"I waited a long time for you. I won't wait even a quarter that long to make you my wife."

Kate takes a big gulp of breath, her chest heaves. And her eyes shine.

"I love you," she mouths.

"Ahhh!" My mom yells from across the booth. Kate jumps.

For a second I forgot we had an audience. But I don't care that my parents saw our conversation. I'm not ashamed to love Kate and want her to be my wife.

Mom claps her hands with delight. "I always knew you two would get together. I just knew if Ethan held out long enough, you would come around."

Kate turns red. It's going to take her a long time to live that down.

"Sorry, sorry, I know you embarrass easily." My mom reaches across the table to pat Kate's hand. "Let's talk about your birthdays. Ethan, you're going to miss it again this year, so I'll have Kate blow out the candles for both of you. But next year the ritual continues."

"Yes, ma'am." I salute her. I'm looking forward to the day when Kate and I can celebrate a birthday together again. It's been three years since we blew out each other's candles.

When it's time to go, we linger over goodbye's in the parking lot. Kate offers to let my parents take me to the airport, but I shoot her a dirty look.

"I don't want to say goodbye to you in a diner parking lot," I whisper sternly in her ear.

My mom, being the very aware person that she is, declines Kate's offer. "We have some errands to run. It's okay. You take him."

Dad leans in for a quick hug, clapping me on the back with a few loud smacks. He's not a fan of long goodbyes. According to him, the best breaks are clean, and he always says goodbye the same way. Quick hug, three claps on the back, and a gruff "I love you, son."

Mom's a different story. I have to unwrap her heavy arms and step back from her. Dad goes to stand behind her, winding his arms around her waist. His purpose is probably to hold her back, but he's doing it under the guise of being a supportive husband.

"I'll call you soon, Mom. I love you, and I'll be home before you know it. Ten more months, and it's finished. I'll never have to go back again."

We climb in Kate's car, still waving and saying goodbye. The sun pours in my open window.

"I'll come by soon to visit," Kate promises my mom.

She nods, sniffling, trying to smile.

"I'll call you when I get to Germany," I tell her. I've already said this a dozen times this morning, but reminding her doesn't hurt.

Her smile is weak. She's crying too hard to talk anymore. As a unit my parents take a step back.

I wave as Kate puts the car in drive and heads for the 101.

***

THE AIRPORT COMES INTO VIEW, and suddenly, it looks like the enemy. Its goal is to take me away from Kate and send me to a desolate land filled with people who want to do me harm.

"I liked this place a whole lot more when I was here ten days ago." My dislike grows as Kate takes the ramp up to the Terminal Four parking garage.

Kate's voice is soft. "Me too."

She finds a spot on the fifth level and parks. Neither of us make a move.

"I don't want to get out." I stare out past the half wall of concrete at the mountain range in front of us. It looks too much like the place I'm headed.

"So don't." There's challenge in her voice.

We both ignore her statement. Being AWOL is the last thing we need.

Just ten months. If anybody can do it, Kate can. She's strong and loyal. *Kate can Master it.*

I turn my gaze from the mountains to her beautiful face. "This has been the best trip. Way better than all my other trips home, combined." I tug gently on the ponytail hanging over her shoulder.

"That's only because I let you kiss me this time." She tries to smile, but it doesn't develop into a real grin.

"That certainly had something to do with it." I hope my joke disguises how bleak I feel.

I listen to her laugh, work it into my memory, even though I already know all her laughs by heart. I'm adding this exact moment to my memory bank, cataloguing the view of the brown mountains, coupled with the smell of Kate's sweet scented lotion and the feel of the cool air as it flows from the air conditioning.

How am I supposed to say goodbye to her? She's taken me to the airport plenty of other times, and our goodbyes were always sad then, too, but this one is different.

"How do we do this, Ethan?" Kate's on my wave-length, as usual.

I think for a minute, then say, "I have a plan."

Kate loves plans. She likes parameters she can exist within.

"I'm going to get my bag out of your trunk, and leave it next to your car. After that I'm going to get back in my seat, kiss you, whisper a few sweet nothings in your ear, and say goodbye. Then I'll pick up my bag and walk inside." I raise my eyebrows at her, silently asking if she agrees.

She nods and looks relieved.

I do exactly what I said I would do. She pops open the trunk and watches in the rearview mirror as I remove my duffel and set it up against the side of the car. Then I get back in and sink into the seat with an audible thud.

"So." I turn to her, but I stop talking when I see her face. Her features are taut as she tries to hold herself together.

"Please don't cry, Katie."

"I'm not crying."

Liar.

I don't argue. Instead, I reach for her face, gently cupping her cheeks in my hands.

"I'll be back before you know it. Ten months, that's it. Then it's game on. Me and you." My voice rings with conviction.

Tears slip down her face, and I have to fight my own urge to cry. Kate needs another plan.

"Let's take a vacation when I get back. We can spend some time alone together. No distractions. We could go to Mexico? Or maybe Park City? It'll be winter when I get back."

Kate looks at me, a little pout pulling on her lower lip. "I know what you're doing. It's working."

I kiss her with a passion that consumes me. The fire in me fills her, the car, the whole damn airport. Every part of me is aflame as I kiss her. All the while, I silently pray it won't be the last time. And if it is... I've taken measures to make sure she's cared for.

She's breathless when I pull away. My mouth drifts over her cheek and to her ear. "Wait for me. I'll come for you." Tears sting my eyes.

"Stay," she murmurs.

If only I could.

"We'll get through this, and then it's me and you, forever. I love you." I'm trying to be strong, but a tear sneaks out and rolls down my cheek.

"I love you, Ethan."

"The time will fly by, and I'll be home soon. I love you," I say it again, because *oh my God,* I finally can.

"I love you, too." Her trickle of tears is now a gush.

I kiss her one more time and get out of the car. I swing

the duffel over my shoulder and walk. Each step moves me farther away from her, and closer to the danger awaiting me.

I don't look back. My situation has been decided, chosen by me three years ago. I knew what I was signing up for. I have a duty to uphold. I'm nothing if not loyal.

9

KATE

NINETY-ONE DAYS MARKED OFF ON THE *WAITING FOR ETHAN* calendar. Two hundred four more days to go. Time has taken on a whole new meaning to me now that I'm counting it. Every sunrise and sunset is quantifiable.

The first few days after he left were the hardest, but I began to feel better as my life slowly settled back into routine. I've been an all-star at work. I was running every morning until it got too hot. I visit Evie and James, I go shopping and hiking with Harper, and to dinner with my mom. I have Skype dates with Ethan on Mondays and Thursdays, unless he can't make it. Which happens frequently.

His emails are daily unless he's on a mission. Sometimes they're long and read like love letters, and other times they are short and sweet. I cherish every one of them.

Today is Thursday, so I've been antsy all day waiting for the work day to be over with. I have a six p.m. date with my boyfriend, and I can't wait. I did my work with one eye on the clock at all times, watching the minute hand move at a tortoise's speed. Finally, after an interminably long day, the clock struck five, and I hurried away from my desk.

The second I get into my apartment, I change out of my uncomfortable work clothes and toss down leftover chicken enchiladas from two nights ago. I hand Harper a plate of food and head for my room. I'm settled on my bed with my laptop, but I'm ten minutes early, so I kill time by perusing the day's news.

At six on the dot, I open up Skype and wait for Ethan.

Two minutes later, I get what I've been impatiently waiting for all day. One click of a button, and Ethan's face appears on my screen. He's smiling, but I can see by the set of his eyebrows something's bothering him.

"Hi, babe." His deep voice reaches through the computer and into my chest, triggering the warm feeling I always get when I hear it.

I wave enthusiastically. "Hello to you!"

"How are you?" Ethan asks. "How was work?" For the millionth time, I'm thankful for technology. It's as if he's here. Almost, anyway.

I smile as I take in the sight of his black hair and golden caramel eyes. In seven months Ethan will be here, and we can finally start the life we're meant to share.

"Thursdays are always long."

"Because you can't wait until it's Friday?" Ethan loves probing me. The familiar flame of embarrassment creeps onto my face, heating my cheeks. I really need to stop it with this embarrassment crap. I have nothing to be embarrassed about. As always, Ethan takes notice of my enflamed cheeks.

"Why are you blushing?"

"Because my impatience on Thursdays has nothing to do with excitement for the end of the work week. I feel the same impatience on Mondays. All day long I know I'm going to see you, and I watch the clock, and every minute that passes feels like an hour."

Ethan grins. "I watch the clock, too."

"We'll only be watching the clock for a little while longer. Thank God."

"I know." The little flare of annoyance I noticed at the beginning of our call comes onto his face again.

"Something is bothering you. Care to share?"

A short sigh rushes from him. "I'm leaving for a mission today. They just sprang it on me, and they won't tell us how long we'll be gone, so I might miss Monday's date. Hell, I might miss Thursday's too. I have no way of knowing." Ethan exhales loudly. "Sorry." He adds in a smaller voice.

"You don't have to be sorry. I understand. Besides, it won't be for much longer, you know? A handful of months, and this will all be over. No more missions, no more Skype dates, no more nights apart." *And what a glorious thing it will be to close the miles that separate us.*

His irritation lingers, so I distract him with stories of gossip around my office.

"Crazy, right?" I've just divulged the latest scandal circulating the cubes.

"Better than a soap opera. Tell me about our birthday dinner last night. Did my mom make two cakes or one?"

"Two, of course. And we cut a slice out of your cake and put a candle in it. I blew out mine and yours."

"What did you wish for?"

"Not telling," I sing-song.

"Aw, come on. I didn't get to blow out your candle, so technically you can't make a wish on my cake if I can't make a wish on yours."

"I made two wishes, one for each of us. Just like I did last year when you missed our party. And the year before that."

Ethan frowns. "Next year I won't miss it."

I beam. Having Ethan home for our traditional joint birthday party will be the very best gift. *Speaking of gift...* "Thanks for my present. I love it." I pull the gold necklace away from my throat and study the inscription on the front of the bar. *Me & You.*

"It looks beautiful on you."

"Thanks. Your gift should arrive soon. Hopefully you won't be gone too long on this mission. I'm excited for you to see what I got you." He's going to love the fancy knife I picked out with his dad's help. It has all the little tools he'll need (according to his dad) plus an incredibly sharp knife. And I had his initials engraved on it. That part was my idea.

Ethan looks upset again, so I blurt out the first question that comes to mind. "What is the first thing you want to do when you get home?"

"Kiss you." His answer comes right on the heels of my question.

"Well, duh." I laugh. "What do you want to do *after* that?"

"Hold your hand. Smell your hair. Kiss you again. Not necessarily in that order." Ethan offers one of his brightest smiles.

My heart flip-flops at the prospect of what he's talking about. "All right, all right, you scored some points with those answers."

Ethan makes a fist and playfully pumps it in the air in front of him. "Yes."

"Ethan, do you think if I snapped my fingers twice you could come through my computer and be here, in my living room? I would like that very much, thank you."

"If it were possible, I would've already done it." He glances at the watch on his wrist and sighs again, this time louder than before. "I have to go. I need to be ready to leave in fifteen minutes. I hate this." The sad look on Ethan's face makes my heart twist.

"Go keep me safe, and before you know it, we'll be having another Skype date."

Ethan grins. "Don't forget Nick will be out there next week."

"I haven't forgotten. Just email me all his info, and I'll be the best tour guide there is."

"Consider it done." He looks at his watch and sighs again. "I'll be home soon, and then we can be together. I love you." He says it without pageantry, and yet the emotions behind the words are evident on his face.

My heart soars. *How did I get so lucky?*

"I love you too." With one stiff, reluctant finger, I hit the end button. Ethan's lopsided grin is frozen on the screen for two seconds before it fades to black.

I close the computer and lay back against my pillows. Eyes shut, I picture Ethan's myriad expressions during our call. His laughter at my stories and frustration with going on this mission. I open my eyes when the whir of the ceiling fan's blades lifts a paper off my bulletin board and scrapes it against the wall.

I watch the blades rotate until they make me dizzy. *How many days will I have to go before I talk to Ethan again?* It's only been five minutes, and already, I miss him. If I sit around and check my email all day long, I'll go crazy. I need to make plans. I need to have things to do, so I'll still be a sane person when Ethan returns from his mission.

The gym.

That's it. They swipe fifty dollars from my checking account every month, I might as well go. *Okay, this is good. Gym.*

I hop off my bed and grab the gym bag hanging on the back of my closet door. When it's packed, I place it directly in front of my bedroom door. I might trip over it, but I won't forget it. I officially have a hot date with the gym after work tomorrow.

***

"So, you don't know when you'll hear from Ethan again?" Harper looks at me, her expression incredulous as she scoops a mound of guacamole with her tortilla chip.

"It's not like it'll be a year." My eyes strain with my effort to keep them from rolling. I look around the Mexican restaurant and back to Harper.

"It just seems like it would be really hard to not have any idea where he is." She points out the obvious without looking at me.

"No, it's great, I love it," I say under my breath.

Harper either doesn't hear me or ignores me. With unparalleled focus, she builds another tortilla-guacamole mountain. She's still chewing her first creation, so she hands the food to me.

"Have some guac. You're being punchy."

She's right, as irritating as that is. All my big plans to stay busy aren't proving to be enough to keep me from sulking. And it's only been forty-eight hours since I last spoke to Ethan.

"I'm worried." I conjure up the image of Ethan in his helmet, his Kevlar vest, and fatigues.

He's safe. That's what I tell myself. Because he has to be. Anything else is inconceivable.

In my head I cloak his image in a prayer for his safety.

"Kate, put the food in your mouth," Harper instructs, her eyes wide with annoyed exasperation.

I do as I'm told, but my stomach wants to reject it. My core feels sick. Heavy.

I shake my head, like somehow that's supposed to stop the worry. "I'm sure he's fine. He didn't talk about this mission like it was anything special. It's probably just like every other one he's been on." My words are meant to reassure me, but they don't.

"Probably," Harper agrees quickly. "It's great that Ethan's looking out for our safety. I, for one, feel very safe eating all this wonderful Mexican food." Harper motions to the rest of the restaurant.

"Don't choke on that chip," I warn as she crunches through another tortilla chip. "He's not here to give you the Heimlich."

My joke causes Harper to laugh, and then she actually starts coughing over her food. She sucks down all the water in her glass to recover from the fit.

I burst out laughing at the sight of my beautiful roommate looking less than poised. She grabs my water glass and downs it.

We're waiting for the check when Harper shocks me.

"I always thought you'd develop feelings for Ethan," she says with confidence.

My eyes narrow. "You lie. Such a thought never went through that pretty little head of yours. You've been my roommate for three years, and not once did you argue when I said Ethan was just my friend." Harper loves to argue. And she loves to talk. There is no way she would've kept quiet.

"I thought it, I just never said it. It was so obvious. Every time he came home, you were attached at the hip. And you couldn't stand when another person, and by person I mean *girl*, expressed any interest, not that he noticed anyone else anyway. You just needed time. A lot more than I thought you would need, but you finally came around."

"Why didn't you ever say anything?" *How could she have kept this to herself?*

"And watch the look of annoyance come over your face? No, thanks."

"What look of annoyance?" My voice raises incrementally. I'm pissed.

"Uh, the one on your face right now." Harper answer is flippant, like this is no big deal.

"You deserve the look right now." My tone is stern, intense. *What if she had told me? Would I have realized I loved Ethan a long time ago?*

Harper shrugs as though the topic already bores her. "Okay," she agrees. Too quickly.

"You should have told me."

Harper holds her hands up in a defensive position. "Fine, fine. I should have told you. But I would've lost my friend to a guy. I need you to be my wingwoman. My partner in crime. Not coupled up the way you are now." Her top lip curls.

Why is my relationship so distasteful? She's the one going on date after date, trying to find the man who puts all other men to shame. And not for the sake of love, either.

I stay quiet when the server appears and drops off the check.

"This is really your fault, you know." Harper tosses her hair over her shoulder, her tone calm. "You made it clear you believed there was nothing more than friendship coming from your side."

I already feel bad enough about what I've been putting

Ethan through for ten years. I don't need to be told yet again, so I ignore her.

"Are you ready to leave?" I pull cash from my purse and toss it on the check.

"Yes." Harper grabs her purse too. "If I tuck my chin to my chest, will you give me a good shove to the back so I can roll out of here?" She points to her stomach and puffs air into her cheeks.

We climb in Harper's car and head to the mall. Harper wants a new dress for work, and she's talking about how her closet needs a refresh. I'm finding it hard to pay attention.

I wish I knew what Ethan was doing at this very moment. I picture a barren desert, Ethan's combat boots, and his smile. *I want him so much.* My heart feels the yearning like a physical ache.

Harper continues to prattle on about the type of fabric she wants, but her voice fades into the music coming from her car stereo. I pretend to listen, nodding my head sporadically.

I stare at the brake lights in front of us, but what I really see are Ethan's eyes and the intensity that burns behind them when he looks at me.

Two hundred and two more days to go.

10

ETHAN

I'VE BEEN IN THIS HELLHOLE FOR TWO MONTHS. PLAYING superheroes and bad guys was the highlight of my day when I was a kid. My pretend games didn't include men who wanted to blow me up. Last week, that happened to a guy I knew from basic. I saw him that morning at breakfast. Everything seemed normal, just like every day...just like today. And then...well, armored Humvee's can only provide so much protection when a civilian steps in front of you wearing a bomb.

Shit has been getting really bad over here. Today's mission has me nervous. I want to protect my country. And I'm not afraid to die. I'm just afraid to be without Kate. And to leave Kate without me. *Life won't be that cruel. We're meant to be. The lucky ones.*

I'd feel worse if we were going by vehicle. Orders are to meet at the helicopter. It's unusual for us to fly, and there have been whispers all morning about the reason. I don't care. If I'm in a bird, I'm safe from suicide bombers. It isn't until I arrive at our meeting point that I learn what we're doing today. *Aerial scout*, he said. Which makes me wonder what is coming up that requires an aerial scout.

Me and nine other men strap into our seats. The helicopter's blades are a loud *thump thump thump*. Soon we're in the sky. I look down at the craggy rocks and sand. The landscape is just as ugly from the air. Desolate and forsaken.

We're fifteen minutes in, cruising over a rocky mountain, when a deafening sound blasts through the helicopter. My body slams against my seat. Pain spreads through the back of my head. I try to focus on the pilot, but fuzzy spots cloud my vision.

Through the cursing and yelling around me I make out the pilot's words. "We've been hit."

And then comes the second blast. The sound is all around me, filling my throbbing head. The chopper shudders, throwing me back again. Sharp pain ricochets through my jaw as my teeth crack together. Thank God Nick isn't with me. He needs to do what I asked of him. We can't both die, or else—

The helicopter bounces, and it's like being in a ride at a fair. Twisting, shaking, turning. I know what's below us.

We won't make it.

I won't make it.

Katie girl, I love you. I'm sorry. I won't come for you. I love you.

The helicopter drops. The screams of men fills my ears.

I love you Katie.

The free fall continues.

I love you Katie.

Spinning. Just a few seconds from impact. My eyes squeeze shut, and I see pictures of the life I was supposed to have. Kate in a white gown, smiling. Kate holding an infant in her arms. Kate, gray haired and wrinkled, blowing out the candles on my birthday cake. She looks up at me, her face radiating with happiness.

Her lips are moving.

I love you too.

Impact.

11

KATE

FRANTIC POUNDING.

Where is it coming from?

Awareness creeps into the bookstore my dream-self is standing in. The loud noise rolls through the bookshelves, and I look around in irritation to see who's creating it.

More pounding.

My eyes open. No more bookstore. Just my dark room. I glance at the clock. *Two a.m. Saturday night...or, Sunday morning.* More banging.

My covers fly back. My feet hit the soft carpet, and I stumble but keep moving forward. I smack the wall on my way to the front door, and the overhead light in the kitchen comes on. I blink twice at its intensity. The knocking that's more like banging continues. I'm almost afraid to answer it. In my heart I know this isn't good. People don't bang on doors at this hour with good news.

My heart beats a furious, thumping rhythm in my chest.

I spare a quick glance down at my cell phone as I hurry past the little table in the hallway. The face glows with notifications. Six missed calls. My steps stutter, and I grab the wall to keep from falling.

I reach the door and fight the lock with shaking fingers. The three seconds of time my fumbling costs me feels like an hour. The lock makes a loud clicking sound as it finally slides out of the way. The pounding cuts off when I open the door.

A man is half-standing, half-sagging against the door-frame. *Zane.*

His face, twisted almost grotesquely in agony, looks past my head. His eyes are glazed over.

My heart falters. An icy hand claws at it, gripping it with tenacious strength. The hairs on my arms stand upright, and my whole body is tense, waiting. My brain refuses to consider the one thing Zane and I have in common, the single factor that would send him drowning in anguish to my door.

"What?" It's a desperate cry. I reach without thinking, my hands on his shoulders.

He stays silent. His mouth hangs open like he wants to speak, but no sound comes out.

His silence angers me. The icy hand in my chest is reaching out to other parts of my body, having already had its way with my heart.

I glare into his face, my hands still on his shoulders. I shake him once, hard.

"Speak," I yell, the terror I feel making my voice shrill.

Finally, he's moved into action. Tears pour from his eyes.

"Ethan," Zane chokes out. He lets out a guttural cry after he says my best friend's name. "Ethan's dead."

My limbs are shallow. My chest is empty. I'm weightless. This is a joke.

I can't live in a world without Ethan. And I'm still alive. So Ethan must be too.

Anguished cries stream from my throbbing throat. Finally I find words.

"You're lying," I scream.

Deny, deny, deny. Bent fingers bunch the fabric of his shirt.

"I'm not." Zane's hands cover mine. "His helicopter was shot down in the mountains. Every person aboard is dead. I tried calling you. Evie tried calling you. You didn't answer."

I can't... I won't... My Ethan... No.

I think I'm crying but I don't really know.

I think I'm breathing but I don't really know.

My life, my future, my Ethan. *Gone.*

Zane's chest catches my collapsing head. The air from my sobs fills my lungs and pushes against my throat.

This pain... It's new. Pain I've never felt before.

It's massive, consuming, a foul black liquid coursing through my body and filling me. It's all I can feel.

I want it to take me away.

There's a heavy weight on my chest. It pushes me down. Ethan's face looms behind my closed eyes. His bright smile, the look of absolute love in his eyes, the last thing he'd said to me. *I'll be home soon, and then we can be together. I love you, Katie.*

The blackness comes, opening up a hole, beckoning me. I go to it. Anything, *anything*, to take away the pain that rolls over me, wave after relentless wave.

My knees are weak, then everything is dark.

***

MY MOTHER'S HERE. I smell thyme and onions. *Polenta soup.* It's the same thing she made for me after my dad died.

I open my eyes. And then I wish I hadn't. At least with my eyes closed, I can pretend Zane didn't come to my apartment in the middle of the night. I glance at the clock. *Twelve hours ago.*

"Sweetheart?"

My mother's voice, so thick with her concern. I turn my head to it.

"What?" My own voice, so frail and meek.

She stands in the doorway. "I made food for you. You need to eat. You haven't eaten a thing all day."

"Not hungry," I mumble. *Ethan is dead.*

She frowns. "You need sustenance, honey. You need food to live."

I stare at her, my face blank. *Ethan. Is. DEAD.* I want to shriek at her, at God, at the whole damn world.

I roll over and bury my face in my pillow. I listen to my mother's retreating footsteps. *I don't want your soup. I don't want anything.*

I remember what happened. I fainted. And then I woke up on the couch, and the pain was so sharp, I was sure there was a knife inside my body, stabbing my heart from within. Then I fainted again.

Now I'm in my bed, and the pain isn't stabbing me. It's different, more like a choking black fog. It fills my insides, billowing out into all the fissures and hidden corners of my body.

I can't breathe.

The sobs choke me again.

My heavy head lifts from the pillow, and I force myself to slow down, taking tiny breaths whenever I can fit them in.

When I get up to go to the bathroom, I hear Harper talking to my mom.

"I just can't believe she passed out like that. I barely caught her head before it hit the ground. I didn't even know what was happening, I'd just come from my room and saw her and Zane, then she was falling." Harper sounds amazed and proud of herself.

"Well, I'm certainly glad you got to her in time." My mother's voice sounds dull. *She's devastated too*. And yet she's here, tending to me.

I want to tell her thank you, but I'm overcome by exhaustion. My eyes throb. The sobbing and emotional distress have emptied me.

I leave the bathroom and crawl back into bed. Fervently I pray for the blackness that took me away last night. Soon I'm watching the onyx curtain fall over my mind, and then it's dark again.

***

MY MOTHER STAYS until it's late, hovering, watching, waiting for me to be human. Harper keeps coming into my room and prattles on about useless, unimportant things. In my mind I tell her to get the hell out, but my mouth stays shut.

When I wake up Monday morning, I call my boss to let her know I need time off.

"Lynn, something terrible has happened. I'm going to need some personal time to deal with it." I want to hit myself for using those words. *Deal with it. Deal with it?* My world is broken. Shattered pieces of the life I knew surround me. How could something like that ever be dealt with?

"When will you be back?" Lynn asks. Her voice is all business. I fumble for my answer.

"I don't know," I whisper haltingly.

She clears her throat loudly into the phone. "Why don't you take this week off? Come back next Monday."

It strikes me as a bizarre suggestion, one I would laugh at if I could remember how to take a laugh from my chest and move it up through my throat.

One week. Just seven days and suddenly, I'll be a functioning part of society again?

My sigh into the phone is just as loud as hers. "Two weeks, Lynn. I need two weeks."

My voice is in my ears, and it doesn't sound like me. Hot anger rips through my chest. I *hate* the words coming out of my mouth. I *hate* the reason I have to ask for time off.

"All right." Lynn doesn't hesitate.

I end the call without waiting for her to respond.

My thumb rubs over the smooth, cold glass, gliding over my background picture. I'm smiling, and Ethan is looking at me.

I want to hurl my phone at the wall. My hand raises above my shoulder. But I don't do it. This phone is a link to Ethan. To pictures, text messages, and emails.

I fall and let my bed catch me.

Lynn wanted me to come back in a week. I blink up at the ceiling, wondering how she could think of work when Ethan is dead. This world is not the same anymore. Can't she feel it too? Can't everyone feel this loss?

But the clock keeps ticking. Each minute passes at the same pace.

Not for me. My clock stopped ticking when Ethan stopped breathing.

**

I've LIVED six days in a world without Ethan.

I hate this world.

This world is evil, a seductress who entices with promises of true love and then curls her pointed fingernails and stabs the hopeful hearts placed in her wicked palm.

Six days without a future.

Six days inside a mind filled with terrible, scary thoughts. And a million questions.

What happened in his final seconds?

Did he have time to say goodbye to someone?

Did he pray?

Did he know what was happening to him?

Did he think of me?

And then comes the realization that I'm even asking these questions at all, and *oh, my God, Ethan's dead.*

Six days in this bed. I hate these watercolor floral sheets. Too bright. Garish. *But Ethan laid on them with me.*

I shower every day, but only to please Harper. If she weren't pulling me from bed and shoving me under the running water, I'd lie under my sheets and keep praying for God to kill me.

I don't say any of this to Harper. She wouldn't understand. She talks about normalcy and getting back to a routine. *You've been knocked down but you need to get right back up.* It's exactly what my father would have said. *Sorry, Dad. Kate can't Master this.*

I stare at Harper and say nothing. I let her pull me from bed and walk me to the shower. *She thinks she knows.*

She knows nothing.

Pain doesn't wash away. The bubbles disappear down the drain but the hurt is on the inside, devouring me.

The hot water runs out, and I'm on my knees, sobbing silently with my face pressed into the tile floor. *This is normal now.* When I get out, Harper is there, assessing me.

"Why are you shaking?" Her eyes squint, her question more of an accusation. "I made sure your water was hot."

"It ran out."

"And did you get out?" Her tone is patronizing.

"Yes." Lie. I push past her.

"Your mom is bringing over dinner. She's worried about you."

"Why?" I ask, dropping my towel to the ground.

Harper doesn't bat an eye. She's used to this by now. On day one when I dropped my towel, she gasped. Old Kate liked privacy. New Kate doesn't care about anything anymore.

I pull on underwear. Harper hands me the bra hanging from my desk chair.

"I told her you haven't been eating."

I have no desire for food. I lie in bed, smelling the frozen dinners Harper makes, and my stomach turns.

Harper sighs. "She'll be here soon."

I nod, pulling my head through a white T-shirt. *Ethan's shirt.* Left in secret in my room on the day he last left Phoenix, a note attached. *When you wore this shirt, I knew you had feelings for me.* I've worn it every day since he died.

"Why don't you put on something else?" Harper pulls open a drawer and looks through my pajamas.

"I'm good." I climb back under my covers.

"Did you hear me say your mom will be here soon?"

I nod.

Harper's exhale is a long, annoyed sound.

I keep my back to her until I hear the door fall into the frame.

My mom arrives a few minutes later, food in hand. She doesn't leave the food in the kitchen this time.

"Sweetie? I brought you dinner." She holds out the casserole dish.

"No, thank you."

"Kate, you've got to eat." Her voice is gentle, but there's a stern edge to it.

No, I don't.

I don't say anything, and she walks out. She's back quickly with a plate full of food. I roll over to face the wall.

"I'm going to put this on your nightstand. You have to get hungry sometime."

The plate bangs down onto the wood. The tinny sound of silverware follows. The bed moves under me, and my mom touches my shoulder.

"Can you roll over please?"

I do as she asks.

Her eyes fill with worry as she takes me in. She scratches her neck, like she's trying to cover up her unease at the sight of her heartbroken daughter.

"Have you talked to Evie and James yet?"

My forearm lifts to cover my eyes. I wish my answer was yes.

"No." My voice is tiny. "How are they?" *Stupid, stupid question.*

"Not well. Evie's looking forward to seeing you tomorrow."

I turn my head away from her, squeeze my eyes, and dry heave. It happens every time I think about tomorrow.

Her hands are on me, on my face, pressing my cheeks and forehead. "Honey, what's going on? Are you sick?"

"Not sick." I look back to her distressed face. "This is

what my body does when my brain remembers what tomorrow is."

"If there was anything in there to come up…"

"It would be on my bed."

She looks pained. "Kate, this isn't good. Ethan would hate this."

I hate this too.

I shrug.

"Do you want to talk yet?"

The shake of my head is barely perceptible. I'm sure she knew what my answer was going to be.

"I know a thing or two about losing the love of your life," she says softly.

I can't talk. Even to her, the woman who lost her husband. My father. I can't talk because what's inside me now is nothing but a dark, deep nothingness. An abyss. I can't see around it, under it, or beyond it. The darkness is me and I am the darkness.

Evie and James don't need my darkness.

My chest feels heavy, pushing me down into the mattress. Soon my body will move with sobs that shake my center and make my legs and arms slack.

"Mom, can you please go? I need to be alone."

I roll over so I don't see the hurt I'm certain is in her eyes.

"I'll see you tomorrow." She sounds disappointed. "Your brother's coming in the morning. Can we take you?"

"I have a ride." *Get out, get out. It's coming.*

"Okay." She sounds hurt. "I love you."

"Love you," I mumble.

My door closes just as the first sob takes over. Knuckles pressed to my lips silence the sound.

Say goodbye to Ethan.

Twenty years together.

One day to say goodbye.

My stomach contracts. This is more than a dry heave. *I swallowed water in the shower. I ate three bites of Harper's yogurt this afternoon to get her out of my room.*

Weak arms lift me up, and I twist just in time to bend over my nightstand. The cascade lands on the plate of food my mother left behind.

Spent, I lie back down and wipe my mouth with my forearm. Old Kate would already be flossing, brushing, and gargling. New Kate doesn't care about stomach acid and its effects on tooth enamel.

My legs curl into my chest. What if my shattered heart and I left everyone behind? I could leave this world and go find Ethan. My reason for living no longer exists. Why should I?

My whole body wants to follow the darkness. What would it take? One of my kitchen knives slicing across the right spot on my wrist... My neck squeezed tight by a shoelace... I don't know how to make a slipknot, but I could learn.

Fear ripples through me. *Suicide?* I can't. I remember my Sunday school teachings. If I want to be with Ethan again, I can't go in search of him.

I cry, my eyes aching and burning, until the only blackness I can have falls over me.

12

KATE

Goodbye, Ethan.

Is that what I'm supposed to say?

I look into the mirror and say it out loud. My voice is a whisper. I try it again.

"Goodbye, Ethan." This time my voice is louder.

"Are you talking to yourself?" Harper's standing in the entrance to my bathroom, mouth turned down.

"No," I mutter. *I'm talking to Ethan.*

"It looks like a bomb went off in here."

I look around me. Dirty clothes litter the ground, used towels hang haphazardly from the curtain rod. The contents of my makeup bag dot the length of the countertop, and I'm leaning against the counter, in the middle of it all. I swing my arm over the mess and send the little pots of color flying across the room. Some hit the wall and tumble down, others go directly to the floor. I barely notice the sound of plastic splintering.

Harper's face remains impassive. She grabs a tube of concealer from behind the faucet and hands it to me. "Make sure you use this. You need it."

I do as she says, plucking makeup one piece at a time from the floor and finishing my routine. How is it that my mind hasn't forgotten how to do this simple thing, when my whole body wants to?

I finish my makeup under Harper's watchful eye. She leaves to get dressed, and I wander into my closet.

What am I supposed to wear to say goodbye to my best friend? Black would be the most traditional choice, but I can't bring myself to do it. I don't want to sit with hundreds of other people and be just another head in a mass of black.

Ethan loved me in red.

My fingers run along the hangers, looking for a dress. It's not black, or appropriate for a memorial. And I don't care. Ethan liked the color and that's all that matters.

The red dress slips over my shoulders, gliding across my skin and falling into place.

I step out of my room. "That's what you're going to wear?" Harper asks, disapproval plain on her face.

I grab my purse and walk toward the front door. "Let's go."

My stomach knots. Every step closer is a step I don't want to take. The urge to turn and run is strong. *I could do it. Take off and go... Anywhere.*

Anywhere that isn't Ethan's funeral.

I wait at the top of the stairs while Harper locks our front door.

Of course I'll go to Ethan's funeral. It's the last place I want to be, but I would never miss it.

***

I REMEMBER THIS SMELL.

Must. Paper. Old carpet.

Church.

My mom and Noah meet me in the foyer. My brother looks uncomfortable in his suit. His brown, curly hair hangs over his forehead.

My mom's eyes search mine. *What is she looking for?*

She hugs me, and her hair smells like pasta. How much more food is she going to cook?

I'm passed off to Noah. My little brother is much bigger than I am. The hug is awkward. He murmurs something about how sorry he is and that Ethan never treated him like an annoying little brother.

My mom takes my hand. "Evie's asked me to take you to the first pew." My feet move with her, but I'm not sure how. It doesn't feel like I'm directing them.

"Here's a program," says a kind voice at the door to the sanctuary. The tri-fold paper hangs in the air between me and the old man with the apologetic face.

"Thank you." I take it and try not to look at the shiny paper with Ethan's picture on the front.

Mom leads me to the front of the church. I keep my eyes on my feet. I don't want to see anybody.

I sit where my mom tells me to. I try not to lift my head. I try not to look. But I do.

A huge, floral wreath lays against an easel, Ethan's picture in the center. Little American flags stick out of the flowers.

"Mom, where's...?" I don't know what to say.

The casket?

His body?

Ethan?

I look back to her. She bites the side of her lower lip.

"Mom?"

"The helicopter was badly burned. They..." She gulps. "They haven't been able to recover everyone."

My stomach flips, turns. Bile rises. My hand clamps over my mouth.

"I didn't want you to find out like this. This week... I wanted to tell you every time I saw you, but you weren't in any condition to hear it."

I close my eyes. My breath is shallow. Ethan's beautiful, perfect body. His soul, so vital to keeping my soul intact. Gone.

Behind me I hear noise. Feet shuffling. Murmurs. Back-slaps muted by thick layers of suit fabric.

"Kate?"

I open my eyes and turn my head.

Evie is sitting beside me. Her eyes meet mine. *Caramel. Ethan's eyes.* Her lips make tiny movements, like she's trying not to cry.

It doesn't work.

I see her tears and add my own.

Her hands are on the back of my head, running through my hair as she holds me.

"Your mother said you wouldn't get out of bed." Her voice is low.

I pull back and look at her, see the dark circles under her eyes, knowing how they match my own.

"I'm sorry," I mouth. It's all I can say.

"I know." Her hand moves to my face. She holds my cheek.

"Excuse me?" says a deep, thick voice.

Evie looks first. "You made it." She stands up.

I look up to find a soldier in her arms. My heart lurches. *Not Ethan.*

But for just a fraction of a second...

Evie lets the soldier go. "I'm so happy to finally meet you. Ethan... Well, he loved you. He talked about you all the time."

The soldier nods and looks at the floor. He clears his throat and brings his eyes back to Evie's face. "I'm so sorry for your loss. He was my best friend." His voice falters. "This, uh... It hurts. A lot."

Best friend?

Soldier?

Nick Hunter.

He looks down at me. My voice is in my throat. *The uniform...* Pain stabs my heart.

Nick takes a knee in front of me. He looks me in the eye. "Kate?" His hand extends between us. "I'm Nick Hunter."

I place my palm in his warm hand. The corners of my mouth turn up like they are supposed to, but it's not a real smile. "Nice to finally meet you, Nick Hunter."

Dimly I remember I'm supposed to be this person's tour guide. It's the last thing I want to do.

Evie puts a hand on my shoulder. "The pastor said it's time to start."

Nick takes a few steps away but Evie's arm shoots out to stop him.

"You sit down here with us. Next to Kate."

Evie takes her seat on the other side of my mother, beside James.

Ethan's dad... His eyes are wide, bugged out, and he's staring down at his hands.

Nick sits down. I should say something, but I don't know what. *I wish he were wearing civilian clothes.* The uniform is making this harder.

I lean back slightly and squint at Nick until my eyes water.

His mahogany hair turns black.

The bump on his nose straightens.

His square jawline rounds.

He turns his face, and his eyes peer into mine, the confusion in them clear. His blue eyes don't change to caramel.

I turn my face forward. I should be mortified. But I'm not. I don't know how to recall that emotion. Two hands fall on my shoulders and squeeze. I look back and into Zane's eyes, brimming with tears. Emotion, so strong and sad, passes between us. We stare at each other for another moment, until the pastor and the choir come out.

The pastor speaks of Ethan's accomplishments and his heroic service to the United States. The choir sings *Amazing Grace* while a slideshow of pictures plays on a screen above their heads. Part of me wants to close my eyes as Ethan's image clips by. As much as it hurts to see his face, over and over in so many expressions and varying points in life, watching it is hypnotizing. I sit, mesmerized, as our history flashes before me.

Seven years old, waiting for the bus stop on our first day of second grade. We're each holding a lunch box, and my arm is slung around Ethan's shoulder. We beamed for the camera. Ethan was missing a tooth.

The slideshow continues on like that, each picture stabbing a new wound in my heart. All the pictures, even the ones without me in them, are familiar to me. Every step of the way, throughout most of his life, I was there.

It's all here in front of me. The Christmas he got a guitar, the ski trip with his parents and Zane, the broken leg from falling out of the big tree in my back yard. The pictures zip by, taking us from high school and into college. To everyone sitting behind me, the pictures are still images, but to me they are so much more. I don't see just one moment captured in time. I know the moments leading up to the click of the camera and remember what happened after the camera was put away.

And then, the very last image. Ethan's Army picture. So handsome in his dark green Class A's, his beret perched just so on his head. No smile in this picture. He looks intimidating and strong. Worthy of the responsibility handed to him. A responsibility for which he would give the ultimate sacrifice.

***

I RIDE with my mom and Noah to the veteran's cemetery. Ethan's parents, me, my family, Zane and Nick sit on the benches under the ramada. Other attendees stand in a semi-circle around the structure. A bugler, outfitted in dress blues, plays Taps. The sound, so similar to a trumpet, seeps into my skin and flows through my veins, leaving a haunting feeling in its path. My shoulders jump as the rifle volleys are shot. I shade my teary eyes from the sun when the Air Force does a fly over, one aircraft missing from formation. Two soldiers fold up an American flag in a very precise and methodical way and present it to Ethan's parents. A few words are said, a final prayer is offered, and then it's over.

After, I stand off to the side of the covered pavilion, watching people leave and averting my gaze every time someone makes eye contact. I don't want to talk to anyone. Their platitudes don't help.

Trent and Harper stand together, chatting. Harper laughs and tosses her hair.

What is there to laugh about right now? Nothing is funny.

The quiet and solitude of my bed calls my name, but I want to talk to Evie and James. They are besieged by well-wishers, so I wait. My foot slides off the concrete pad and dips down into the sandy dirt. With the toe of my shoe, I make swirls in the dirt.

"Hanging in there?"

I look up into blue eyes.

By a thread, I want to say.

"I guess so." I nod. "You?"

Nick shrugs. The movement doesn't look like much under the weight of the fatigues. "Nothing can prepare a person for this."

My eyes burn as they fill. "Nothing."

I pull a tissue from my purse and dab my eyes and nose. Nick surveys me.

"I feel like I already know you," he says after I've stashed the tissue in my purse. "Ethan talked about you all the time."

Because he loved me more than any man has ever loved any woman. And now he's gone.

I sniff. "He talked about you, too. Lots of fun nights in Europe." I work to keep my voice light. Shallow stabs assail my chest as I recall the animation on Ethan's face when he told his stories.

Nick laughs once, his smile wistful. "Guilty." He holds his hands up in surrender.

"Have you moved here?" Remorse creeps in. I'm supposed to be helping this guy adjust to life here. I told Ethan I would. But that was before the rug was snatched out from under me.

Nick's hands go into his pockets as he rocks back on his heels. "Day One."

I can't muster any semblance of a smile. "Welcome to the Valley of the Sun."

"This isn't exactly what I thought my first day would be like."

"Life is not what I thought it would be like anymore."

Nick reaches for me, touches my forearm. His eyes are sad.

"Are you waiting for the Shepherds too?" I ask. I can't take his sadness. I'm inundated by my own.

"I'm going home with them."

"You are?"

"Evie insisted. I called her a few days ago to let her know I would to try to make it here by today." He shakes his head. "I cut it pretty close. I ran full speed to make my connection in New York."

"That's—"

"Kate, are you ready to leave?" Harper interrupts us. She smiles her pretty girl smile at Nick.

"I'm waiting for Evie and James."

Harper doesn't look at me. "Hi," she says to Nick. "I'm Harper Robinson. Kate's roommate."

Nick takes her outstretched hand. "Nice to meet you. Nick Hunter."

"Did you know Ethan?" Harper's voice goes soft, and her head tilts. *I will flip a lid if she uses Ethan's funeral as a time to flirt.*

I walk away. I know Harper well enough by now.

Evie catches me as I'm looking for my mom. "Promise me you'll start getting out of bed?"

"Promise." *Just not until I have to go back to work.*

"Can you come over for lunch on Monday?"

"Yes." I don't hesitate to agree. "What day is it today?"

"Kate..." Evie frowns.

I hold up a hand. "Please. I just don't know what today is. That's all."

"Today is Saturday. June twenty-first."

"Thank you."

"Everything okay?" My mom's voice reaches us before she does.

I see Evie look at my mom, shaking her head almost imperceptibly. *Almost.*

"Harper's ready to take me home, I think." I look over to where I left Harper and Nick. Nobody is there.

"Kate's coming over to have lunch with me on Monday," Evie says to my mom.

"That's great." Mom sounds relieved. And happy. "Can you stop at our house after?"

I nod. She grins.

A waving arm catches my attention. Harper's standing halfway between the pavilion and her car, one hand on her hip.

I hug both women and catch up to Harper.

"Kate, I have a date tonight. Let's go." She snaps her fingers and starts walking.

"You have a date tonight?" Dirt and tiny rocks kick up as I hurry to stay in step beside her.

She gives me a side-eye. "It's Saturday. Of course I have a date."

"But... it's... Never mind." *I'd rather be alone anyway.*

We reach her car. I pause with the door open and look around. Thousands of small rectangular headstones lay flush with the ground. *And one of them is Ethan's.*

Zane catches my gaze. He's standing under a tree with his hands in his pockets. I wave at him, my arm moving slowly. He nods at me. It's too far for me to clearly see the look on his face.

"What are you doing?" Harper half yells, half whines.

I look down at the car. Her exasperated face looms over the passenger seat.

"Nothing." I get in.

Harper puts the car in drive and complains about the dust on her dress, but I'm not listening. We are one of only a few cars left in the cemetery.

Ethan's memorial is over.

But I know the truth.

This isn't over.

For me, this has just begun.

13

NICK

"Home sweet home," Mrs. Shepherd announces as we pull into the driveway. She gestures to the two story house as she glances at me through the rearview mirror.

Everything about her seems tired. Her voice, the expression on her face, even her arm gestures heavily.

Mr. Shepherd turns in his seat to look back at me. His eyes are bloodshot. "We're happy you're here, Nick. You can stay as long as you like."

I nod tersely, trying to get ahold of my grief long enough to thank them appropriately.

"Thank you, Mr. and Mrs. Shepherd," I manage. "It's generous of you to offer your house."

Mrs. Shepherd shakes her head. "Call us Evie and James. After all, we're practically family. And we're happy to have you here. We have plenty of space..." She trails off, glancing up at the house again.

Oh no. I can't stay here. I'd just assumed they had another room in addition to Ethan's. Staying in Ethan's room? That's not going to work.

I hate to bring it up, but I'm a direct person, and it will be better for everyone if they know right away how I feel.

Evie and James are already climbing from the car, so I follow them out and around to the popped trunk.

James reaches for my bag, and I reach out a hand to stop him, partly because he doesn't need to carry my bag, and partly because I'm not entirely certain I'll be staying here after all.

"I've got it, James. Thank you." Pausing with my hand wrapped around the handles of the duffel, I look at Ethan's parents.

Today might have been the first time I met them, but it wasn't the first time I've seen them. Ethan had their picture tacked up on the wall in his room in Germany. Right next to all those pictures of Kate.

Beautiful, broken-hearted Kate. She was another person I met today, but feel like I already know.

She's also the reason I went through with the plan to move here. When Ethan died, that plan almost derailed. If it wasn't for the agreement we made, I would have gone home after exiting the Army. But staying the course doesn't mean I have to sleep in Ethan's room to accomplish what I came here to do.

"Evie and James, I just, uh..." I glance up at the house, at the neatly trimmed lawn, then back to them. "If Ethan's room is the only one available then I think I should find somewhere else to stay. I appreciate your generosity, I really do, but staying in his room..." My sentence peters out. It's hard to put words to the pain and anguish parked in my chest. Mere words seem to cheapen my pain.

Evie's eyes widen. "Oh, Nick, no. We have a guest room. We would never put you in Ethan's room. We would never do that to you. Or to us, for that matter." She looks over at James. His hands are tucked into the pockets of his blacks pants, and he stares down at his feet. "For right now Ethan's room needs to stay the way it is. He was the last to sleep there, and I never got around to washing the sheets after he left."

I get what she's saying. She needs his smell to stay there, on those sheets, for as long as possible. My mother would do the same.

I lift my bag from the trunk and sling it over my shoulder. "In that case, you've got yourself a houseguest."

"For as long as you need," she reminds me, leading the way up the driveway and to the front door.

It's nice, but I won't be overstaying my welcome. I might have come here for a specific reason, but I'm going to settle in here. I'll find a job and get my own place. I'll make a life for myself.

Aside from my mom, there's nothing for me back home in Connecticut, and Phoenix seems as good a place as any to start over.

I'm not certain what life after the military holds for me, but I'm willing to find out.

***

THANKS TO THE ARMY, I've been a lot of places. I've met a lot of different people, and learned how much exists outside of my upbringing. A whole world is out there, and I'm just a tiny speck in its existence.

And yet, the feelings of one person can consume them, until their feelings become their whole world. When that happens, a person forgets how many other people exist in the world. They are the one, the only, their pain unique only to them.

Tonight, sitting around the Shepherd's dinner table, we were three different people consumed by emotion that felt like it belonged to only us.

Evie tried to make conversation, but it was half-hearted. Not that anyone could blame her. I tried to be a good house-guest by responding, but found it hard to engage with any authenticity. And James was pretty much silent. He nodded his head when he was supposed to, but didn't utter a word. After taking a few bites of his food, he pushed his plate away, waited until we'd finished, then strode away from the table and out the door leading to the backyard.

I watched him go into the little shed at the back of the yard, and thanks to the tour Evie gave me earlier, I know he was disappearing into his workshop.

"Well," Evie had said, and I knew she was about to say something to excuse James' behavior, not that she needed to. In my opinion, a man who has just lost his son is allowed to act how he wants.

I stood, stacked the dinner plates, and carried them to the kitchen. Evie tried to shoo me away, but I told her I was on dish duty for the foreseeable future, and she backed away.

After that I went back to my room to unpack and lie down.

Now it's three-thirty in the morning and I'm wide awake. It'll take a while for my body to adjust to the new clock I'm on.

I rub my eyes and roll off the double-bed, coming to standing and looking around.

A dresser against one wall, a matching nightstand, and

oil painting of a countryside on the wall. It's definitely not the sparse, military bedroom I'd gotten used to.

Oddly, I miss it. Or maybe I miss the familiarity. I'm sure that will wear off.

Pulling a shirt on, I leave the room in search of the bathroom. When I'm done in there, I take a left instead of a right.

It's not too hard to find Ethan's room. It's the door Evie didn't open during my tour last night.

I pause with my hand on the doorknob, take a deep breath, then push it open and flip on the light.

"Geez, I'm sorry," I say, startled at the sight of Evie sitting upright on the bed, her legs criss-crossed.

Her hand flies to her chest in her surprise, then she pulls it away, using it to wipe her cheeks.

"It's ok." Emotion makes her voice tremble. She tries to smile at me, but it's all wrong.

I take a step back but she stops me.

"Don't go. I need to get back to my own bed, anyway." She swings her legs over the side of Ethan's bed and stands. Before she passes me, she stops at his dresser and brushes her fingertips over a framed picture.

From where I stand in the doorway I can't see what the picture is of, but Evie smiles sadly at it.

"It may sound crazy, but seeing the broken hearts of those who loved Ethan most is oddly soothing. He was so loved while he was here. I don't know if there's anything more a mother could ask for."

She pulls her hand away and passes me, lightly squeezing my shoulder as she goes.

I listen to her retreating footsteps and when the sound disappears, I step all the way into the room and close the door softly behind me.

I'm curious to know what picture she was looking at, so I start there, picking up the photo off the dresser.

Kate.

A younger Kate, her cheeks more filled out, her eyes bright. She might actually still look like this. Today probably wasn't an accurate reflection of how she normally appears. Today she looked...well, like hell.

I turn, setting the picture back down on the dresser and taking in the rest of the room. It's a young man's room, with baseball posters and hooks where baseball gloves and hoodies hang.

It's exactly how I pictured his room. We'd had so many conversations about life where we were from, and I knew his love for baseball. And Kate. It's not surprising to see both themes dominating this space.

Crossing the room, I open his closet and push aside his shirts. At some of the clothes, I can't help but laugh. There are brands he might have worn four or more years ago before he joined, but never would've worn as recently as six months ago.

We did some shopping on our weekends off in between deployments. I remember what he bought, and it didn't look anything like these shirts with their logos printed on the front.

I'd never wear anything I wore from the time before I joined the Army. Or act the way I acted, either.

I was an angry kid looking for fights, and starting them when I didn't find any. I thought I didn't need anybody, or anything, and even the people I called friends weren't really my friends. They were people who populated my moment, but not my journey.

Ethan was different. He was on my journey. He was the brother I never had, the best friend I never had.

My eyes grow tight, and I blink back the moisture. I'm not good at crying. In fact, it's one of the last things I'd elect to do. Since Ethan was killed, I've cried more than I have in my entire life.

I wipe my eyes on my shirtsleeve and shut the closet door. My eyes sweep the room one more time before I leave, turning off the light and closing the door behind me.

When I get back to my room, I pull out my lap top and run an internet search for EMT job openings. My ultimate goal is to be an ER doctor, and I'd like to stay in the field of medicine while I'm in school. There's one opening to fill an immediate need, so I upload my application and hit send. Then, I go to the Arizona State University website and apply to be a student, starting in January. I'll go to the DMV when it opens later today and get an Arizona drivers license and change my residency to Arizona.

I feel a little better now that I've accomplished those tasks, but I've still got that big task hanging over my head.

The promise that brought me here in the first place.

As I change into workout clothes and slide on my running shoes, I think about Kate. Not the Kate from all the pictures I've seen, but the Kate I met yesterday at the funeral.

I expected tears. I expected grief and anguish. But the hollowness, the desolation, the vacant eyes holding no hint of the soul that lay beyond all that?

I did not expect it.

That promise I made is looking like it's not going to be so easy to keep after all.

14

KATE

Harper is gone. I'm curled up on the couch after the funeral, staring at a picture on the wall.

There's a knock on my front door. I don't get up.

"Kate, I know you're home." It's a man's voice.

Trent?

I open the door. He's standing awkwardly, wearing an expression like he's somewhere he wishes he weren't.

"Why are you here?" I ask.

Trent pushes a white paper bag to my chest. His eyes quickly scan my body, the corners of his mouth turned down.

"Nice dress." He walks in.

I close the door. The bag crinkles as I fold my arms in front of myself. "Why are you here?"

"You know you need to eat, right?" He throws a look back at me as he walks to my living room. I follow.

"Yes, I know." Of course I know I need to eat, I just lack the desire to actually do it.

Trent sits on the couch I just vacated. "So maybe you

should. You're wasting away. How much have you had to eat in the last seven days?"

"Nothing I do is any of your business." There's no need to play games anymore. Trent doesn't like me, I don't like Trent. We're no longer linked by Ethan. No further need to play nice.

Trent points to the bag. "Eat."

I open it and find a wrap and a salad. I'm not hungry, but I have the feeling the sooner I eat, the sooner Trent will leave. I sit down on a chair across from him and pull out the plastic containers and a fork.

"Why are you doing this?" I ask.

His looks at my dress again, his face flat. "Because you look too thin."

He watches me take a bite. It's awkward, so I toss the TV remote on his lap.

He turns on a channel I never watch, but right now, I'm grateful for the five men arguing about a baseball game.

I finish my food. All of it. I didn't taste it, but I ate it.

"Thanks for dinner." *I'm ready to be alone now.*

Trent uncrosses his foot from his knee and leans forward. "Is Harper planning to grace us with her presence?"

"She's on a date. Why?"

"Just wondering." He studies me. "Someone needs to be here with you. I'm putting you on suicide watch."

I shake my head. "You can go."

His jaw clenches. "I'm not here because I enjoy your company. Ethan would have wanted someone to take care of you, and that's what I'm doing."

"Somehow I don't think Ethan would have chosen *you* for the job." My comment is snide, and I don't care. My grasp on sanity is slipping.

"You're welcome. For the food." Trent stands and stomps to the door.

"Feel free to call Harper tomorrow morning to see if I've killed myself." If only the sarcasm was realism. I follow him to the door.

"I could do it for you and put you out of your misery," he mutters as he steps through.

Would you please? I can't do it.

With one foot I hold open the door. He turns back to me, his pinched mouth showing his obvious contempt.

His hands come out of his pockets and fold across his chest. "Kate, I don't like you."

For a people pleaser like myself, this should be terrible news. But I already knew this, and I no longer care.

I cross my arms too. "Trent, I don't like you either."

He stares at me, I stare at him. He pivots on one foot and walks away. *That may be the last time I see him.*

With the door closed and locked, I go back to the couch. I'm alone again, with just my pain for company.

I sit until the setting sun leaves me in darkness.

Tequila. I walk to the kitchen, flipping on lights as I go. On tiptoe I reach back to the farthest corner of my pantry. My fingers snake around the smooth, cool glass. Bottle in hand I reclaim my seat on the couch and take a long drink. The amber liquid sets my throat on fire. *Damn, that hurts.* I tip the bottle up again.

Ethan... I need you. Please. You can't be gone. I need to see your face. My memories aren't enough.

But they are all I have. Memories. And pictures. I have so many pictures.

I put down the bottle, stand up, stumble, and catch myself. *Lightweight.* My feet are unsteady as I cross the room to grab the photo album off my bookshelf.

I sit back down on my couch with the mammoth book. My hand drags across the dusty cover and over the soft fabric of my dress, leaving a swipe of grayish brown against the red.

This is masochistic. But pain is what I'm looking for. I want to *ache*.

On the inside cover of the album, written in my mother's scrawling script, is the word *Summers*. With that one word, I can smell coconut-scented sunscreen, hear the melody of the approaching ice cream truck and the cacophony of cicadas, recall the utter seriousness of rushing through breakfast to beat Ethan to our meeting spot under the orange tree in his front yard. Summertime meant three months of freedom to build forts, ride bikes, have movie marathons, and stay up until our eyes drooped. And the evidence of it all is sitting on my lap.

So many pages. So much time spent together. My tears splash on the plastic that covers the pictures. It's excruciating. *Just like I want it to be.*

The more pages I turn, the more I understand. This album is a tale told through pictures. One by one these memories come together to show me all the years Ethan's love for me was unrequited.

Tequila.

The grubby, missing tooth pictures steadily change, and that's when I see the truth of it all. We grew older, became teenagers, and even though I still considered him my best friend, I wasn't as close beside him in the pictures anymore. Our body language changed, and in those teenage years, mine was very different from his. Where his body turned toward me, my body turned away. It makes me remember all the times I'd turned him down but continued to keep him as my best friend. I knew he was in love with me, and even though I told him I didn't love him like that, I still behaved just as I always had, in whatever way made him fall for me in the first place.

"I'm a horrible person," I whisper.

More tequila. My insides are on fire.

For years Ethan waited patiently, and I brushed him off at every pass. My favorite line was, "You're my best friend, and I don't want to ruin that." At the time I'd really believed myself. In reality I was just too stupid to see what he'd offered to me.

My heavy head tips back, and I let the edge of the couch support my neck. The ceiling swirls. I close my eyes to make it stop.

The lyrics of a song I haven't heard in years float through my head. *I need to hear that song right now.* Fuzzy eyes see my phone on the coffee table. Clumsy hands grab it. After a few attempts to type in the name of the song, I find it and buy it. *Whiskey Lullaby.*

The strains of the haunting music go through me, piercing straight to my heart like an arrow. The tequila bottle doesn't stray too far from my lips as I listen. I hit the repeat button before the song ends. I alternate between taking sips of the liquid fire and turning the pictured pages, an illustration of my history. The pictures grow fuzzier and fuzzier, blurred by tears and tequila.

My eyes close. I'm sixteen and sitting in Ethan's car. He's turned on the child lock.

"Why are you trapping me in here?" I look up from my ice cream when he doesn't respond. His face is pale. He looks nervous.

"What's the matter with you? Are you going to be sick?"

No response.

"Let's go inside." I gather my stuff.

"Can you, um...?" He coughs. "Can you just wait for a minute please?" He reaches out and wraps his hand around my wrist.

"I guess." He's scaring me. He's never acted this strangely before.

Ethan's chest rises and falls with one deep breath. "I want you to know how much your friendship means to me."

My eyes narrow. Since when does Ethan start out a sentence like that?

He continues. "I have something to tell you, and it might come as a surprise. So, brace yourself."

I'm frozen. I have no idea what he's about to say.

"I like you. As in, more than a friend." His upper teeth bite down on his lower lip. He keeps his gaze through the windshield.

Silence sits between us, making a place for itself right there in the cup holders. It stretches on.

He's looking at me now.

"Kate?"

My stomach is somewhere near my knees. I take a deep breath, feel it lift back into place.

"You're my best friend," I say, "and I don't want to ruin that." It was the first time I would say those words, and certainly not the last.

"A guy can try." He shrugs and grins. Beneath the nonplussed exterior I see how much work it takes to cover up his disappointment. "Still friends?" He smiles as he asks the question.

"Always." I look into his eyes, and I want to cry. I've disappointed my best friend.

"You ready for our party?" He presses a button, and the child lock disables.

"Ethan, I..." I don't know what to say, so I stop talking.

"Kate, listen. I don't like you. I can barely even stand you, okay? Let's go celebrate our birthday, and I'll pretend I can tolerate being in the same room as you. Got it?" He grins and holds up a hand for a high five.

I slap his hand. We go into his house for our party, and all I can think is, *Ethan has feelings for me.*

Tears free fall. Ten years later, and here I am, desperate to go back in time and smack sense into my younger self. *You love him! Forget about how it could mess things up. Let go of your control for once in your stupid life and follow your heart. Take a risk.*

I've never hated myself more than I do right now.

Ethan is dead, and it's over.

Through the thick haze of drunkenness my brain registers a different noise making its way through the music. My head is leaden as it swivels. Two figures stand at the entrance to the living room. I hear my name. *I think.*

Harper's hands are on her hips. Her mouth opens wide. I lift a finger and pretend to poke the center of the hole her mouth makes.

"What's the matter?" I hear my own slurring.

She glances from the open bottle of tequila to the photo album on my lap. She turns to the man beside her and says something I can't hear.

"Would you mind speaking up?" I'm being obnoxious.

Harper and the guy disappear, and only Harper comes back.

"Seriously, Kate? I've never seen you like this. How much of that bottle did you drink?"

"I dunno." My stomach lurches. "Harper?"

"Yeah?"

"I don't feel very good."

"Shit. Get up!" Harper yanks me onto unstable feet.

The kitchen trash is closest. I bend over and emit the contents of my stomach. Harper holds my hair and cusses. She keeps saying "*disgusting*" and uses every synonym for the word.

When I'm done, Harper leads me to my room.

Away from my phone, still playing the song.

Away from the pictures.

Away from purgatory.

She leaves with an irritated look. I brush my teeth and lie down in bed, dread filling my throbbing head. Tomorrow when I wake up, I'll have to face the rest of my life. And the loss of the person I never imagined life without.

15

KATE

A DAY LATER AND THE REMNANTS OF MY HEADACHE ARE STILL hanging around. At least drums aren't pounding in my head anymore. Yesterday was a blur. I slept the entire day, waking once in the early evening to call Lynn. I left a message letting her know I would return to work sooner than expected.

Harper keeps telling me to get out of bed. *Do something,* she says.

I don't want to do anything.

Going to work will please her. My first small step toward recovery.

Like recovery is attainable. Maybe it is for some people. But not me. My heart and soul have been torn to shreds and scattered throughout my body. Even if I could put them back together, I wouldn't recognize them.

I don't know who I am inside but I know I'm not the Master of Everything anymore.

***

BEFORE I LEAVE my apartment I look at my phone, a small part of me hoping Evie has called to cancel. She hasn't. And neither has my mother. I'm going to spend an entire afternoon in two places I don't want to go.

Nausea builds when I make the familiar turn onto my old street. Why didn't I suggest we have lunch somewhere else? I grip my stomach with one arm. I used to love coming here. But not today. *And maybe not ever again.*

Ethan occupies every inch of this place. His spirit is here, wrapped around every tree trunk, whispering through the leaves.

My tires spin over the same asphalt we scraped our knees and elbows on. My chest drags in air, then loudly expels it.

Keep it together.

I pull into the Shepherds' empty driveway and get out. Fallen oranges dot their front yard. I pick one up and throw it. It hits the tree trunk and splits open. I'm walking to pick it up when something bumps my thigh.

I look down to see an orange rolling away from me. Then I look up to see Evie waving from the porch.

"That was your game, wasn't it? Pretending oranges were snowballs?"

"And now I'm remembering they hurt." I rub my thigh.

One corner of Evie's mouth twitches, like she might smile. "Ethan probably didn't throw them at you very hard."

Didn't. Past tense.

She waves her hand. "Don't worry about the broken one. Let the birds have something to eat."

I walk to the porch.

She smiles warmly and hugs me. "I'm glad you came." She lets me go, and I follow her inside.

Tears fall over my eyes without warning. It's all too much

for me. The familiar smell of Ethan's house, the familiar smell of Ethan's mom.

She sees the tears even though I've turned my head, pretending to look at the painting on the wall next to us.

"I know it's hard." Her cheeks glisten.

"Everything I do, everywhere I look, everything I taste and smell, it all reminds me of him. And it all hurts. It's like a knife stabbing my heart." *That's the tidy version.* I won't tell her the pain is so great it feels debilitating. I won't tell her the monumental effort it took to drag myself out of bed this morning. I won't tell her about the torture I'm experiencing even now, looking into her lovely, heartbroken eyes.

She strokes my hair and says nothing. She knows.

"Let me feed you. I hope you're in the mood for lasagna. I have about twenty casseroles—not that I'm complaining—and we need to start eating them. We might have to buy another freezer just to keep them." She peeks into the oven as she speaks. "Food seems to be the answer for many of life's biggest moments. When someone dies, when someone's ill, when a baby's born, people respond with food." She smiles wryly. "Especially casseroles."

I nod. "Giving food says, 'Don't worry about the everyday things like grocery shopping or preparing meals. Go ahead and grieve'." I had experience with this. There was enough food to feed my mom, my brother, and me for a month after my dad passed.

Evie smiles. "Does that mean once the food is gone, it's time to stop grieving?"

I laugh involuntarily, but the sound isn't happy. "Not by a long shot."

Her gaze wanders out the kitchen window toward the pool and James's wood shop. *What is she thinking?*

She spins around suddenly, walking to the wine rack on

the counter. She selects a bottle and pulls two oversized red wine glasses from the cabinet above her. "I think I'll have wine with lunch. Would you like some?"

"Please," I answer without hesitation.

She puts me to work pouring the wine while she removes the lasagna from the oven and portions it out. We move to the dining room with two plates of steaming pasta and red wine. I can't tell her that after how I felt yesterday I should be taking it easy today. It's obvious she wants to take care of me. We eat in silence, our utensils making the only sound in the house.

I want to fill the silence with conversation, but I don't know what to say. Instead of forcing chit chat, I focus on eating.

When I finish, Evie reaches for the spatula.

I protest with a stiff hand.

"Eat, Kate," she says before I can decline. Her tone is no-nonsense. "You look like a skeleton. Harper must not be taking care of you." She slides another square of lasagna on my plate.

"Harper's gone a lot."

Evie places a second slice on her plate too. Again we eat in silence. The lasagna is delicious, and I'm stuffed. I set my fork down on an empty plate for a second time.

"Don't even think about trying to talk me into a third piece."

She laughs as I sip my drink.

"Good wine." I lift up my glass, looking through the ruby liquid.

"Ethan found it when he went to France with Nick. They had it in a restaurant, and Ethan said it reminded him of me." She looks wistfully at the bottle.

"It's generous of you to share it." I gesture to the half-empty bottle. "I don't think I would have."

"I was saving it to have the night Ethan was supposed to be home for good." She taps a finger nail against her glass, sending a lone tinkling sound into the air. "I thought we might as well share it, in honor of him."

I reach over, replacing the cork in the bottle. "Let's save the rest for James. He'll want to have some of the wine Ethan once enjoyed."

Evie shakes her head sadly. "No, he won't. I asked him to have lunch with us today, but..." She pauses, her eyes grow shiny. "He's not dealing with things very well. He think's Ethan's death is his fault."

My gasp is loud.

Evie holds up a hand. "I know, I know, it sounds crazy. But James was in the military, too, a long time ago, and when Ethan talked about joining...well, James was very supportive."

I shake my head. "That doesn't make him responsible."

"I've tried telling him that, but the wall has already gone up. He won't even go into Ethan's room." Evie toys with the edge of her napkin. "He spends all day in his wood shop."

"Does he have a lot of orders?"

"Yes. No. I don't know." She shrugs. "Maybe making rocking chairs is cathartic. It was supposed to be a hobby."

"I'm sorry. I hope things get better." I don't know what else to say.

"C'est la vie." Her expression is forlorn.

She gets up from the table. "Other than the fact that I love you and want to see you, I asked you to come here because I have something to give you. You can say no, if you're not ready for it. Someday you'll want these things, but I understand if today is not that day."

Instantly I feel sick. I can guess what she wants to give me. *Ethan's things. There's no way... I'm not ready.* But I know myself, and I know I won't refuse them. I nod my silent acceptance.

I follow Evie from the table, then wait at the foot of the staircase as she goes to Ethan's room and returns holding a large box. "These are just some things I thought you might want. An old sweatshirt from high school, some pictures of you two, letters you wrote him when he was at summer camp, things like that. You don't have to say yes or no right now, but it's here if you want to take it when you leave." She sets the box on the floor next to the front door.

I swallow the huge lump in my throat and blink back my tears. The pain settles like a weight on my chest, but by now that feeling is familiar. I follow Evie to the couch, where we spend two more hours talking. I'm grateful for the box of tissues she places between us, especially when she starts talking about birthday parties.

"We were so lucky you two shared a birthday. Those joint birthday parties were some of my happiest moments. Watching you guys blow out the candles on each other's cakes, making wishes for one another, instead of yourselves..." She pauses, remembering. "Who's idea was it to do that?"

I swallow hard, reaching for another tissue. "Who do you think?"

Her lips pull to one side of her face, wistful. "His heart was gold, wasn't it?"

I can't respond. My brain can't even form the words. I focus instead on wiping my face. *Last year his birthday wish for me came true. I fell in love with him.*

"Chocolate cheesecake!" Evie yells suddenly. "I think we need it, right now."

Evie brings out a box and two forks. She opens the box and sets it between us.

"Don't think, just eat."

I take the fork and obey. The cake is creamy, rich, and delicious. I'm eating my feelings, and it's not all that bad. Maybe my mother is on to something.

After another hour I tell Evie it's time to leave.

"Are you sure?" Her words come with a frown. "Nick should be back soon. He borrowed my car to go look at apartments."

I glance out the large front window and across the street to my mom's house. "My mom's waiting."

Evie pulls me into her when we reach the front door, and we're both crying again.

When I look into her eyes, I see Ethan in the caramel color. It's somewhat comforting. His beautiful eyes are still in my life, even if they don't belong to him.

"I'm going back to work tomorrow, but I'll visit soon." I hug Evie again.

"I love you, Kate. I thought you were going to be my daughter-in-law." Her arms are still around me as she says it.

"I love you, too. You would have made a great mother-in-law." My chest is tight. I step back and bend down to pick up my purse and the box with Ethan's things. I gaze at Evie over the top of the box. What do I look like right now? I feel so many things inside, and I have no idea which emotion has made its way onto my face.

Evie sighs, the sound bearing the weight of her sadness. "Bye, Kate."

"Bye, Evie."

I try not to think about what I'm carrying as I stop at my car to deposit the box. Holding his belongings in my hands feels like a gut punch. I wipe my eyes and walk across the street to my mom's house.

***

"Mom, I don't want to talk, okay?" It's the third time she's asked, and the third time I've refused.

She won't let it go. "You need to talk about this. Don't shut down."

The concern in her eyes only irritates me further. "Quit looking at me like that."

"Like what? Like I love you and want what's best for you? Sorry, I'm not going to stop." Her arms cross in front of her.

I've only been here for half an hour, and already I want to go back to my apartment. If I left now I would hurt her feelings.

"Noah didn't stay long." I don't have to ask if he's gone. Noah's visits are always short.

Mom pushes aside her hair and frowns. "He wanted to surprise you at your apartment, but I told him you probably didn't want company. He went back to Oregon last night." She shakes her head, her frown deepening. "I don't know what it is about him. He can't stand to be here."

I keep going with her train of thought, just to keep her from going back to Ethan. "Maybe it reminds him too much of Dad."

Her eyebrows pull together in confusion. "Doesn't he want to be reminded of Dad?"

"I have no idea. Why don't you ask him?"

"Did Evie give you a box?" Her tone is nonchalant, like she didn't just abruptly change the subject.

"Yes. And before you ask, no, I don't want to go through the box right now."

Her face falls. "You need to start dealing with this, honey. The only way to do that is to face it head on. I have some knowledge in this department, you know."

Then you should know to leave me alone right now.

I take a deep breath to calm myself down. "Mom, grief is very personal, and I'm not going to handle it the same way you handled it. It's only been nine days. Besides, I am moving forward. I'm going back to work tomorrow."

"Good." She nods her support of my decision.

I sense an opening to set up my exit, and take it.

"Speaking of, I need to leave soon. I need a good night's rest." I point to the dark circles under my eyes.

"Can you stay a little longer?" Her eyebrows rise with hope.

I glance around the kitchen and remember she's alone now that my brother has left.

"I can make tea," she offers.

I nod. "Sure."

It's not like I have anything to rush home to.

***

I HOLD it together when I step out of my mom's house and see Ethan's house across the street.

I hold it together when I head to my car in the Shepherds' driveway and remember all the times I bounded across the street and knocked on their front door. *Can Ethan come out to play?*

I hold it together all the way to my car. And then I sit in the driver's seat and see Ethan's box in the passenger seat.

Ethan sat in that spot when he was here. Now his *belongings* are there. I hate the word *belongings*.

I hit the steering wheel.

Over and over.

Pain spreads through my palms and over my knuckles, but I don't stop.

The car door opens, and I'm lifted out.

My breath catches in my throat. I'm in someone's arms.

Nick.

His hair brushes my shoulder as he leans forward, bending to gently set me on my feet.

I use my forearm to wipe my wet face. He pulls the bottom of his shirt away from his body and offers it to me.

"No way." I shake my head and a tiny bit of laughter escapes. It takes me by surprise. Laughter. *That's what it feels like.* How quickly the mind forgets.

Nick eyes me. "You should really pick a fight with someone who can at least fight back."

I shake out my throbbing right hand. "I'll consider that next time."

"Want to talk about anything?" His face is hopeful. *Why does everybody want me to talk to them? Nobody needs to see what a mess I am.*

"I'm good. Better go." I turn back, pausing in my open car door. "I have to work in the morning. Thanks for, uh... Thanks." My face flames.

Nick stands in the driveway and stares at me as I reverse and get the hell away from the place that used to hold happy memories.

16

JULY

HI KATE,

You wouldn't believe what happened to me a couple weeks ago. I was coming out of the house where I'm staying and there was a girl fighting her car. Well, technically she was fighting her steering wheel. Anyway, I broke up the fight. I think she'll be okay. I don't know about the car though.

Phoenix has been cool. That's not true. It's really hot. And shitty. It's hard for anything to be good right now. You might not know this, but I lost my best friend. He was killed fighting a war. I wasn't there for him. I was in Germany doing my exit interviews. I talked to him that morning before he left for his mission. He had to get off the phone with me so he could Skype with his girlfriend.

I've been looking for an apartment. There's a lot of nice stuff out here. Then again, pretty much everything is nice when you're coming from where I've been.

I hope you had an okay week.

Nick

P.S. That girl who fought her car— Did I mention she was you?

. . .

Mom, voicemail:

"Kate, it's your mother. This is my third call. Why aren't you answering? I've talked to Harper. I know you're ignoring me."

Mom, voicemail:

"Katherine Rae Masters, I'm beginning to get upset."

Mom, voicemail:

"I thought you were doing better. You had lunch with Evie three weeks ago. You talked to me after. I thought... I'm worried about you."

THERE's a buzzing sound on my nightstand. I grab my phone and open just one eye. I can't open the other. It hurts too much.

Sarah Maxwell: *Where are you? Lynn asked me if I've heard from you.*

What the hell? I force my pounding head up to look at the clock.

Ten. On a Monday morning. *Shit.*

I just need my Tylenol. Then I can call Lynn and tell her I'm too sick to come in.

On my dresser are two pills and a note.

You are hilarious when you're drunk.
Take these, you're going to need them.
H

When did I talk to Harper? I don't remember seeing her last night. But I do remember sitting on the couch and pouring a fourth drink. After that... Nothing.

*Doesn't matter...*because last night, I kissed Ethan. The more I drink, the more real Ethan becomes. And last night he was alive, vital, and in my arms. I smelled his clean, woodsy scent. Tasted his tongue, his pink lips. Felt stubble on his cheeks.

The alcohol brings him to life. *I'll never have to be without him again.*

A peaceful feeling flows through my veins and warms me. I've discovered exactly how to keep Ethan alive. And it's good I did.

Either I was going to die or Ethan was going to live.

Lucky for me it's the better of my two choices.

***

WHEN I COME out of my room, I find Harper in the living room, lying on the couch with her computer on her lap. Her head's propped up on a pillow, and she's typing. Her fingers stop moving when she sees me.

One side of her mouth turns up. "Well, well, well. It's about time you woke up. Did you take the medicine?"

I nod. I don't know what I said last night, and I don't want to admit it by asking her.

"I need something to eat. And coffee. And water. I need a lot of things." I walk to the kitchen. Behind me I hear Harper set her computer on the table and follow me.

"I like drunk Kate."

I ignore her and start the coffee. How can she like me

when I'm as drunk as I was last night? I'm the very worst version of myself. *But it's so worth it.*

Harper leans an elbow on the counter and watches me slice a grapefruit. "Why aren't you saying anything?"

"I'm not sure what to say. I got really drunk last night and didn't call in sick until ten."

"What did Lynn say?"

"I told her I'm sick. I think she knew I was lying." I bite my lip.

Harper dismisses my words with a wave of her hand. "You *are* sick. Look at you. Bags under your bloodshot eyes. Blotchy skin. Definitely sick."

Thanks a lot. I already know how bad I look. And it's not just from last night.

I eat my grapefruit and keep my comment to myself.

Harper plucks a wedge from the cutting board. "As long as you recover by tomorrow night." She sinks her teeth into the fruit.

I look up in alarm. Harper's watching me expectantly, a smile on her face. And I have no idea what she's talking about.

"Remind me again what tomorrow night is?" I focus on eating as though it requires intense concentration.

"Hah!"

My shoulders startle at her victorious laugh.

"I knew you didn't remember last night." She looks smug.

"Fine. I don't remember. Can you please fill me in?"

She walks to the fridge and picks out a bottle of sparkling water. I watch her grab a glass and pour. Slowly. My patience gives out when she grabs a lime and a knife.

I snatch the lime from her hand and pull it to my chest. "Why was I was so hilarious last night?"

She huffs. She's used to me playing her games. *Old Kate.*

She shakes out her long hair. "You were impersonating yourself and Ethan when you guys were younger."

My groan is loud. I don't even know what I would have to impersonate. I set the lime down on the counter.

"Show me." I don't want to know, but I also really, really do.

Harper sets down her knife and claps her hands once with excitement. "Yay, I love charades."

My life is not a game.

Harper clears her throat and shakes out her arms, then sings like she's warming up. "Me me me me me meeee."

I cross my arms. "Enough."

I'm terrified of what Harper is about to say. But I need to know. I need to know what my drunken thoughts are. Because I certainly don't remember them.

"Ethan, let's study for finals. I'm a prissy rule follower, and I must study at least two hours a day." Harper's voice is falsetto. *I don't sound like that, but okay.* She jumps and turns around, facing the direction she just came from.

"Kate, I don't want to study. I want to tell you I love you again." Her voice is deep now. She does the jump and turn.

"No, Ethan. We can't be more than friends because I say so. Even though I love you too. In a few years I'll realize we should be together. Just hang tight." She jumps and turns.

"I'll just sit here and wait for you to change your mind. I'm loyal. In the meantime, I'll join the Army."

Jump and turn.

"Ethan, that's a great idea. You go fight the bad guys, and we'll wait until the day I decide I'm finally in love with you. But first I'll date a few guys and make you really jealous."

Jump and turn.

"Kate, that's perfect. I love watching you try to deny your

feelings about me by dating other people. Just let me know when you're ready."

Jump and turn. Hand waving manically.

"Ethan, oh Ethan. I'm ready. I'm not stupid anymore. Now it's time for us to be in love."

Jump and turn.

"Awesome, Kate. I've been here all along, but the wait has been swell. Let's be in love now."

Jump and turn.

"Oh, Ethan, let's be together forever, like a real fairytale."

Jump and turn.

"Oh, Kate, sorry I can't. I have to get on the helicopter and die and leave you behind forever. Too bad you didn't love me earlier. Maybe I wouldn't have joined the Army. Well, see ya later."

No more jumping, no more turning. She doubles over, her laughter filling our small kitchen, making it smaller.

My chest is tight, my eyes burn. Why did I say all those things? Why did I say anything at all? And how is any of this funny? My broken insides are no laughing matter, even if I was drunk and talking crazy. Why can't she see that?

Harper recovers and looks at me. "Well, fine. It was funny last night when you were hammered and jumping around."

I can only nod. I have no idea how to respond.

Harper looks at me, exasperation plain on her face. *Does she really expect me to find it funny?*

She grabs her water glass and points at the living room. "I have emails to send. I'm double checking everything for tomorrow night's party. The one you agreed to go to." She looks at me pointedly.

There's no way I'm going to a party tomorrow night, but

I'm not telling her right now. She'll start spouting trite clichés like, *'Get back on the horse'*.

If I hear her say that one more time...

She's back in her place on the couch when I pass her on the way to my room.

"By the way, I deserve an Oscar for that reenactment." She doesn't look at me as she speaks. She's typing again.

Old Kate's temper would have flared at that comment. But new Kate doesn't care. New Kate doesn't feel.

17

AUGUST

Hi Kate,

Ethan warned me it would be hot here during the summer. Getting into my car is awful. Tomorrow I'm having the windows tinted. In Connecticut my windows didn't need tint. In AZ, it should be mandatory.

I got a job. My experience as an Army medic qualified me to be an EMT here in the civilian world. Ultimately I want to be a doctor. I'm starting classes at ASU in January. I didn't take school seriously before I joined the Army, but I will now.

Hope you're doing okay. Maybe write me back this time? Your mom and Evie are worried.

Nick

P.S. Your mom is really funny.

Mom, voicemail:

"I was hoping you'd answer. You answered my call last week. I think I'll just keep calling you every week."

. . .

MOM, voicemail:

"Another week, another unanswered phone call. It's a good thing Harper answers her phone, or I wouldn't know that you're okay. Whatever your version of okay is."

ZANE, voicemail:

"Hey Kate. I'm back from Idaho. Classes start tomorrow, just wanted to give you a call and see how you're doing. Take care."

"KATE, I've got your wine. The one you keep going through at breakneck speed."

Harper's voice reaches me in my bedroom. I find her in the kitchen, unloading groceries.

I open the pantry door and start putting away dry goods. "Thanks for grocery shopping. I'll give you some cash."

"I'd prefer it if you'd just start cooking again."

I swallow and look away. I have no desire to cook.

"Fine. I get it. You're still not ready to start acting like the Kate we all know and love."

She picks up the wine bottle and pushes it to my chest. "Take your wine and go hide with it. Get drunk like you do every night." It's a mean comment, but she speaks in such an even tone that it's hard to be certain if she meant to be rude.

I take the bottle. "I thought you like drunk Kate." *I should be mortified right now, but I'm not. Why is that?*

"I like drunk Kate when she's funny." Her hands go to her hips and her head tilts as she looks at me. "You're not funny anymore. You're...sad."

I walk to my room. No glass necessary. This sad, pathetic excuse for a person drinks wine from the bottle.

The wine bottle comes in the shower with me. When the

hot water runs over my shoulders I twist off the cap and take a big drink.

When I get to work in the morning, I'll take three pain relievers from the stash in my desk drawer, and I'll make it through the day. Then I'll come home and do it all again.

Work, drink, repeat.

***

Two weeks later Harper sends me a text as I'm leaving work.

Harper: Are you going to be at home tonight?

Me: Of course I'm going to be at home tonight.

Harper doesn't tell me why she asked, and by the time I get home I forget to care. I'm sitting on the couch with her after dinner, waiting an acceptable amount of time before I can announce my escape to my room. My eyes grow heavy. Soon I'll be asleep. *Just get to your bed so you can hold the pillow he slept on.*

Harper makes a noise, and I look at her. She rolls her eyes. *At my sleepiness?* She mutes the TV, throws the remote on the table, and turns to me.

"We need to have a heart to heart."

"About what?" I ask, even though I'm sure I know the answer. She's finally going to ask me how I'm doing dealing with Ethan's death.

"You need a pep talk."

What?

"And what exactly do I need to get pepped about?"

Harper crosses her arms, all business. "Returning to life." She states it so matter-of-factly.

Returning to life? I shake my head, confused. "What are you getting at?"

"You've been moping around here, not going anywhere or doing anything. It's been two months since Ethan died. It's time to get on with your life."

I sit, silent and unmoving, trying to absorb her words. She's never been sensitive, but this is a whole new level.

"See, you're thinking about what I said. I knew talking to you was the right thing to do."

I want to smack the smug look off her face.

I shake my head, trying to calm myself down. I'm not sleepy anymore. "The right thing for you to do would be to actually be my friend and help me as I grieve for whom and what I lost. How could you even suggest that it's time for me to move on?" My voice raises as I talk until I'm a notch below yelling.

"Whoa, calm down." Harper holds her hands out defensively. "If you want to wallow in self-pity, then so be it. Don't say I didn't try to get you back on your feet."

I open and close my mouth several times before I'm able to put together a response. When I do, it's bubbling from my loosely tethered temper.

"This conversation is over. I can't say I'm shocked by your insensitivity, but I'm surprised you're being so heartless." I get up from the couch and head to the kitchen to clean up from dinner.

Harper follows, continuing to talk even though I said we're done. "I miss Ethan, too, okay? I'm sad, too. But I'm not going to crawl into a hole and die."

I stare at her from my place at the sink, my jaw dropped down in astonishment.

"You weren't the one in love with Ethan." I slam a plate

into the dishwasher and hear it crack. "It's not all about you, Harper. For once, this is about me."

As I say the words, I begin to understand why Harper's being so callous. This *pep talk* is starting to make sense.

Harper's used to being the center of attention, and right now, she isn't. People are talking about me, and losing Ethan, and how awful that is for me. Harper recently told me just exactly that. She said every time she hangs out with any of her friends or sees anybody who knows me, they ask about me. Surely that would irritate someone who is the center of her own universe—*and make her jealous.*

Of course Harper is eager to right the ship and get the focus back on her, where she believes it belongs.

"That's not at all what this is about. I just want you to move past it." Her hands are on her hips.

I close the dishwasher and wash my hands. "Whether you know it or not, this is all about you. Everyone still loves you, Harper. You're still the person they all want to be friends with. Pretty soon everyone will be bored of my sad fate and stop asking you about me. In the meantime, I'll continue to work through each day the best that I can. And you can keep any future pep talks to yourself."

I walk to my bedroom and shut the door, ending the conversation for good.

18

SEPTEMBER

Hi Kate,

This is my third email. If you don't respond in two weeks I'm coming to look for you. Getting your address will be easy.

If that happens, I'll be coming from my own apartment. I moved out of the Shepherds' house a few weeks ago. It feels pretty good to be on my own. It was nice of Evie and James to let me stay there, but... It was hard. Ethan measured his height on his door frame. Some of your measurements are on there too, but way below Ethan's. Shorty.

Two weeks, Kate. Two weeks and I'm going to come looking for you. You're shirking your tour guide responsibilities. And I need to know where I can get the best tacos.

Nick

P.S. Ethan asked me to look out for you. But you're making it really hard.

"Honey?"

My mom's voice comes through my bedroom door.

Crap. I get out of bed and look at my reflection. Under eye bags? Check. Pajamas? Check. Greasy hair? Check.

And it's six on a Saturday night. She'll have a field day with this.

"Come in."

Her head peeks around the door first, then she walks in all the way. What was she looking for before she decided to commit to a full entry?

"Hi, Mom." I watch her take me in. "What are you doing here?"

She tries to hide her shock, but I see it anyway. She has a terrible poker face. Her lips purse, her eyes get bigger.

"I was in the area. My financial planner is nearby. I honestly don't know why I need one, but your father liked him a lot." She leans into my dresser mirror and fiddles with her hair. "I guess I keep him because the appointments remind me of your dad."

She flips back around, her face hopeful. "Is there anything you do to remind you of Ethan?"

Her voice is soft, cautious. She's treading lightly, like I'm an agitated animal. *Don't poke the bear.*

"No," I hear myself say. *Unless you count getting drunk every night so that my brain conjures up memories and has vivid dreams. Then, yes.*

She studies me. I want to shrink into my bed and hide under the covers. I don't want to talk any more.

When she takes my hands I almost cry. *Almost.* I could do it. Right now. I could open up and let her in. Tell her I don't have a heart anymore. That I don't feel anything. *Anything.* I live only for the nights when my world transforms and I'm whole again. That's when Ethan is alive, and *we exist.*

I choke back the words. Letting them out could be a step toward recovering. And if I do that, I'll lose him. *Again.*

My mom steps back and drops my hands. Her lips press tightly together as she regards me. I wait for her to say more, to ask me again to open up. Her lips part.

"Want to get dinner?"

I'm so relieved by her invitation that I accept it. *As long as we leave Ethan out of the dinner conversation, I can go.*

Her lips twist into a half-smile. "Would you mind taking a shower?"

I laugh. Not a real laugh. An involuntary chuckle. Something in my brain knows this is funny, but my body doesn't feel the happiness that comes with laughter. It's an automatic response. My mom doesn't know that, though, and she laughs too. The hope is back on her face.

"I'll be out in ten."

"Don't rush." Her face is lit up. "I'll look for a good place while you're getting ready."

I grab an outfit from my closet and walk to the bathroom.

When I pull on my jeans I realize how long it's been since I've worn them. It's been work clothes and pajamas for almost three months.

I come out of the bathroom and find my mom bent over the open drawer of my nightstand. "What are you doing?"

She jumps. The drawer bangs shut.

"Umm, I was just, uh..." She blinks a few times in a row.

"What were you trying to find?"

"A journal."

I roll my eyes. I haven't kept a journal in years.

"Honey, I'm worried. Give me a break. You're my daughter. You won't talk to me. It's been three months since Ethan died."

Not three months. *Two months and twenty-seven days.* I turn away from her words.

"Kate, please. You need to talk to me. You need to talk to someone." Her voice breaks on the last word. "I'm scared for you."

"I'm fine. Okay?" My tone is harsh. "I'm fine."

"I'm your mom. I love you more than anyone else. And I know how it feels to lose the love of your life. If there's anybody who could understand what you're feeling, it's me."

"Stop, Mom. Just stop!" I walk to the dresser and attack my wet hair with a comb. It hurts, but I don't stop. "I don't want to talk. And I don't want to get dinner, either."

She crosses her arms and stands straighter, eyes piercing me. My brother calls it her Showdown Stance. It makes me feel like I'm in high school again. "Nick said he's sent you three emails. Why don't you respond to him? He could help you deal with things."

Unless Nick can make me dream of Ethan like my good buddy vino, I'm not interested.

I shrug again.

"You haven't talked to Evie."

"No." I look down at the tan carpet and push my big toe in between the fibers.

"She's been calling you. Just like I have. We're both worried about you."

"I'm fine," I mumble.

"She wants to see you."

I want to see her too, but I can't. I can't risk losing Ethan. Evie will want to talk. She'll try to make me feel better. And if I do, he'll go away. *Not happening.*

I have to say something to get Mom off my back. "I'll call her." I move around my mom and grab my purse off the bed.

"I changed my mind about dinner. Let's go." I start for the door.

"One day, you'll heal. Promise." Her whisper reaches out, finds me where I walk ahead of her. I'm not sure if she meant for me to hear her. But it doesn't matter.

She's wrong.

19

OCTOBER

"I'M HERE. DON'T YOU KNOW THAT I'M HERE? I HAVEN'T GONE anywhere."

He's leaning over me where I lie in my bed, wearing a blue shirt the color of a cloudless day.

"You look sick." Concern steals the smile from his face. "What's wrong?"

Tears slide out of the sides of my eyes. "You're dead."

Ethan shakes his head. "No, I'm not."

I CAN'T FOCUS. Not after the dream I had last night. And Lynn is going to be very unhappy if I'm not prepared for the meeting. I was supposed to send my notes to Sarah yesterday. I sit back in my chair and stare at the blank computer screen. *Ethan said he was alive.* My mind replays the dream again. And again. And again. In all my other dreams Ethan never says those words.

At five minutes to eleven Sarah walks into my little space and leans down. "I never received those notes on Reynolds and Leyva." She looks at my computer, like perhaps they will be on it, waiting to be printed. I look down at my shoes. I can't see Sarah's frown but I'm certain it's there. She sighs. "Let's go to the meeting."

On heavy feet I walk beside her. *This is so unlike me.* My nervous stomach churns.

We sit in our normal seats. Lynn starts the meeting like she always does. We take turns discussing our current workload in the same order we always go in. Everything works like clockwork, until Lynn turns to me.

"Kate, what do you have for us today?" Her cool eyes gaze at me expectantly. *I used to be her star.* The thought saddens me.

"Well," I take a breath, my brain scrambling. "Reynolds and Leyva are back with a request to paint them as a law firm for the people. They feel they've gotten away from the smaller cases that are their bread and butter, and they need to remind the public they are still the 'guys on the ground'. Their words." *That was pretty good. Hopefully Lynn glosses over my brevity. And the fact I don't have an action plan to share.*

Lynn props an elbow on the arm of her chair and rests her chin on her fist. "What about the other issue with Reynolds and Leyva?"

I gulp.

"What other issue?" I arrange my features into a concerned, confused look. It's not too hard. The consternation I feel is genuine. My embarrassment is genuine, too.

Lynn's expression doesn't change, but the disappointment is there in her eyes. "Reynolds and Leyva are considering creating their own PR department. Their email stated this."

Shit... How did I miss that?

I want to look away and drown in my mortification, but her dismayed eyes hold me. After a few seconds she bends over her paper and jots something down. I know it's a note about the most current state of the client, but I wonder if she's added something else. Something like, *Kate is distracted and showing poor performance.* She looks back at me. "They've been your client for three years. You need to show them why it's more valuable to stay with Simone. Make them see why you're better than an in-house shop." She says it, and I wonder if she really believes that I'm better, or if I only used to be.

I nod my head vigorously. "I can do that."

Lynn regards me for one more moment before she moves on. I look away too, only to meet a bevy of stares. Some curious, some befuddled, and some smug.

I'm one of the last people to leave after the meeting is over. Sarah's waiting for me when I walk out. She looks at me with sad eyes.

"I say this out of love: Get it together." She turns and walks quickly in the opposite direction of her cube. I shrink back into the conference room and close the door, the tears flowing.

Another person who is *right*. My mom wants me to talk to her about what I'm going through, and she's *right*. Harper wants me to move on, and in a twisted way, she's *right*. Sarah wants me to get my professional act together, and she's *right*. But they don't know what I know. They don't know that Ethan comes to me at night, in the darkest part of my grief, and kisses my tears.

I won't give that up. Not for anything. And I don't care that it's not right.

I know what I have to do when I'm finished with work today.

***

THE SUN IS low in the sky but I think I can make it up and down Camelback before nightfall. I lace up my tennis shoes and start on the trail.

I'm here for one reason only.

If there's any chance Ethan is alive, this mountain is where I'll find him. When I get to the top and the breeze lifts my hair, I'll feel him.

I make good time, despite how out of shape I am. The path is familiar, and the reason why I know it so well is painful.

I make it to the top and walk the perimeter of the large peak. *Where are you, Ethan?*

I go to the flat rock, the one I sat on with Ethan dozens of times. My eyes close. I inhale deeply, the smell of dirt and sweat filling my nose.

The last time we were here together, you kissed me. I sat here, and you kissed me. Please come back to me. You told me if I waited, you would come for me. I'm here. Please come for me.

Nothing.

My eyes squeeze tight. Why can't I feel his touch on my hand? His fingertips on my shoulder? *You said you're not dead. You said you haven't gone anywhere.*

I wait.

Nothing happens.

I wait longer.

Finally I open my eyes. I'm alone on the mountain. The bottom of the sun touches the top of the horizon.

"Where are you?" I scream, my voice falling to the houses and cars below me. My hands swipe at my cheeks. I look at them, see the dirt on my palms streaked from my tears.

He's not here.

Because he's dead.

Stupid. So stupid.

I go too fast on the way down, trying to beat the setting sun. I'm not surprised when my foot slides on loose dirt and I fall. Hot pain rides up my leg.

I grunt and stand. I try to put weight on my foot. It's okay. I think it's okay. I take a step. Pain shoots up.

"Shit," I mutter, reaching to my back pocket for my phone. It's not there. I look around and spot it a few feet away. I sit down and reach, but my outstretched arm isn't long enough. I crawl, wincing at the gravel digging into my knees, and get my phone.

"Harper, thank God," I say when she answers.

"What's up? I'm working."

"I need help. I fell on Camelback, and I think I sprained something."

"Are you on the trail right now? It's almost dark!"

"I need you to come get me." I reach for my water bottle that rolled to the side of the trail and take a long drink.

"Can't. I'm running an event for a very needy woman. If I leave she'll throw a fit."

I balk at her refusal while I'm still drinking and end up coughing on the water. I recover and toss the bottle aside, my panic rising.

"I need help!" The sun seems to dip lower with every word I speak.

"Call Nick. He's probably the only person strong enough to carry you off the trail."

"I don't have his number." My voice breaks, the stress seeping through.

"I do. I'll call him."

"Don't, I'll—"

Harper hangs up.

I sigh and carefully turn over to sit. In the rapidly waning sunlight, I study my ankle. It doesn't *look* injured.

I stand. It doesn't feel horrible. It hurts, but it's not excruciating. Maybe I can hobble down.

I step.

Pain ricochets through my ankle and up my leg, and I drop, my body falling sideways. Needles stab my left arm. "Shit. God, that hurts."

My upper half is off the trail, arm resting on a low-lying cactus. A burning sensation moves over my arm. Using just my right hand, I hoist myself up and shift my body away. My left arm screams, but I use it anyway to move myself all the way back onto the trail.

The sun goes down fast in the desert, and I'm already losing light. Using my phone's flashlight, I study my arm. Thick, waxen cactus needles stick in the tender flesh. I'm able to remove a majority of the needles with my fingers, but there are a few that won't budge.

I hiss in frustration. I want to hurl my phone.

Keep trying. You have nothing else to do. Except sit here and wait for a rattlesnake to bite you.

I'm using my teeth to pull out the last needle when my phone rings. I stare at the ten digits for a moment before realization dawns.

"Nick?" My voice is shrill.

"Where are you?" His voice is strong. Not panicked.

"On Camelback mountain. Don't go out of your way. I can call Zane. I'm sorry Harper interr—"

"I'm already here. Yell for me."

I look out into the dark, even though I know I won't see him. "Umm...okay. What should I yell?"

"*Help* is traditional. But let's try something else." I hear the scrape of sandy dirt moving. *He's walking.* "Yell your favorite color."

"Pink," I call out.

"Ketchup or mustard?"

"Mustard."

"You have to yell it."

"Mustard," I yell.

"Vanilla or chocolate?"

"Strawberry."

"Yell it."

"Sorry. Strawberry!" I turn my face up and belt out the word.

"I heard that one. I'm getting closer." He breathes loudly into the phone.

"You sound like a hurricane."

"What?" he asks. More huffing.

"You're breathing into the phone. It sounds like a hurricane."

"You try running on a trail."

I glance down at my ankle. "I did. That's how I got into this mess."

"Good point. I'll slow down."

I turn my head. There's light from the city in the distance, but it's not enough to let me see anything close to me.

"Do you like eggs scrambled or over-easy?"

"Scrambled," I shout.

"You don't have to yell anymore now that I've heard you. I know your approximate location."

A warm blush hits my cheeks. "Okay."

"We're going to play a game where I ask you a question and you answer without thinking."

"Isn't that what we've been doing?"

"You've been avoiding me. Yes or no?"

"No." I pause. "Yes. But not on purpose."

"You read my emails. Yes or no?"

"Yes."

"You wish you hadn't agreed to be my tour guide. Yes or no?"

"Yes." I bite my lip.

"You miss our best friend. Yes or no?"

"Of course."

The sound of gravel crunching reaches my ears. And it's not just through the phone.

"Is that you?" My heart beats faster. An arc of light shines out across the mountain near me. "Do you have a flashlight?"

"No."

"What? Who the hell else is out here right now?" What if it's a crazy person? What if they drag me away before Nick can get to me? What if—?

Nick appears around the curve of the trail.

"It is you!"

Relief makes me sag back on my arms. The left one protests, even with the absence of cactus needles.

"What's on your head?"

Nick hangs up the phone and jogs the last ten feet.

When he reaches me he bends down so we're eye to eye.

"It's a headlamp. I wanted to keep my hands free."

"Do you keep one lying around?"

"I had it in Afghanistan."

"It's...interesting." I want to laugh at the band around his forehead.

He smirks. "You can laugh at me later. Are you ready to get out of here, or did you want to do a little star gazing?"

"Screw the stars."

He places one arm under my bent knees, the other around the middle of my back, and lifts me into the air.

"I'm going to take it slow. If we both fall it'll be bad news."

I nod. I haven't been this close to anybody in months. Harper doesn't hug me. Even when she knows I'm struggling. *Which is all the time.*

I hold my head away from his body, but my nose turns in. I just want to smell him. Maybe he smells like Ethan.

I sniff slowly, so I don't make any noise. *He doesn't smell like Ethan.*

Nick smells like sweat and some kind of body wash.

I peek up at his face. His jaw is very square. And his nose looks like it's been broken before.

"Are you doing okay down there?" He keeps his eyes ahead.

"You've had a broken nose. Yes or no?"

A flicker of something goes through his eyes. "Yes."

"You're having a hard time dealing with Ethan's death. Yes or no?" His eyes stay focused on the terrain as he asks me the question.

I suck in a breath. "Yes," I whisper.

Nick steps down hard off a rock and my teeth clatter. "Sorry. I'll be more gentle."

"With your questions or how you're walking?"

He stops and looks down at me. His blue eyes crinkle at the corners, apologetic and sad. "Both."

"Thank you," I say as he starts walking.

He doesn't ask another question until we're back at the car. "Do you have ice packs at home?"

I nod.

"Do you have a wrap for your ankle?"

"Yes."

He looks surprised. "Really?"

"I have a whole first-aid kit. Fully stocked."

He opens the passenger door of my car and helps me into the seat. "You're ready for everything, aren't you?"

Not everything. Nothing can prepare a person for heartbreak.

He gets in the driver's seat and looks at me. "Keys? Please don't tell me you left them out there." He peers through the windshield at the mountain.

I reach into the glove compartment, grab the keys, and hand them over.

He turns on the car and backs out.

"What about your car?" I point as we pass the only other car in the parking lot.

"You can bring me back for it in the morning. Assuming your sprain isn't too bad."

"Are you staying the night with me?"

"I can get an Uber."

My hand protests before my lips speak the words. "Stay the night. I don't want you going any further out of your way."

Nick drives out of the trailhead, and I give him directions. Before the mountain disappears from sight I look back at it. *I can't believe I was up there in the dark.*

"Kate?"

"Hmmm?" I look at Nick. The headlamp rests in his lap.

"Ethan and I had an arrangement. If I died, he would take care of my mom. And if he died, I would take care of you." Nick turns to look at me. "So that's what I'm going to do. I just thought you should know." He looks back to the road.

Tears well up in my eyes. I bite my knuckles and stare out my window.

***

"This is a nice apartment," Nick says when we walk in. He looks around. "Very...feminine."

From my place in his arms I turn my head to see what he sees. Lots of mirrors... *Harper's idea.* Candles everywhere. *Harper's candles.* A lot of ivory and light pink. *Harper.*

"Thanks. You can probably put me down now." I point and flex the toes below my hurt ankle.

Nick frowns. "I don't think you should be holding your own weight yet."

He strides to the couch and puts me down. "I'll be back in a second." He goes to the kitchen.

Only his upper half is visible above the half-wall. He opens the freezer, then some drawers, a couple cabinets, and I hear glasses clink.

"Why don't you ask me where stuff is?"

He looks up at me and then looks back down. "I'm learning."

"Learning?"

"Yeah." He walks around the wall and back to me, arms full.

"Lie back," he instructs.

While I'm doing that, he grabs my hurt foot and places it on two pillows.

"Keep this elevated."

I nod, watching him wrap a bag of frozen peas in a kitchen towel. He adds the frozen peas to the top of my ankle.

"I have ice packs in there."

"I saw. Peas are better. Try not to move. It needs to stay on there." He studies my ankle, then looks around. He leans back, grabs a pillow off the loveseat, and gently tucks it under my head.

"How do you feel?" he asks on his way back into the kitchen.

"Embarrassed." I sigh and push the hair out of my face. "I can't believe that happened. I've hiked that mountain a hundred times."

Nick walks back to the couch. "Why were you up there so late?"

I look away.

"You don't have to tell me. It's okay. Here."

I look back. In one hand Nick holds a water glass, in the other, a bottle of pills. "Anti-inflammatory. Two or three?"

"But if I take those..." *I need to see Ethan.* If I take those I can't drink.

"If you take these...?" Nick's eyebrows rise on his forehead.

"Nothing, nothing." I hold out a hand.

Nick places the pills in my palm and helps me sit up. He hands me the glass of water.

I don't know if I'll see you in my dreams now. The thought is soul crushing.

I swallow the pills individually, each one heavy like a stone. When I'm done Nick takes the glass. I lie back down.

"Tell me about Connecticut."

I close my eyes as Nick talks. His voice is deep and smooth.

"...green. Different than the green here. The green back home is like the original color from the crayon box. Here it's more olive green."

His words start sounding far away.

"...and the roads are way better out here. It's so easy to

get around. And the Mexican food. Don't even get me started. I never knew what I was missing..."

When I open my eyes again I'm in my bed. Nick's pulling my sheet up around me.

"Sorry," he whispers as he pulls the comforter over the sheet. "I was trying not to wake you."

"It's okay," I mumble.

"Go back to sleep. I'll see you in the morning." He turns toward the door.

"Nick?"

He pauses, looks back at me. "Yeah?"

"My favorite color isn't pink." I yawn and close my eyes. "It's green. Connecticut green."

His retreating footsteps sound far away.

***

SOMETHING TICKLES MY EAR. My eyes open. Blonde hair hangs in my face.

"What are you doing?" I ask, my voice scratchy.

Harper backs away so I can sit up.

"He is way hotter than I remember. Please tell me he's single. Scratch that. I don't really care if he has a girlfriend." She sends furtive glances out to the living room the whole time she talks.

I rub the sleep from my eyes. "Can you please settle down?"

"I don't know if I can. Have you seen that body?"

I scowl. "Of course not."

Harper scowls right back. "Quit acting like you don't have eyes since Ethan died."

My chest tightens. "Fine. Go jump him. Attack the guy

who recently fought in a war. While he's sleeping. Tell me how that works out for you."

And there it is. The eye roll. She's perfected it in recent months.

"Why are you wearing that awful shirt when a super-hot guy is sleeping on your couch?" She pulls back the cover to see the rest of what I have on.

I look down. Old plaid boxer shorts. Frowning, I pull the 5K Alzheimer's Run T-shirt away from my chest. *He dressed me. Oh, my god.* I sit up and rub my eyes.

A throat clears. It's not mine. It's not Harpers.

"Sorry to interrupt." Nick stands at the entrance to my bedroom. And he doesn't look sorry at all. Instinctively my arms come up, crossing over my chest. I breathe a little sigh of relief when I feel the bump of the spaghetti strap tank top I wore underneath my shirt yesterday.

"It's fine," Harper coos. Her face softens. She glides to my dresser and leans against it, striking a pose in her nightgown. "Thank you for rescuing Kate. I knew you were the right person to call."

Nick's face doesn't change, even with Harper's preening. "Of course. I'm sorry I didn't remember you at first."

My throat constricts with contained laughter. Harper doesn't bat an eye. She gives him a sympathetic look.

"You've been through a lot these past few months. It's understandable. Kate's barely been able to get out of bed. It's a good thing she has to work, or she'd develop bedsores."

Nick looks at me. "How are you feeling?"

"I haven't tried to walk on it yet. Obviously." I point at the bed I'm still sitting in. "We should probably go get—"

"Nick," Harper breaks in like I wasn't even speaking. "Let me make you breakfast, to say thank you for everything you did for Kate last night. If you're waiting for her to make you breakfast, you'll starve. Kate doesn't cook anymore." She pushes off from my dresser and walks out of the room, passing him where he stands in my doorway.

He strides to my bed and sits down on the end. Now that Harper's gone his expression has softened. His eyes look kind.

"Can I examine you?"

I think about the clothes he put me in last night, how he's already seen me half-naked. I gulp. "Yes."

I take my legs out from under the covers and stretch them out. There's a twinge of pain in my ankle, but it's not as bad as it was last night.

Nick re-positions himself on my bed so he's cross-legged and facing me. He picks up my injured ankle, turns it one way, then the other. His expression is serious.

"Mild swelling. You could get an x-ray to check for ligament damage. But it's probably just a sprain. Don't go hiking for a while. Let yourself heal." He holds up a bandage. "I'm going to wrap you. Just in case. If anything it will be a good reminder for you to take it easy."

I nod and watch him as he watches me. Gingerly he picks up my heel and begins wrapping my foot.

"Did you change my clothes for me?" A flush creeps onto my cheeks.

His face is impassive. "You were passed out, and your clothes were filthy."

The flush on my cheeks turns into a flame. He finishes the wrap and looks up.

"I'm a professional, Kate. I was an Army medic and now I'm an EMT. And I respect you."

His words lessen my embarrassment. Only a fraction, though. "Thank you."

He leans back on his hands, eyes not leaving mine.

"Are you going to let me be your friend?"

"Friend? I thought you're supposed to be some kind of keeper." *It's so Ethan to appoint someone my caretaker. That was always his job.*

Nick frowns. "I'd rather be your friend. Keeper makes me think of a zoo animal."

My nose scrunches. "Well, in that case…"

Nick leans in, hand stuck out between us. "Friends answer their phones. Deal?"

Answer the phone.

Interact.

What will I lose?

"Kate? Don't leave me hanging." Nick pushes his open hand closer.

I gulp. The first inch of fissure splits into the walls I've built. I don't want to heal, but I know I can't maintain this lifestyle. Drinking like this… Ethan would hate it. *But how else am I supposed to keep him?*

My hand reaches out. *If I feel Ethan slipping away, the agreement is void.*

"Deal."

Our intertwined hands are poised in mid-air.

"For the record," Nick's eyes glint with triumph, "I'm glad I finally got the chance to start making good on my promise to Ethan."

Nick smiles, and I see why Ethan liked him.

20

NICK

I can't help my grimace as I settle into the front passenger seat of the ambulance. It feels like a dry sauna after being parked in the sun.

"Bet you wish you stayed in Connecticut."

The comment comes from Chad Woodley, the driver and my first friend in Arizona. He chuckles at the face I'm making.

I shrug. "Come December, I'll be happy to be here and not there."

He nods, starting the engine and putting it in reverse. "That's what we tell ourselves all summer long. Just get through summer and it's smooth sailing until next summer." He glances at me as he pulls into the street. "You'll see."

I bite into the sandwich we've just stopped for and try not to be annoyed by the sweat I feel dripping down my neck. At least I get to eat. Chad has to drive, *and* he's hot.

I swallow my bite and ask, "What do you do here when it's not hotter than the inside of an oven?"

"Eat every meal outside. Take my kids to the park. Go hiking. On my days off when my kids are in school I like to hike Camelback. It's beautiful up there. Difficult hike, too. I'll take you up there."

I nod, but I don't tell him I was up there last night. Not that I got the chance to enjoy any of the hike, since it was pretty dark and I wasn't exactly going along at a leisurely pace.

"Sounds good," I tell him, finishing off my sandwich.

He starts talking about his kids, but I'm only half-listening. My mind is on the reason I was on Camelback Mountain last night.

I'd just gotten home from work when Harper called. She went on about how Kate thinks she's in trouble, but Harper thought she was just being dramatic. I knew right away how wrong Harper was. Kate and the word *dramatic* don't go together.

First of all, Ethan wouldn't have been in love with someone like that. Second, none of his stories about Kate made her seem like a person with a predisposition for drama.

After interrupting Harper and getting her to tell me where Kate was, I hung up as quickly as I could. Harper was in the middle of telling me about the woman whose party she was throwing when I told her flat out that I needed to hang up.

I said goodbye without waiting for her response.

Harper might be Kate's roommate, but she gives off bad vibes. I like to think I'm pretty good at reading people, and everything about Harper tells me her intentions are to the benefit of her only.

It didn't take me long to reach the place where Harper said I'd find Kate. It was easy enough to find, considering it's a massive mountain in the center of Phoenix. I don't know what I was expecting, but it wasn't something so big. I'd thought to grab my headlight on my way out the door, but even with that I wasn't so sure this rescue attempt was going to go smoothly.

The first few hundred yards on the trail were easy, but then the mountain pulled an about-face. The terrain turned rocky, and vertical to the point I'd had to use the rails installed to help people along.

That's when I called Kate. Luckily for both of us she wasn't too far up the trail. Once I cleared the vertical section I moved faster, and it wasn't too long after that I found Kate.

She looked tired, worn out, but not too bad considering the pain she was in. I like to think her mood was helped by our conversation as I made my way up the trail.

I lifted her in my arms, and the smell of something floral and sweet washed over me.

She gazed up at me, searching for something, but I can't say what. I still don't understand that look on her face.

Or why she has been ignoring me the past few months. I've been giving her space, knowing how hard this all is on her, but she's used up all the space I'm willing to give. I have a job to do, and she's not going to keep me from doing it any longer.

She agreed to be my friend, and that's all I really need to make sure I accomplish what I came here to do.

Chad is still talking about his kids. He speaks about them, and his wife, with reverence. It makes me hopeful. One day, I want to do the same. I want a messy house full of kids and a wife who gets down on the floor and plays with our kids. I want someone whose face I feel supremely lucky to wake up next to. I want someone who will fight with me and call me on my shit.

She'll be a fierce protector of our children, but so tender-hearted that she'll kiss the pain away from their injuries.

She'll be everything my mom wasn't.

We pull back up to the station and Chad parks the ambulance. Our next task will be to clean and restock the back of the ambulance following our last call.

Just in time too, before I have any more of a chance to think about the kind of parent my mom was before she put down the bottle.

21

KATE

Two weeks later I'm sitting at work when Nick calls. As promised, I answer my phone.

"It worked," he says in lieu of hello.

"What worked?"

"Your phone."

"I told you I would answer." As hard as it is, I tear my eyes from the email I'm writing.

"How's the ankle?"

"Healed, I guess. No pain. I've stayed off it, like you told me to." It wasn't too hard to follow Nick's instructions. It's not like I do much these days.

"Good. So here's the thing. I need cooking lessons. If I bring over some stuff, will you teach me how to make it?" His voice is hopeful.

"What makes you think I know how to cook?" My panic level rises. I haven't cooked in four months. I live on sandwiches and salads. Things that can be assembled. Cooking was Old Kate.

"That morning at your place Harper said you don't cook *anymore*. And Evie told me you used to cook all the time."

I stay quiet.

"So, here's what I'm proposing. Every Thursday night I bring over food and you teach me how to prepare it. Weekly lessons."

My teeth work my bottom lip as I pick up a pen and start doodling on a piece of paper on my desk. "You know there are instructions and videos all over the Internet, right?" I sketch a tiny carrot.

"I'm a visual learner." *This guy has an answer for everything.* I draw a small banana.

"Do you have a recipe you want to try?"

"Risotto."

I draw little grains of rice. "You're starting with risotto? I thought you were going to say something easy, like pasta."

"I like a challenge."

"Risotto it is."

He hangs up after we agree on a time. I look at my pathetic excuse for a drawing. *Ethan was always the better artist. My thing was words. Fitting them together, arranging them so they flowed in a smooth undulation.*

Sarah appears at my side. "I heard you say risotto, and now I'm hungry." She glances at the paper on the desk in front of me. "Nice drawing. Very... third grade."

"I skipped art class." I ball up the paper and toss it in the trash.

"Want to get lunch? I mean, can you?" Sarah lowers her voice. "Are you taking lunch anymore?"

My eyebrows pull together. "Yes, why?"

"Well, um, I um..." Sarah picks at a pleat in her skirt and clears her throat. "You've been late every day this week, so I wasn't sure."

"When you saw me this morning, I was coming from

Lynn's office. I wasn't late." *Monday through Wednesday, that's a different story.*

It's because I've been playing chase with an elusive, ephemeral dream. A few months ago, all it took was a couple glasses of wine, a fountain of tears, and there he was. *But not this week. Or last week. Not once since the night I fell on Camelback.*

"Good." Sarah looks relieved.

I look back at my computer screen, the cursor blinking right where I left it before I answered Nick's call. "Let me finish this email."

"Meet me in the lobby." Sarah leaves my desk.

I nod, already typing my response to a client who needs to publicly respond to salmonella found at one of their factories. *I'm going to work on your apology and corrective action statement. Expect an official statement by EOB.*

I grab my purse from my desk drawer and hurry to meet Sarah.

***

I'M on my knees peering into a kitchen cabinet when Nick knocks.

Standing, I shake out my hair, which I know is wild from my search efforts.

I pull back the door. "Hi."

Nick smiles, a brown paper bag in one hand and a bouquet of sunflowers in the other. He holds out the flowers.

"These are for you, obviously."

I take them, staring at the soft yellow petals. "These are

beautiful. Did Ethan tell you sunflowers are my favorite?" I step away from the door, and Nick walks in.

"You have a picture of a field of sunflowers on your dresser mirror. I made the leap."

I follow him to the kitchen, where he sets the bag on the counter.

"Thank you." I pull a vase from under the sink and set it in the basin.

"You're welcome. How was your day?" He pulls items from the bag. *Arborio rice, mushrooms, peas, chicken stock, red wine.*

I get out two wine glasses, then turn on the water and push the vase into the stream. "It was good." I don't plan on telling him about my tardiness at work. My Ethan dreams, and how I attempt to obtain them, are my little secret. "How about you?"

"After I talked to you, we responded to a bad car accident." He rubs his forehead, like he's trying to scrub away the memory. "All because a young girl was texting her mom."

My mouth drops open. "That's terrible. Is she going to be okay?"

He drops his hand and sighs. "I don't know. I did what I could do for her."

"I'm sorry. That must be really hard to handle."

"It is. But it's what I want to do. Eventually I'll be the doctor who stitches these people up." He winks at me, trying to lighten the somber mood.

"Do you want to go into emergency medicine?"

He nods as he folds the paper bag. "I think I'm good under pressure and..."

He cuts off abruptly and reaches past me to shut off the running water.

I turn around to the sink and see the vase is full of water and the sunflowers are floating in the basin.

"Oops." I make a face.

He laughs. "Are you sure you can be trusted in the kitchen? Maybe Evie doesn't know what she's talking about."

I really don't know if I can be trusted or not. My limbs don't feel like they work the same anymore.

"I guess we'll have to see." My voice is small. I dump half the water out of the vase and add the flowers.

Nick touches my elbow. "Hey, I'm sorry. I was joking. Evie said you're an amazing cook."

Drying my hands on a dish towel, I meet his apologetic gaze. "It's okay. I haven't cooked since Ethan... You know." I swallow hard. "And I can't find my deep saucepan or my favorite bamboo spatula. I don't know what Harper's been doing in here, but she doesn't put stuff back where it goes." I'm talking fast, and my throat constricts.

Nick opens the bottle of wine he brought and hands me a glass. "Here. I think you need to relax a little. We'll find that stuff."

I take it and sip.

Nick pours himself a glass. "Ready to cook?"

I hold out my hand, palm up. "Recipe?"

He shakes his head. "No recipe."

My eyebrows pinch. "Nick, this is cooking. We need a recipe."

"Do you already know how to make risotto?"

Slowly I nod. What is he getting at?

"Then you don't need a recipe. Trust yourself."

I take a deep breath. Cook dinner without a recipe? I've never done that.

"You know I could just get my phone and grab a recipe from the Internet in ten seconds, right?"

Nick smirks. "Consider this a challenge. Can you cook without following a recipe?" He extends a hand.

My lips twist as I consider. Recipes are like rules. And I've always liked rules. *You followed the rules and tried not to fall in love with your best friend, and look where that got you. And him.*

"Challenge accepted." I shake Nick's hand.

He smiles. "Let's begin."

***

"Best. Risotto. Ever." Nick nearly groans the words as he puts another bite in his mouth.

I take the spoon from his hand before he can take more from the pan. "No more double-dipping."

I'm serving up two portions when the front door opens.

Harper steps in, sees me and Nick, and her eyes grow wide. Slowly she walks to the entry table and deposits her purse and keys. Her surprised eyes never leave me.

"Kate, are you cooking?" she asks, astonished.

I put down the pan and grab another bowl. "Do you want some?"

Harper walks over and peers into the pan.

"It's good," Nick vouches. "I promise. I tried it."

She inhales. "Of course it's good. This is Kate Masters we're talking about."

Nick's eyebrows pull together in confusion, and he looks at me. I roll my eyes. The last thing I need is Nick believing the same tired thing everyone else believes. And it's so far from the truth. *What if they all knew? Perfect little Kate*

Masters, Master of Everything, drinks herself to sleep every night in hopes of conjuring up her late boyfriend.

"Yes, I want some." Harper shoots a smile at Nick. "I'm starving. I had to go to a cocktail reception for a company I planned an event for last year. Hors d'oeuvres can only get a person so far."

I spoon some into the third bowl and hand it to her. Nick pours her a glass of wine, and we sit at the table.

After we've each had seconds and the bottle of wine is gone, Harper sits back and sighs.

"Kate, I've missed your cooking. Does this mean you're going to go back to Old Kate? I really miss her."

I blink at Harper's beautiful face. How could I ever go back to my old self? I've been ripped to shreds by a cruel monster named Fate.

"Did you know Kate made this without following a recipe?" Nick glances at me. "Have you always been this talented in the kitchen?"

"Yes." Harper answers for me. "Kate's good at everything. She was excellent at it since the moment she decided she wanted to learn. Ethan was only too happy to be her taste tester. Until I moved in and took over the job." Harper and Nick laugh.

My breath sticks in my chest. Pain slices across my heart. I don't want to remember, but I do. Ethan sitting on the kitchen counter, legs dangling, greedily demanding more of whatever I made. *Damn it, this hurts. This is why I've stayed numb for so long. Why is my numbness fading?*

Nick watches me, but Harper's still talking.

"You okay?" he mouths.

I smile and nod. What can I say?

Just when I'm starting to wonder if this is going to be a long night, Harper announces her exit.

"Well, this has been fun. I'm going to be rude and leave without helping with the dishes. I'm meeting someone for a drink." She stands and goes to her room.

I look at Nick and shrug. "She doesn't spend much time at home. She's very outgoing."

"I gathered that."

Is that disappointment I hear, or am I imagining it? *Please let me be imagining it. She would not be good for him.*

Harper sails back through to say goodbye. She's wearing a blazer and a skirt. A very short skirt.

"Don't wait up for me."

"I'm going to bed early tonight. I need to get to work on time tomorrow," I say to her disappearing back.

Nick squints like he's studying me.

"You mean you've been having trouble getting there on time?"

I reach across the table and stack our empty bowls. Loudly. "That is *not* what I said."

The front door closes. I feel his eyes on me.

"Why aren't you getting there on time?"

He takes the stack of bowls from me and carries them to the kitchen.

I follow him and perch at the sink. "It's really not your business." I turn on the water and begin rinsing.

"I told Ethan I would look after you. If you're struggling, he'd want me to help." Nick's voice is soft.

"Ethan's not here." *And he's not in my dreams anymore either. Where is he?*

"That's my point, Kate." He reaches over and turns off the running water for the second time since he arrived. "He's not here to take care of you. He made it my job, and I don't take that lightly."

My hands jerk into the air, water drops flying. A few hit

Nick's cheeks. They roll down like tears, and he doesn't wipe them.

"Do I get a say in this?" A flare of anger rises. "What if I don't want a caretaker?"

"I think you need one," he says quietly.

My fingers grip the edge of the sink. "I don't. I am just fine."

"Are you?" Nick shifts, crossing his arms in front of his chest. "You can't get to work on time? Why is that? I can only think of one reason. And the Kate I know—"

"You don't know me!" I turn to him as I say it.

Nick's jaw tenses. "I know what Ethan told me. You're serious, hard-working, and you like to follow rules. You think you're supposed to be perfect, because your Dad had crazy high expectations."

My cheeks are on fire. I can't believe Ethan told him all that.

"So, for somebody who otherwise meets or exceeds expectations to be late for work, something must be going on." Nick's eyebrows move up on his forehead. "An illness, perhaps?"

I bite the inside of my cheek. My eyes stay locked on his.

"You're stubborn. And you have a temper. Those are things I've learned on my own." His chin lifts, like he's challenging me to argue.

"I think it's time for you to go." My voice is low. I'm focusing on the coffee maker in the corner. "Thank you for the flowers."

There's a long pause while he does nothing. Then he walks to the door. He pulls it open and stops. I turn to meet his disappointed eyes.

"You don't know me as well as I know you," he says. "I won't stop trying. I might be the only person, besides you, who gave Ethan a run for his money in the loyalty department."

The door closes, and my tears fall. Nick doesn't understand. Nobody could possibly understand.

Tonight I'm going to bring Ethan back.

22

KATE

ETHAN DID NOT COME TO ME LAST NIGHT.

I drank enough that he should have. But he didn't.

And I made it to work on time, just like I said I would.

I may have thrown up three times in the bathroom, but I was at my desk by nine.

Now, in the weekly meeting with Lynn, the spinning in my head is finally slowing.

"I have very big news for all of you." She gazes around the room, eyes dancing. "You are probably wondering why I've called in the whole staff, and not just the reps."

I look around, realizing for the first time that all the assistants and the receptionist are in here, crowding the space and leaning against the walls.

Lynn continues. "Simone PR will be merging with a marketing company. This merger is going to make us more influential and effective in the marketplace. Now our clients will be able to go to one company for their marketing and PR needs." Lynn's red lips pull back in a huge smile, exposing a lot of teeth. I've never seen her so happy.

"Which marketing company?" someone in the room asks.

"Maxim Marketing."

My stomach turns as the air fills with murmurs of excitement. Hasn't fate been cruel enough? Now I'm going to be subjected to *him* every day?

This cannot be happening.

"Okay, team. Thanks for coming in. I'll keep you apprised of any developments. For now, expect this to merger to conclude the first week of December. That gives us roughly five weeks. This year's holiday party will also be a celebration of the joining of our companies." Lynn looks at the faces seated around the table. "Reps, I need you to stay here for our normal meeting. The rest of you, meeting is over."

My elbows rest on the table top, and my hands hold up my chin. When everyone has left, Lynn gets excited again.

"Isn't this wonderful news? This has phenomenal upside. So much new business from existing Maxim clients." She claps her hands in quick succession.

People around the table bob their heads excitedly and offer congratulations.

Lynn beams. "Does anybody know someone who plans parties? It's a short time frame."

My hand goes up. "My roommate. She's incredibly talented."

"Send me her info." Lynn taps the piece of paper on the table in front of her, adopting her serious face. "Let's talk business."

She looks to the person directly on her left while I take a deep breath.

In my mind I see the person I dislike more than anybody in this world. Blond, blue-eyed, and hateful. *Trent.*

In five weeks, Trent and I are going to be coworkers. The last time we saw each other we declared our mutual dislike for each other.

I don't need a crystal ball to know this won't go well.

***

I DRIVE HOME from the office, my mind filling with scenarios where I work side by side with Trent. When my mom calls, I pick up the phone, ready for a break from the what-if's.

"Hey, honey, it's me."

"I know," I chide gently." Your name and picture come up on my phone when you call."

"Oh, right. Duh." She laughs. "How are you?"

"Hanging in there." *I made it to work on time today. Go me.*

"I ran into Nick at the Shepherds' today. He was helping Evie rearrange furniture and—"

"Why didn't James do it?"

My mom sighs. "I don't know if I should say anything."

"Mom..."

She sighs again. "He's having trouble. That's all I'm going to say. You can let Evie tell you, assuming she wants to. Anyway, I saw Nick, and he said you fell on Camelback and sprained your ankle." Her voice fills with concern.

"I'm fine. It was a minor sprain. No special treatment necessary. And it was almost three weeks ago. How was Nick when you talked to him?" My lips purse as I wait for her answer. I feel bad about the way things ended last night.

"He was fine. Why?"

"Oh, um, he had to work on a young girl who was in a car accident. He seemed upset by it. Just wondering if he's doing okay."

"He didn't say anything to me. He was only telling me about your fall. And that you're cooking again." Her voice is calm, but I know her so well, I can hear the barely contained excitement bubbling beneath.

"I wouldn't say I'm *cooking* again. I *cooked*. Once."

"Do you know what this means?" The excitement has broken through. She sounds almost dreamy.

"No."

"It means you're coming back to us. The Master of Everything is—"

"Don't say that."

There's a long pause. Then, "What's wrong?"

"I don't want to be the Master of Everything anymore." My hand flies to my mouth. If I'm not Ethan's best friend, if I'm not the Master of Everything, who am I?

"Oh, thank God. Finally." Now my mother sounds more overjoyed than she did twenty seconds ago.

"Seriously?" I'm confused. *She loves how much I've achieved. She seemed so proud at all my ceremonies.*

"I've been waiting a long time for you to rise above that nickname. It never did suit you. But your dad was certainly proud of it."

Dad never hugged me harder than when I was being recognized for an achievement.

"Yeah, well..." I clear my throat.

"Why do you think all this is happening? The cooking again and the distaste for your nickname?"

"I have no idea." Maybe it's because I laid in bed for three months with nothing to do but watch my life splinter.

"Well, whatever it is, keep doing it. You'll be your old self again in no time. Minus the nickname, of course."

Right. My old self. As if she'll ever come back. "Will do, Mom."

"I can tell you're ready to get off the phone. Just really quick, tell me if you're going to a Halloween party tonight."

I wrinkle my nose. "No way. I don't even have candy to hand out."

"Good. Then I don't have to tell you to be safe."

"I'll be perfectly safe inside my apartment."

"Maybe you can start a journal? First entry tonight? I think it would help you sort out your feelings."

"We've been through this."

"When your dad died, my therapist had me start a journal. Writing down all the things I was feeling, even if they seemed silly, helped me work through them."

Her words register slowly. Finally, I say, "I didn't know you saw a therapist."

"You were twenty-one. You weren't living at home, so you didn't see how hard things were for me. Just give it a thought, okay?"

"Sure, sure," I say, to mollify her. My creative writing hand stopped moving across papers a long time ago. A memory flits into my mind. Ethan asking me about my stories on the second day of his last leave.

I cherish the memory, even if I don't like Mom's idea.

We say goodbye, and I hang up.

When I get home I go immediately to the kitchen, check my stash of wine, and see that it's low. Last night's attempt put a big dent in my supply. I grab my keys and head to the store.

***

"Hey, Harper." She's sitting on the couch when I get home.

I move quickly to the pantry and deposit my restock. I'm not really hiding it, but I'd rather not advertise either.

"Go check your bedroom." Harper turns on the sofa, hops onto her knees, and leans on the back of the couch.

I narrow my eyes and walk to my bedroom. Everything looks the same. And then I see what's on my bed.

I shake my head. *No way.*

"No way," I yell to Harper.

She comes to my room and crosses her arms.

"I'm not taking no for an answer. First you went hiking and then you cooked. You're almost your old self again, and you loved Halloween, the chance to dress up and be someone else. Come on."

Why does everyone want me to be my old self? I don't *want* to be that person. That stupid woman who didn't wake up to her own feelings until it was too late. That ridiculous woman who broke Ethan's heart over and over. Who would want that woman back?

Harper wraps an arm around my shoulders. "Say yes."

A chance to be someone else for the night? If I put on the costume can I also pretend to have a heart? It sounds tempting.

I look down at the outfit on the bed. "I'm not wearing that."

Harper smiles. She knows she's won. "Fine, put a cardigan over it. Just promise me you won't button it."

I eye the sexy school girl costume. It's so unoriginal. "What are you wearing?"

"Sexy nurse." *Also unoriginal.* I stop myself from rolling my eyes.

Harper removes the costume from the hanger and puts it in my arms. "Try this on. I'll make a quick dinner, and we can start getting ready."

She leaves my room and I lay the costume back down on the bed. My eyes run over the plaid skirt and the white collared shirt that will knot above my belly button.

From the second I put on the skirt, I know it's too tight. It zips, but not without effort. The shirt fits okay, minus the fact that half my stomach is visible. I'm not trying on the knee-highs. I know what those look like.

"Dinner is rea...dy," Harper stutters the last word. She cocks her head to the side, frowning. "We're having salad. Don't want to be bloated tonight."

I cross my arms. "Just say it."

"I wasn't going to say anything."

I look down at the outfit and back up to her. "I can't wear this."

She studies my mid-section. My hands crawl over my stomach to cover it.

"No, you cannot wear that." Her lips pull to one side as she considers. "Use the white shirt you wear to work. Tuck it in, so it will look cuter."

I do as she says. Harper puts her arm around my shoulders and turns me to the mirror. "If you stop drinking so much, you'll drop the weight. It's all that sugar in the wine."

She removes her hand from my shoulder and starts walking. "Let's eat. The sooner we leave, the sooner we'll be celebrating."

I look in the mirror one more time before I follow her. I don't need this costume. I could go as a shell. A shell of a person who once housed a heart, a life, a personality. She had likes and dislikes. Feelings. And I wouldn't even have to change my clothes.

***

"THIS IS GOING TO BE EPIC." Harper grabs my hand and starts up the long driveway of the ludicrous house. I was expecting an incredible home, just based on the streets she was taking to get here, but not something this insane. Two giant iron gates are pulled back to allow for partygoers to enter, and once we're through them I feel like maybe this party was a bad idea. The feeling grows with every step we take toward the stone house that never seems to end.

Harper sails past the line of bedecked people waiting to walk through the front door. Two men with a clipboard sit at a table outside.

"There's a list to get into a house party?" My voice is bewildered.

Her smile is so excited it makes her eyes crinkle. "Crazy, right?"

She walks up to the table with authority. "Hey guys! What a turn-out."

"Lookin' good, Harper," one guy says.

"Oh, well, you know. Just a little something." Harper shrugs and turns in a circle.

The guy who complimented her gets up from the table.

He opens the burnished metal front door and gestures us in. "Have fun."

Harper stops in front of him and places a palm on his chest. "There's a third in my group."

"He's already here." The guy throws a thumb over his shoulder. "Anthony gave him shit about not being with you, but they got it figured out."

Harper laughs. "Anthony's doing his job then."

"Something like that." The door closes.

"How do you know those guys? And who's the third in your party?" I ask as I yank on the bottom of the skirt, trying to make it magically lengthen.

"I hire them for security for a lot of my events." She takes my hand, and we snake our way through throngs of people. I open my mouth to ask my second question that she left unanswered, but she stops to wave at a guy across the room.

"I have to talk to Marc. Go find the bar. I'll catch up with you." She disappears into the crowd.

I turn in a circle, trying to get my bearings. The house is huge and people are everywhere. I take a step and bump into someone. I look up and gasp. The person I've bumped has full skeleton make up and an intricate top hat. He grins, showing huge, crooked teeth, and keeps going.

I continue to jostle and be jostled until I reach the stairs. I climb to the fifth step. From there I see over people's heads to the bar set up outside and a DJ on a platform in a different room.

I climb down the stairs and keep to the edges of the room, so I field fewer elbows than last time. I pass Harper, where she's engaging a man I've never seen before in a lively conversation. One hand is on his bicep and the other waves in the air while she speaks. He laughs, his attention rapt. *The queen is on her throne.* Here, Harper is in her element.

I make it to the bar and order a drink. When I pull out money to pay him, he points to a sign hanging from a large glass canister. *All proceeds go to No Child Hungry.*

"I didn't realize," I say, but he's already moved on to someone else. I drop the money in the jar and walk away. Harper didn't mention this was a charity event.

At the back of the yard is a water sculpture that looks like a wall. I'm drawn to it, imagining it sounds peaceful and tranquil. Very different than the loud music being spun by the DJ. A set of chairs sits in front of the water. Nearby, a fire pit is surrounded by couches. *I choose the water over the fire.*

I sit on the edge of a chair and stare into the water as it slides over the multi-colored metal wall. As I sip my drink, I count the different shades I see in the metal. Mostly shades of green and blue, some yellow interspersed throughout the piece. I could never be that creative.

You used to be creative.

Ethan wanted me to write again. And my mom wants me to keep a journal. But it's been so long. I'm sure all the creativity in me was wrung from my body as I twisted and turned myself inside out to be the person my dad wanted me to be.

I sigh and shake my cup. The ice cubes in my glass tumble together.

Time for a refill.

"Can I get two of those?" I say to a different bartender. He's dressed like a sailor.

"Sure thing." He winks at me. "I guess that means you're already here with someone?"

"She's here with me," a deep voice says from behind.

I whip around to the owner of the voice.

My whole body stiffens, and I gasp.

23

KATE

ETHAN.

No, not Ethan. *Nick*. Dressed in fatigues.

My fingers are at my throat, as if somehow that could help my body get more air.

"Are you following me?" I want to look away, but I can't tear my eyes off the uniform.

Nick squints, defining his cheekbones. He looks arrogant, like that's something he would never do. "I'm not following you."

My eyes narrow. "I already told you I don't need a caretaker."

Nick tips up his beer, eyes on me the whole time. "Harper invited me."

"*You're* the third person in Harper's group?"

He nods slowly.

I look away. "Original costume."

"Yours is just as original."

I wrinkle my nose. I hate what I'm wearing.

I take a deep breath and turn back to the bar. I smile my thanks at the bartender for the two vodka and sodas sitting in front of me. I toss my cash in the jar and pick up one drink. Nick watches me, and I keep my eyes on him as I drain the entire thing. It's stronger than the first one, and I want to grimace, but I refuse to let Nick see through my show of defiance.

He shakes his head and looks away. I swipe my second drink off the bar, some of it spills on my hand, and I stomp to the house.

I can do what I want, Nick Hunter. I don't have to make you happy. I don't have to make anybody happy.

Instead of going in the back doors, I stomp off to the side of the house, where it's darker and less populated. I pause beside a window. My brain feels fuzzy.

"Taking a break from wine?" The same deep voice comes up behind me again.

"Go to hell." I lean up against the wall next to the window, hoping to get my bearings.

"You're out of control."

"You don't know what you're talking about." *If I can just get drunk enough and drown myself in memories, Ethan will come back to me. I know he will.*

Nick steps in front of me and places one hand on the wall next to my head. He leans in, his eyes intense, locking my gaze to his. "My mother was a drunk. I watched her tear her life apart with alcohol. That"—Nick points at my drink—"won't heal your pain."

"That's not my objective," I grumble.

Nick scrutinizes me. "If you were given the chance to have Ethan back for five minutes, what would you do?"

The question catches me off guard. Five minutes with Ethan... There's so much I want to do. To say. I set the cup down on the windowsill beside me.

"Only five minutes? How about ten?"

He shakes his head no. "Five."

My eyes close and I think.

"Don't think," I hear him say. "Just answer."

I open my eyes. Nick's gaze bores into mine.

"I would kiss him like I knew it was going to be our last kiss." My lips tremble, and I close my eyes. "I would touch his face and smell his skin."

"Finally." Nick breathes the word. "This is perfect, Kate. You're stoic all the time. Show some emotion. I know it's in there."

I open my eyes. Nick's face is pained. The words pour out of him. "You're dying on the inside. Do something to revive your soul."

I need Ethan. Only he can revive me. I reach for Nick's shoulders and pull. We're so close I feel his chest expand with his surprised intake of breath.

Our faces are almost touching. My heart hammers in my chest.

He doesn't move.

I lift my mouth to his cheek, dragging my lips toward his. At the corner of his lips I hesitate. I'm drunk, but I know what I'm doing. *Kind of.* My mouth continues another inch, so our lips are touching only a fraction. It's just enough for me to take a small portion of his lower lip and pull it between my teeth. He groans and turns into my face.

His mouth is on my mouth.

Ethan. This could be you.

Our lips mold and mesh, yielding to tongues and gasps for air. My fingers rake up his head and back down, running through his hair. My body presses against his. His uniform feels stiff where it touches my skin. I kiss down to his jaw, my face goes lower, and my nose presses into him. I inhale. *The smell is wrong.* Nick stiffens.

He backs away from me. My hands drop. When I look up, I see blue eyes.

Blue eyes.

Not Ethan.

"Who were you kissing just now?" Nick grabs for breath, his voice empty and thick at the same time.

I stare down at my hands. I'm too ashamed to look him in the eye. "Ethan," I whisper.

Nick takes another big step away from me. "That's what I thought."

"Hey!" A voice bellows. Harper sashay's over in her nurses costume. Her chest is puffed out. *Like anybody could miss the cleavage she's displaying.* "What are you two doing hiding over here?" She glances from me to Nick with suspicious eyes.

"Talking." I pick up my cup and drink. *What did I just do?*

Nick's lips move to the side in disapproval. "Go easy, Kate." *Those disapproving lips were on my lips.* My insides are a scary jumble. I want to scream, run, do *something* to shake up the utter humiliation and regret building in my chest.

Harper waves away his warning. "Don't worry about her. She drinks every night."

I sway, just a little.

"Is that right?" He directs the question at me.

Harper steps closer to Nick. "So, I heard Anthony gave you a hard time tonight. Tell me more about that." She puts her arm through his and turns him toward her.

"I'm going to find the bathroom." I walk away before they can stop me.

The line for the bathroom takes forever. There are probably ten more bathrooms in this massive place, but I'm not up for an expedition. I wait, listening to the laughing and talking from the girls in front of and behind me. Their conversations are carefree. *Isn't this place so crazy? What are we doing tomorrow? What classes are you taking this semester?* When it's my turn I hurry into the bathroom, eager to leave the carefree talk behind.

When I'm done, I exit with my head down, hoping to avoid overhearing any more jovial conversations. I pause when I've reached a corner of a room, and pull out my phone to order a ride.

"Excuse me?"

Irritation rides through me. I look up, ready to tell Nick to leave me and my pathetic self alone, but it's not Nick's face I'm looking at.

"Yes?" I look at the guy standing in front of me. I think he's dressed up as a tennis player. He has a white sweater tied around his shoulders. No racket though.

"Hi. My name is Michael." He gestures to the DJ. "Do you want to dance?"

What? Me? No, I do not want to dance.

Nick and Harper come into sight behind the guy's head. Harper has her arm wrapped around Nick, and she's right up against his side.

Nick looks annoyed. Harper beams.

I look back at the guy to tell him no.

"Everything okay here?" Nick breaks in.

I glare at him. "Everything is fine." My voice is harsh.

The guy puts his hands up. "I was just asking her to dance. I didn't realize she was with someone." He looks nervously at Nick.

"She's not. She'll dance with you." Harper says excitedly. She lets go of Nick and hurries to my side, pushing me forward.

What the hell, Harper?

My hand comes up in frustration, but the guy mistakes it

for my acceptance. He grabs my open palm and pulls me away. The crowd swallows me up immediately. I turn back just before I lose sight of my companions. Nick's mouth is in a straight line, arms folded at his chest. Harper looks happy. She turns to him, and her mouth is moving, trying to get his attention.

Suddenly I feel angry. I'm mad at Nick for thinking he knows my personal hell. I'm mad at Harper for making this decision for me. And I'm furious with myself for letting her.

***

"I CAN MAKE it up myself. Promise."

But Michael won't hear of it. He's been a total gentleman since he pulled me to the dance floor. He's continued to be a gentleman after he insisted he see me home. He barely touched me when we danced, which I appreciated. No bumping. No grinding.

I'm very, very drunk. Maybe that's why Michael insisted on following me to my front door. He wasn't positive I could actually make it up.

After some fumbling, I manage to open the door and step inside. I'm vaguely aware Michael's walking in behind me. *Where is Harper?* I lost track of her and Nick. *Please don't let them be here together. Please tell me Nick didn't fall under her spell.*

I need water. My mouth is dry. My head's already starting to hurt. I grab two water bottles from the fridge and hand one to Michael.

"I'll be right back." I teeter off to my bathroom. I need my trusty Tylenol.

When I walk out of the bathroom, I find Michael standing in my dark bedroom. *I might be drunk, but I know I told him I'd be right back.*

The light from the living room filters in just enough that I can see his face. He smiles at me, but it's not a nice smile. It's cocky. Over-confident. "The cat-and-mouse game has been fun, Kate. But it's time to be done with all this innocence crap."

He grabs me and yanks my arm. I trip and fall into him. My head hits his shoulder. My palms come up to his chest, and I push off him. But I'm weak. Too drunk to be coordinated. Michael takes my chest palming as a sign of submission.

His hands are on my cheeks, and his face is coming toward me. *No no no.* I turn my face to the side, and Michael's lips miss their target.

"What the hell? I've been buying your drinks for the last two hours. You owe me at least a kiss."

He puts his hands on my cheeks again, this time squeezing, and forces my face to stay still.

He pulls back to look at me and grins. I feel sick inside. *This is the worst mistake I've ever made.*

Michael's face looms in my vision, inching his way to me. I brace myself for contact.

And then he's gone. My cheeks tingle as the blood rushes back in. I hear grunting.

I can't see anything well, just bulky shapes moving. My hand shoots out and smacks the wall switch.

Light floods the room.

Michael is pressed up against the wall opposite the one I'm leaning on. Nick's forearm pushes against his throat.

More grunting. Michael's condescending smile is gone. His eyes bulge.

I rush over and put my hands on Nick's shoulders, pulling him and getting nowhere. "Stop! Don't get into trouble. Not over this guy." My voice shakes.

"He was going to hurt you." Nick's teeth are clenched.

More grunts from Michael as he puts up a useless fight.

I move so I'm beside Michael on the wall. I search for Nick's gaze, but he won't look at me.

"Nick, you have to stop."

Finally he drags his gaze to meet mine. His eyes are wild.

"Let go," I plead.

He drops his arm and takes a step back.

Michael doubles over. His loud gasps are a soundtrack to this awful scene.

Oh no. My stomach. So sloshy. I bolt to the bathroom and barely make it to the toilet in time. My head spins and my body heaves.

Reality creeps in as the contents of my stomach empty, over and over.

I'm out of control.

I feel my hair being picked up in sections. Nimble fingers gather it and wind an elastic around the thickness. A cold cloth falls over the back of my neck.

"Is he gone?" My tiny voice trembles.

"Don't worry about that asshole," Nick growls.

He brushes the little hairs from my forehead. His touch is gentle compared to the angry tenor in his words.

I vomit again. I'm mortified.

After it's over I gingerly scoot away from the toilet and lean my head against the wall. I'd really love to press my cheek against the cool tile on the floor, but apparently I have a few shreds of dignity remaining.

I open my eyes a tiny bit, hoping Nick isn't looking my way. I meet his blue eyes. *Crap.* My face flames with embarrassment.

His mouth twists into a small smile. "You're blushing."

My head bends toward my knees. "You would be too if you'd just puked in front of me." My response is muffled.

"How about tomorrow night I get really drunk and throw up? Then we'll be even."

I groan. "No thanks."

"Here."

I look up. He's holding out my toothbrush, loaded up with toothpaste.

I thank him and take it, but I feel like a supreme idiot. After a minute he helps me stand so I can spit and rinse. *I've officially spat and puked in front of this man. Maybe I should just pee in front of him right now and cap off this fantastic night.*

I wipe my mouth and see my reflection. Messy ponytail, courtesy of Nick. Mascara starting to run. Skin pale from vomiting. And I'm still in the lame school girl outfit.

"I'm going to change into pajamas. Stay here. I'll just close my closet door."

When I come out, I feel a tiny bit better. My overhead light is off, and the lamp next to my bed is switched on.

Nick's sitting on the end of my bed. His shoulders sag. *I've disappointed him again.* He's only trying to keep up his end of an agreement, and I'm making it nearly impossible. I'm sure he wonders why Ethan loved me so much. I want to tell him about how I used to be a whole person. *I promise Ethan had a reason for loving me.*

My bed shifts when I sit next to him. I twist my hands in my lap. "I'm sorry about tonight. I want you to know, what happened with Michael... I've never brought anyone home with me before. I didn't even invite him in. I was just too drunk to realize he was following me." It's vital that he know this. If Nick thinks this behavior is the norm for me after Ethan died... It couldn't be further from the truth.

Nick doesn't look at me. He runs a thumb across the top of his left hand, over and over. "I'm sorry you had to see me like that," he finally says. "It's been a long time since I've been in a physical altercation."

I frown. It didn't look like it. Michael wasn't a small guy, but Nick handled him with ease. He looked frightening. Intimidating. Michael's the only person I've ever heard gasp for breath.

Not including myself. I push the thought out. I don't want to remember the morning after Ethan died.

"Thank you. For getting Michael off me." My face burns red. I can't believe I got myself into that situation.

"He was forcing himself on you." Disgust twists Nick's face. "What kind of guy does that to a girl?"

A tear rolls down my cheek. It drips off my jaw and disappears into the cotton of my pajama pants. "I'm so thankful you came in and stopped him. If you hadn't..." I pause, cringing. It's too easy to picture Michael's face coming toward me.

Nick shudders. "Listen, I'm not trying to tell you what to do. You get enough of that from Harper. But do you ever think about getting over Ethan?" Nick turns and shifts his leg on the bed so he's able to face me. He looks unsure of himself. Unsure of my reaction.

I laugh once, without mirth. "You know, I really hate that term. How am I supposed to 'get over' Ethan? Like the love of my life is someone I should just forget about?" More tears roll down.

Nick stares at me, his own lower lip trembling.

"Have you ever loved someone so much that you knew

your soul loved them too? Not just your heart, not just your brain, or your body? Your *soul?*" My shoulders move with my sobs.

Nick shakes his head slowly. "No." He chokes on the word.

"That's how I loved him. Then it was all ripped away. Suddenly. I'm in love with someone who's not alive to love me back." I clutch at the skin above my heart. "Inside my chest is a heart that beats and loves and aches for someone who's not *alive.* How am I supposed to get over that? How?" I stop to gulp in a breath. My face is wet and I don't have a tissue and I don't care. I'm saying words I haven't said to anybody, and I feel so free.

Nick folds me into his arms. His grip is tight, and I feel tiny. *He's so warm.*

I sit in the circle his arms make and let myself be consoled. Seconds, minutes, maybe hours go by. I don't know. All I know is that I'm crying, and so is he. Unlike me, he's quiet. Small, muffled sobs into my hair.

At some point I feel Nick shift and lift my body. He sets me down in my bed and pulls the covers around me. Our eyes meet once, briefly. He turns around and leaves my bedroom.

24

NICK

I LOST MY TEMPER TONIGHT. IN FRONT OF KATE, NO LESS.

That guy deserved what he got, and maybe even more, but I hate that it was me delivering his punishment. I'm not that guy anymore. Those days are behind me. Or so I thought.

I saw him manhandling Kate, his hands squeezing her cheeks, and the terror in her eyes. After that it was only rage and action, my arms working independent of rational thought.

Apparently elapsed time between fights doesn't matter, because I went right back into strike mode like it hadn't been years since the last one.

And, just like before, the sudden flow of adrenaline has left me famished.

I'm driving now to the all-night diner I found during my shift yesterday. We were on our way back to the station after transporting a kid who passed out at school to the emergency room, and I spotted the diner on the corner. It reminded me of my favorite place back home, and its sign clearly stated, *If you're awake, we are too.*

I'd tucked that little piece of knowledge away, not knowing I would need a middle of the night reprieve so soon.

My thumb taps the steering wheel in time with the music coming from the radio, and I think about Kate.

She kissed me tonight. My chest constricts as I think about her lips on mine, the way she bit my lower lip, how she paused just before she reached her destination, her breath hot on my cheek.

But it was a kiss not meant for me. The intended recipient was Ethan, as messed up as that sounds.

I didn't know it at first. I actually thought she was kissing me. But then she dropped her nose to my neck and breathed deeply, and her body that had melted into my arms suddenly solidified.

That was when it hit me, and I felt as stupid as stupid gets.

I was kissing Kate. Kate was kissing Ethan. Not me.

It stung.

And my reaction was more confusing than anything else. Since when do I like Kate like that? I mean, yeah, she's attractive. Anybody with eyes can see she's beautiful. And she's a good person. And she's way funnier than she gives herself credit for. When she makes a joke, her eyes crinkle at the corners while the rest of her face remains stoic. She's so nice. Maybe even too nice. I wish she'd let out all that pent up anger, maybe even direct it at the people in her life who deserve it, like Harper.

Tonight, though, she wasn't afraid to tell me like it is. She let me have it at that dumb costume party Harper dragged us to. Was it because she was well on her way to being drunk? Probably. But it means she's comfortable enough with me to show me the parts of her she hides from nearly everyone else. Starting with her temper.

Deep down, a fire burns in Kate.

Shit.

Maybe I *do* like Kate. More than I thought I did. More than I *should*.

She was Ethan's girl. I can't have feelings for her.

I park and walk in to the diner. A woman dressed in a white button-up with an apron bends over the counter, propped up by her elbows. She sets down the paperback she's reading and eyes me.

It takes her less than two seconds to decide I'm not going to give her trouble. My guess is that in a job like this, at this time of night, she's no stranger to drunks and plain old assholes.

"Take any seat you like," she calls out, waving her hand around the place.

The only other customers are a guy with long white hair gathered into a ponytail who sits at the far end of the countertop, and a couple in a corner booth, their backs facing the rest of the room.

I choose a seat away from both parties and nod when the server sets down my menu.

"What can I get you to drink?" She peers down at me, and now that she's closer, I can see that she resembles my mom. Same dark hair and strong cheekbones.

"Water and decaf coffee, please."

"On it's way," she tells me, leaving the booth and swinging around the counter. In a moment I hear the crack of ice and the clinking together of glasses.

By the time she sets down the cold water and hot coffee, I know what I want.

Setting one hand on the back of the booth beside my

head, she tips her chin up and asks, "What are you eating at two o'clock in the morning?"

"A BLT with avocado and fries," I answer. She nods and walks away, writing down the order on a pad as she goes. Once she gets behind the counter again, she passes it through the window to a grubby looking cook. He glances my way, so I raise a hand and wave.

His only response is a slight nod of his head, but I'll take it.

When my coffee is nearly to the bottom, the server, whose name I don't know because she never told me and she's not wearing a name tag, comes over to refill my cup.

"You look like you need to talk," she says as she pours.

"Is that right?" I look up at her. Her shirt has some kind of smeared food in a spot just beyond where her apron covers. Ketchup, maybe?

"I've been at this a long time, and I know when someone is full of something they just need to say. They just have this look about them. And you"—she eyes me—"you have that look."

I take a sip of the burning hot coffee and nod. "Yeah, I guess I do."

She slides into the seat across from me and folds her hands on the table, her gaze expectant.

"What about your other guests?" I look over at the man, then at the couple.

"That's Richard. He's been coming in a few times a week for the past ten years. He can refill his own coffee if I'm not there to do it. And that couple paid an hour ago. The last time I went over there, their hands had disappeared under the table, so I'm not going over there again."

I chuckle and run a fingertip over the rim of my coffee cup. "Probably a good idea."

"So?" She adjusts her seating and leans forward on her elbows, waiting for me.

"The story isn't exactly a happy one," I warn. It's only fair to let her know what she's getting herself into.

"You wouldn't be here at this time of night if it was," she counters.

I smile at her honesty. "What's your name?"

"Glenda, like the good witch."

"I'm Nick."

She lifts up off her elbows and extends a hand. We shake and she sinks back into her previous position. It's clear she has spent a lot of nighttime hours resting her elbows on countertops.

I open my mouth and start the tale from the beginning. "I just got out of a four year stint in the Army. While I was in, I met another soldier who became my best friend. My brother, really. And he had a girl back home." Kate's face flashes through my mind. "We made an agreement, if something were to happen. I would take care of his girl and he would take care of my mom."

Glenda's eyes fill. "Let me guess. You're here to take care of his girl."

I nod. "I've made a life here, too. I have an apartment and a job. I'm starting school in a few months. But I came to help his girl. Her name's Kate."

"And now?" Glenda leans forward, encouraging the rest of the story from me.

"It's not as cut and dry as I anticipated. I thought I was stepping into a situation with clear cut lines." I shake my head and sigh. "The lines are a mess. It's like tangled up Christmas lights. Kate's in terrible pain, and I'm trying to help her through it like I promised I would, but she's not making it easy." She was so angry at me tonight, before she kissed me.

"Grief can be crippling." Glenda says it like she knows what she's talking about. "In my experience, most people who are grieving *want* to be helped. Nobody likes feeling like their body is hollow. Whatever you're doing, just keep doing it. She'll come around."

A bell dings, and the cook bellows, "Order up."

Glenda rolls her eyes and unfolds herself from the booth. "I cannot figure out why he feels the need to yell that when nobody is here."

She walks away and returns with my food.

"Eat up," she says, sliding the plate on the table in front of me. "A full stomach improves almost every situation."

I tuck into the sandwich and consider Glenda's words. Kate loved to cook, but she hasn't done it since Ethan died. Could that be it? An inroad to the old Kate, the one being crushed by a mountain of grief?

An idea blooms in my mind, and for the first time I feel hopeful.

25

KATE

I GROAN AND ROLL OVER IN MY BED, PULLING MY PILLOW ON top of my head. My eyes hurt. *So much crying last night. Eight hours ago.*

Like a freight train the memory of kissing Nick slams into me. *I thought if I lost myself enough, I could find Ethan.*

But Ethan wasn't in the kiss.

And he's not in a bottle.

He isn't *anywhere*.

He's never been further from me.

Sobs wrack my chest. I press my fist to my mouth, afraid of the sounds I'll make if I allow any sound at all.

My body gives out eventually and I close my eyes. I'm spent.

***

I AWAKEN AGAIN to the sound of my curtains scraping across the rod.

"Why do you have a pillow on your head?" Harper

snatches the pillow away. The harsh sunlight assails my eyes.

She squints down at me. "Why are your eyes red? Were you lying here crying?" Her words come with a trace of disgust, like lying in my bed and crying is a heinous crime.

"What's that?" I point at the drink in her hand.

"Your breakfast. Or lunch, I guess. It's late."

I sit up and take the smoothie from her outstretched hand. "Thanks."

"Someone left you a note." She picks up a small piece of ripped paper off my nightstand and flips it over.

I hold out my hand.

Instead of giving it to me, she reads it. "*Fight. Be meaner than your demons.*" Her eyebrows draw together. "Who left this for you?"

"Nick, I'm assuming." I push my hair out of my eyes. "No one else was here." *Except for that d-bag Michael.* I remember his hot breath so close to my face and shudder.

Harper nods slowly, once. "Now at least I know where he went running off to in the middle of our conversation."

"He ran out on you at the party?" I hadn't considered how he came to my rescue last night. I was just grateful.

"I was putting all my signature moves on him when he yelled, '*Where are Kate and that guy?*' He looked around and ran out the front door." She sticks out her lower lip like a three-year old who has been denied ice cream. "He didn't even say goodbye."

"Oh." I'm not sure what to say. *Thank goodness he went looking for me.* Last night I was profoundly naïve. Profoundly stupid.

She re-reads the words on the paper and hands it to me, then turns around and goes to my dresser.

"Is there something going on between you and Nick?" She asks the question with her back to me.

Shock rolls through me. My mouth opens and closes. Opens and closes. *Did he tell her about last night?*

"What? I...uh...no." I shake my head so hard, my hair swings into my face. Then my head pounds.

Harper pokes through my jewelry box on my dresser. "Crazier things have happened."

She's going to see my blush if she turns around.

I go to my bathroom and turn on the water. "Ethan asked him to look out for me. That's all." The cool water I splash on my face tempers my heated cheeks.

"Good," Harper says. She sounds satisfied. "Because I want him for myself."

My insides recoil at her words.

"He's all yours." I dab my face with a towel.

"Perfect."

I return to the bedroom, grab my smoothie, and drink.

"Do you want to hike Camelback?" Harper asks. "Show that mountain who's boss?" I realize Harper's wearing work-out clothes.

"I don't know if I'm ready to be on that mountain yet."

"Because you and Ethan always went together? That doesn't make any sense. You went a few weeks ago."

"And it was too soon." *I can't tell her why I went. She would laugh in my face. Or have me committed.*

Harper rolls her eyes. "What am I going to do with you, Kate?"

Love me. Be kind to me. See my broken heart and stop acting like it's a defect.

I say none of those things. Harper would never understand words containing so much emotion.

When I don't say anything, she turns to leave. "Your loss.

Sit at home, wallow in your self-made pit of despair. I'll see you later."

I watch her walk out. After a few minutes the front door closes. I stand in the middle of my room and drink my smoothie. How can she be kind enough to think of making me food but rude enough to say all those awful things? And why do I allow it?

I take the last of my drink to the kitchen sink and rinse the cup. The pantry door is cracked open. I start to close it, then open it wide instead. On the shelf are bottles and bottles of wine, lined up like soldiers. Enemy soldiers.

But no Ethan.

My face lifts to the ceiling. "Where are you?"

I hear water gurgling through pipes under the kitchen sink. The wail of an ambulance. The stomping feet of the man above me on the third floor.

But nothing from Ethan.

And why would there be?

I should know.

I return my gaze to the bottles. I step inside the pantry, closer. My fingers caress the smooth glass. The magic elixir inside these bottles was a beacon during my darkest, longest, most excruciating experience. My intake of breath fills my lungs to capacity. When I breath it out, I imagine the black, bleak darkness flowing out of me.

I retrieve the trash can from under the sink and drag it in the pantry. One by one, each full bottle goes into the trash. They fill the trash can. I tie the bag and look down.

"Goodbye." My chest reverberates with the rhythm of my heart.

I change my clothes, put on shoes, and lug the whole trash can out to the dumpster. It's heavy, but I stop occasionally and use my knee to help keep it in my arms. With the side of the dumpster supporting one side of the can, I tip up the other side. The contents crash into the dumpster. The scent of wine mingles with that of garbage and filth.

The empty trash can bumps against my knee as I walk back to my apartment. I picture Nick's advice scrawled on the scrap of paper.

Fight. Be meaner than your demons.

***

IT'S THURSDAY. Cooking day. *Nick day,* according to Harper. To me, this is *see Nick after you attacked his mouth and then he rescued you again* day.

Harper flies through the front door, frazzled. "Is he here yet?" she hisses, peering around the rest of our place. I'm in the kitchen setting out everything we need for tonight's spaghetti sauce.

I shake my head. *If he were here, he would have heard you.*

"Thank God, I need to change." She rushes to her room. I watch her go, blond hair sailing behind her.

All week long I've gone back and forth, trying to tell myself that Harper isn't capable of handling deep, raw emotions and not to expect that of her. But she's supposed to be my friend. Shouldn't I expect some support from her?

It's not just her most recent harsh conversation with me about moving on, or even the pep talk she tried to give me a few weeks after Ethan died. It's all the jabs, the small barbs that sound innocuous but are meant to let me know she disapproves of the way I'm handling myself. This morning she told me I'm lucky my skin is so beautiful, because all the wine I've consumed should have given me permanent rosy cheeks. Last week she looked at my stomach and offered to help me prepare more salads for work lunches. I'm not even certain she means to be insulting. Somewhere, in the twisted inner workings of Harper's mind, she might think she's *helping* me.

I smell her before I see her. The scent of her perfume crashes against the bag of onions on the counter in front of me. My gag reflex activates. I move to the other counter.

Harper passes by the kitchen on her way to the entryway mirror, where she plays with her hair.

"I'm going to leave for a date as soon as Nick gets here."

"Why?" I look up from the stack of plates I've just pulled from a cabinet.

"To show Nick I'm desired by other men."

My jaw falls open. "And that's supposed to make him want you?"

We meet eyes in the mirror. Her smile is patronizing. "Aw, Kate. I could teach you all my tricks if you would start dating again." She whirls around and smiles at me, like she's made a joke and wants me to laugh.

Next subject. "How was work?"

"Crazy busy. Your event is in two weeks, and I'm making sure all my ducks are in a row, so to speak. Lynn is lucky I have so many friends in high places. This schedule was tight. Especially with all the other holiday parties coming up."

I want to groan, but I stuff it down. Somewhere, between the attempts to bring Ethan back and the realization that I can't, I've forgotten about the merger.

"You have an awful look on your face." Harper reaches around me and into the fridge. "Try not to think about Trent. Maybe his office will be far away from yours. Or maybe on the new floor. Didn't you say they're renting office space on the bottom floor?"

I nod. "That's what I'll do. Hope he's on the bottom floor." *Or maybe out next to the trash cans.*

I start working on the onion. By the time I get it peeled and positioned on my cutting board, I'm crying.

Nick knocks on the door. Harper quicksteps her way over and throws back the door, wide smile ready. "Come in."

I keep my watery eyes trained on the onion. *How am I supposed to greet him?* Texting him about tonight's cooking lesson was one thing. Being in the same room with him is entirely different. It's not like I can say *thanks for saving me, sorry I assaulted your mouth and pretended you were someone else. What's the proper protocol here?*

I pretend to be extremely intent on my task, until he says, "Evie gave me a cactus," and my instant curiosity thwarts my plan. I look over my shoulder to where he stands, proudly holding a little potted teddy bear cholla in his hands.

"You better be careful." I sniffle and flick a tear from my cheek, my reservations forgotten. "That's a jumping cactus."

I expect laughter, or at least interest in the possibility that a cactus can jump, but he takes one look at my face and drops the cactus on the counter. In two seconds he closes the space between us, his cheeks taut.

"Why are you crying? Did you cut yourself?" He looks my hands over. Satisfied I'm not injured, he looks back at me. Confusion draws his eyebrows together.

I open my mouth, but Harper answers for me. "Kate always cries when she cuts an onion. She has sensitive eyes." Harper flips her hand around, waving off my tears.

"Next time I'll wear goggles." I'm joking, but it probably isn't a bad idea.

Nick takes a step back. "Sorry. I was afraid you were hurt." He rights the little cactus and brushes the small amount of spilled soil into his hand, then dumps it into the garbage.

"That cactus doesn't actually jump." Harper strides to the innocent looking potted cactus and places a hand half an inch from the spines. "It's a silly story, meant to frighten newcomers like you." She smirks and winks at him.

Nick nods. "Thanks for the heads up. I'm going wash my hands, and then we can get this lesson started."

Harper's at my side as soon as he's stepped into the bathroom. She leans into me. "He is so yummy."

And he doesn't appear to be into you. As shocking as that may seem.

When Nick returns, Harper leans in to the mirror that hangs near the front door and applies her lip gloss. When she's finished she stands up straight and looks at Nick. "Well, as much as I adore Kate's spaghetti sauce, I have a date." Her pouty face is something to be admired. "If you'd be so kind as to save me some, I will be eternally grateful."

"I think we can manage that." Nick's voice is pleasant.

"Can you, Kate?" Harper's smile is too sweet. Is she pointing out my weight? Or just asking me to save her my spaghetti sauce?

"Of course." *I'm just being sensitive.* Harper wouldn't be so mean as to point out something like that in front of someone. And anyways, I'm down three pounds since I stopped drinking.

"See you later." Harper twirls her fingers at us and leaves.

I look at Nick. He looks at me. The silence is loud.

"Hi," I say softly. I'm blushing.

Nick smiles with one side of his mouth. "How do you drown a hipster?"

I blink, surprised. "Are you trying to tell me a joke?"

He nods slowly. "Are you always this hard to tell a joke to?"

I bite back my smile. "Try again."

"How do you drown a hipster?"

I think for a moment, then shake my head. "How?"

"Throw him into the mainstream."

I nod my approval. "Good one."

"You're supposed to laugh at jokes." Nick stomps over to stand at the counter, arms crossed. He's copying Harper's pouty face.

"When the joke is really funny, I'll laugh." I lift a finger to poke his side but drop it mid-air. Probably best to keep my fingers to myself.

"Let's get started." I grab a second cutting board for Nick and set him to work.

He's peeling and chopping the garlic like I showed him when he says, "Harper goes on a lot of dates."

"Does that bother you?" I ask from my place beside him. I'm dicing a green bell pepper.

He snorts. "Why would that bother me?"

I sigh. "You know she's into you, right?" I feel bad for saying anything, but Harper's making it so clear she should really just wear a sign around her neck.

"Um, yeah, I do." He clears his throat.

I set down my knife and look at him. "What was that?"

"What was what?" His voice is defensive.

"Um, yeah, I do," I deepen my voice to imitate him.

He laughs. "You're funny. Maybe you should be the one telling jokes."

"Funny is one of the last things I am."

"No really, you are."

"Spill, Nick."

He finishes the garlic and goes to the sink. "When I

met Harper at the funeral, she made sure to get my number, but she said it was for you, in case you ended up needing me for some reason." He pumps soap on his hands. "Which you did. The morning after I got you off the mountain, she was in your bedroom, and I heard some of what you guys were talking about. Then when she left the room she brushed up against me. And she had plenty of space to get by." He sniffs his fingertips, wrinkles his nose, and adds more soap to his hands. "This garlic means business."

I watch him scrub. "Fresh garlic isn't great for the breath, either. So don't go kissing anyone tonight." My eyes go wide as I realize what I've said so flippantly. Hastily I grab his cutting board and face away from him, sliding the garlic into the pan.

"No problem there." He laughs. "Although I know of someone who might do the honor."

I gulp and look at him. "Who?"

He gives me a side-eye. "Harper. Who did you think I was talking about?" His lips purse together like he's trying to hold back a laugh.

Does he enjoy seeing me red-faced?

I turn back to the pan and add the garlic to the heated oil. "I, uh, I just didn't know who. That's all. Let's get on with this cooking lesson. I'm starving."

By the time we sit down with our plates I know we've already eaten our fair share of pasta straight from the pan.

"This is better than I remember," I say between mouthfuls.

"You didn't use a recipe. Maybe that's why."

Maybe...

We eat in silence, until Nick tells me he met Zane for a beer last weekend. Which makes me realize I haven't talked to him since June. *Since Ethan's funeral.* Add him to the list of people I've pushed away.

"I didn't realize you were friends with him." I wipe my mouth with my napkin.

"He got in touch with me in August, when he returned from Idaho. I've seen him a few times since then. I like him. He has some good stories about Ethan."

"He's a good guy. We've known him forever." I hear the words and realize I've misspoke. "I mean, we knew him forever." My nose wrinkles. *Those words aren't right either.*

I push my plate away and rub my eyes, irritated.

Nick stands and grabs my plate before I can. "I'm on dish duty. You can keep me company."

I follow him to the kitchen. We talk mostly about his job while he scrapes, rinses and puts the dishes in the dishwasher.

I'm sitting on the counter, heels bumping a rhythm against the cabinet below me, when Nick hops up beside me.

He sends an apologetic smile across the twelve inches that separate us. "Don't be embarrassed, okay? What happened at the Halloween party... Some of it was my fault. I'm the one who asked you to revive yourself."

I blush. Sitting this close to him right now, it's easy to remember what his body felt like up against mine. And how painful it was when reality smacked me in the face.

"I just didn't know you were going to use my *lips* to resuscitate yourself."

I blush harder.

Nick laughs. He sticks out a hand. "Are we good?"

I shake it and nod, trying like hell to push away the absurd fact that I know what his lips feel like. "We're good."

He hops down. "I have to go. My shift starts really early."

"Of course, yeah." I jump to the floor. "Have a safe drive home."

He walks to the door, pausing after he opens it. "I noticed there wasn't any alcohol tonight." He holds out a fist.

I tap my fist against his.

He walks away, and I shut the door, leaning against the handle.

Tonight will be the sixth night since Ethan died four months ago that I'll go to sleep sober. It's not an easy task. Sobriety means more intentional thought. Less erratic, all-consuming emotions. But it's given me the clarity I so desperately needed. Ethan is not alive. Ethan is not coming back to me, in any form. And it's something I have absolutely no control over.

26

KATE

"You're going somewhere on a Saturday night?" Harper's voice is snide as I walk past the living room. She's sitting on the couch watching TV.

"Nick invited me over." I set my purse on the half wall of the kitchen and look through the contents. When Harper doesn't respond I look at her.

Her angry eyes are trained on me. "He invited *you*?"

"Why is that shocking?" I grab a bunch of used tissues from the bottom of my purse and toss them in the kitchen trash.

She turns back to her show. "It just is, that's all. He should be inviting me over. What more do I have to do? Haven't I made it clear that I'm available?"

"Maybe he's focused on getting his life together after the Army. Maybe he's not ready to date. I don't know." I say all this to the back of her head.

"*You're* going over there."

"It's not a date." I come back from the kitchen to grab my purse.

She flicks her gaze to me. "Wear something else. That shade of green isn't good on you." She looks back at the TV.

"I'm not your competition," I say quietly, then I walk out the door.

I don't know what's happening, but something ugly is sprouting up between me and my roommate. I'm resentful of how she's been treating me, and she's angry because Nick's not falling at her feet.

I spend my drive recalling all the nasty comments Harper's made since Ethan died. They pile on top of each other, like garbage in a heap, until I'm nearly nauseated with the stink of it. Why am I friends with her? Why would I live with someone who tears me down instead of building me up? By the time I reach Nick's apartment, I think of how nice it would be if it was Harper who had a place here.

Nick's car is easy to spot. He still has a blue and white Connecticut license plate. I pull into the visitor spot next to him and climb from the car, juggling a housewarming gift in one hand and my purse in the other.

"Twenty sixty-two," I mutter under my breath, looking at the sign on the front of the building for direction.

"Looking for someone?" A deep voice asks from behind me.

I whip around, startled. The man is tall and skinny and leering at me in a way that makes me feel gross inside my own skin.

"Yes, she is." Nick's voice is loud, assertive. He's standing on the sidewalk in front of me. "And she's found him." His words are a statement, but he speaks with such authority it could have been a command. *Stand down.*

The stranger holds his hands up in front of his chest. "No trouble, man. You all have a good night." He turns and walks to the building parallel to the one we're standing in front of.

I turn back to Nick. "That's two saves in one week."

"Maybe I can get a second job as your security detail."

"The job would be boring, I assure you." I hand the wrapped present to him.

"What's this?" He holds out the box and eyes it.

"What do you think it is?"

"I'll open it once we get upstairs. Come on," Nick grabs my hand and leads me to the stairs.

"Home sweet home," Nick announces when we arrive at 2062. He drops my hand to open the door.

I walk in and look around. The decor is sparse, and that's putting it nicely. A couch. A TV. And a bookshelf, crammed with books. I walk over, running my fingers over the spines. *It's been so long since I picked up a book.*

"Where did you get all these?" I ask.

"A lot of them came back from Germany with me. Some my mom sent out when she sent my car. And that shelf up there"—he points at the top—"is full of new stuff. New to me, anyhow. I found a great used bookstore nearby."

"Begin Again?" With one finger I pull a title off the shelf.

He grins. "That place is awesome. Do you go?"

"Not in a long time." The scent of old paper sticks in my nose and makes me nostalgic.

"Why not?" He leans his forearm against the side of the bookshelf.

"My mom took me a lot when I was younger. But then my dad wanted me to start trying other things, so I stopped reading for pleasure." I put the book back on the shelf.

Nick's frown tugs on the corners of his mouth.

"You don't talk about your dad much." He pushes off and walks to the kitchen.

I follow. "Do you already know what happened to him?"

"Evie told me. I'm sorry you had to go through that."

I nod. If my dad was here, he'd hate the way I've handled myself since Ethan died. Twinges of disappointment assail my brain.

"What's in the bag?" I ask, pointing at the counter.

"I got something for you." He pulls out a thin book and hands it over.

I eye the cover. Animals... Flowers.

"A coloring book?" My eyebrows rise with my question. I haven't colored in at least fifteen years. "Thanks. I'll make sure to pick up crayons."

Nick shakes his head. "No crayons. The designs are too small and elaborate." He reaches into the bag again. "Colored pencils." He holds up a box.

"Okay. Great." *Kind of an odd gift...*

Nick eyes me. "Coloring is cathartic. It relieves stress and anxiety. Heals the soul."

I hold up the book, dubious. "*This* is going to heal my soul?"

Nick walks to the nearly empty living room and lies down on the carpet on his stomach, facing me.

"Let's try it and see."

I look down at the elephant wearing a beaded headdress on the cover and back up to Nick. "You want to color right now?"

He shrugs. "Why not?"

I don't have a reason. I follow Nick and lie down next to him. The carpet is stiff under my forearms.

The box of colored pencils makes a light, wooden sound when Nick dumps them on the ground above the book. *So many colors*. Way more than I used to have.

"Dibs on page seven." He announces in a playful, warning voice.

I turn to look at him, but when I do, I find his nose is only inches from mine. Too close. I look quickly back to the book. "I guess that leaves me with page eight."

I reach for the gray and start on a bird. We're silent as we work. The only sound that punctuates the quiet are the shifting pencils as we trade one color for another.

I'm halfway done with my page when I notice Nick's pencil has stopped moving.

"What's wrong?" My gaze stays on my page. It feels weird to talk to him and not look at him, but his close proximity necessitates it.

"Why do you color like that?"

My eyes rove over my work, double-checking it. When I find no fault with it, I ask, "Like what?"

He points at the tree branch I'm working on. "You outline first." One of his fingers runs along the brown edges of the branch.

Oh, that. "That way I stay in the lines."

"And what happens if you color outside the lines?"

I roll to my side, away from him, and prop my head up on my open palm. He does the same.

His stare is rapt, like he's genuinely interested in my answer. Too bad I don't have a better one.

"I don't know."

He watches me, lips twisting. "Do you feel like coloring is helping you?"

I flick my gaze to the flock of gray birds and hot pink flowers on my page. "Too soon to tell." I look back at Nick. "What about you?"

"This is for you, Kate. You're the one with the broken soul." His words are spoken softly, but it feels like a punch.

I suck in a quick breath. "Do you always say everything you think?"

He adjusts his supporting hand while he considers my question. "No."

Nick rolls back over and starts coloring again. So do I.

"Try not to outline," he says. His voice is challenging, the same way it was when he asked me to cook without a recipe.

I huff. "I like outlining."

"Just try it the other way."

And I do. I try. But I hate it. I feel out of control. I need a barrier to keep my strokes in line.

"I like my way better." I draw thick, blue strokes along the black outline of the next bird. Ah, yes. Peace restored. When the bird is done I set down the blue and reach for the yellow.

"Kate?" Nick's voice is unsure. Very uncharacteristic for him.

"Um hmm?" I'm focusing on the stamens of a crocus.

"Harper said something at the Halloween party, about you drinking every night... Was she right? Every night?"

My pencil pauses, but his keeps going.

"She was right." I toss my pencil back in the pile.

"And now?"

"I haven't had anything to drink since Halloween. I threw out everything in my apartment the next morning." I roll over and sit up, facing him. Nick does the same.

"I've never been much of a drinker. When Ethan died..." I pause, choking on the words *Ethan* and *died*. I never say those words out loud. Deep breath. "When Ethan died, I found that if I drank, it made me fall asleep faster. I..."

Nick leans forward, waiting. He watches me intently, his face open. *He wants to hear about my pain. He's not afraid of it.*

"In the first week after Ethan died, I could only lie in bed and sob." I bite my lip, afraid I've said too much. Nick looks...caring. *Talking like this feels so liberating.* "The tears overtook my body. I couldn't breathe. I would choke and gag on sobs. I'm sure that sounds dramatic."

Nick reaches for my hand. His fingers weave through my fingers, and he squeezes. "It doesn't sound dramatic. It sounds raw. And real. Keep going."

My intake of breath is loud, and my exhale is just as noisy. "I wanted to die. Literally. I wanted someone to kill me. A world without Ethan seemed so impossible. It still does. I stopped for coffee on my way to work this week, and the place was packed with people just leading their own lives. I wanted to yell at them, remind them all that the world is not the same anymore because Ethan isn't in it. Don't they all know that the world has changed?" I feel tears on my face. Nick's eyes are shiny.

"The night of Ethan's funeral, I got really drunk. That was the first night I did it. I sat on my couch, looked through a photo album of me and Ethan, and drank. When I woke up the next day I felt pain in a place that wasn't my heart. Eventually I discovered if I drank myself to sleep, I would dream of Ethan. I think they were dreams, anyway. If they weren't they were very vivid memories, and maybe made-up scenarios that felt dream-like because I was so drunk." My heart pounds. *I'm telling him everything.* "They were like a lifeline. A way to keep Ethan alive. And they were so realistic. I could talk to him and see him and smell him." I look down at our intertwined fingers, afraid I've overshared.

"You drank every night because you thought it would keep Ethan alive in your mind?" Nick can't keep the incredulity out of his voice. I'm not even sure he tried.

I meet his gaze and nod. The wall I've built around my feelings shatters, and my emotions spill between our bent legs. I've never been so exposed. I feel raw, like a scabbed over wound picked bare. Any harsh words from Nick now will sting unbelievably.

His thumb rubs over the top of my hand, and I realize how gentle his words have been. They don't sting. They soothe.

"And now that you aren't drinking anymore?" The pad of his thumb dips into the space between my thumb and finger.

My lower lip slides back in between my teeth, but my mouth is shaking and my lip bounces out from under my teeth. "He's gone," I whisper, and the tears pour. "The night you rescued me off Camelback. That was the day those... dreams or whatever they were...they stopped." My voice is high-pitched, the anguish riding through it. "I tried so hard to get him back. But...nothing. He's gone." My voice breaks. Sobs push my chest up and down.

"Kate." Nick's voice is strangled. He reaches out to my face, but he drops his hand.

"I can't wipe away your tears. Not when they're for Ethan." As he speaks his own tears flow over his strong cheekbones and drop off his jaw.

We sit and we cry. We cry for the person we lost.

The best friend.

The soulmate.

We cry until we're left with nothing but dry, red eyes.

Nick gets up and comes back with a box of tissues. He places them between us, and we blow our noses, half-laughing, half-sniffling.

"What are you thinking about?" I ask him.

"I think Ethan knew we would need each other."

I dab at my face with another tissue. "He knew."

When it's time for me to leave, Nick walks me out to my car. I pause, the open door between us.

"Thank you for tonight. And not just for the gift." The bag dangling from my forearm crinkles as I gesture with it. "I'm hardly a great companion these days. I guess what I mean is, thank you for sticking with me. I know you're doing it for Ethan, but still..."

"You don't have to thank me for anything, Kate. I'm here because I want to be." He places an open palm on my chest. My breath hitches. The warmth from his hand seeps through my shirt, past my skin, and spreads across my heart. He looks into my eyes, his face serene. "Your wounds don't scare me." His words are calm and strong.

My free hand reaches out, over the top of the car door, and rests on his chest. Beneath my hand I feel his heartbeats.

"Your wounds don't scare me either," I whisper.

We stand that way for a few more moments. Nick pulls his hand back at the same time I do, but our lack of contact lasts for only a second. Our hands meet in the space between us and he catches mine, giving it one light squeeze. He releases me with a wistful smile, one that seems to say, *We're fighting this fight together. That's the only way we'll make it through.* I drive away, my mind grappling with the idea that Ethan has managed to take care of me, even when he's not alive. Ethan loved me enough to wait for me, and he loved me enough to give me Nick.

***

"CAN you even believe the shindig that's happening next weekend?" Sarah takes a bite of her sandwich. The cafe we've gone to on our lunch hour has gotten busier since we sat down and now she has to raise her voice. "They had me at *prime rib carving station*."

I swipe my mouth with my napkin. "I know. Harper's been giving me the inside scoop. There's supposed to be an awesome DJ and chocolate fountains. Drinks on trays, passed hors d'oeuvres. And a big raffle she won't tell me the prize for."

"I still can't believe we're merging with Maxim. Maybe I'll meet the man of my dreams." Sarah makes her voice breathy and places a hand on her heart.

"Just as long as his name isn't Trent." I should send out a warning memo to every female in my office.

"I smell a story," she sing-songs.

I tell the condensed version while we pay the lunch bill. Essentially, he's a jerk. End of story.

We draw out the walk back to work. A slight breeze rustles the palm tree fronds along our path. The air is unseasonably chilly, even with the sun streaming down. My face lifts a fraction to let a little Vitamin D soak into my skin.

"Can I say something to you?" Sarah sounds hesitant.

"Depends." I slide my sunglasses down from the top of my head to cover my eyes. "Is it good or bad?"

"Good."

"Then yes."

"You're different. Just in the last week and a half. You're... more you." Sarah cringes, as if she fears that at any moment, I'll go berserk and start screaming.

I don't answer right away. What's happening to me is something I *don't* want to happen.

And it really does make me want to scream and go berserk. Because what's happening to my heart and mind is *not* okay with me.

"I *feel* more me inside." I say *feel* like it's a dirty word.

Sarah stops suddenly. She puts an arm around my shoulders and curls me into her body.

"You're going to make it," she whispers against the side of my head.

I don't know if I'm more shocked by the impromptu hug or the raw emotion from Sarah. Two things Harper has yet to extend.

Maybe it's unfair of me to expect that from her, but the harsh truth is that Harper isn't capable of those things. And she's not going to change.

27

KATE

THE SUN DIPS BELOW THE HORIZON JUST AS I PULL INTO A parking spot. The lights of the bookstore spill onto the sidewalk and over me as I walk past the long display window. It has been years since I've stepped into this place, but when I open the door and the bell chimes, I'm eleven years old all over.

"Welcome to Begin Again," says a smiling woman behind a counter.

I say hello and look around for the person who invited me here.

I find him standing between Psychology and Self-Help.

"I didn't take you for a self-help kind of guy."

Nick looks up from an open book in his hands. "The self-help section of the library got me and my mom through her addiction."

My hands go to my hips. "Is that why you've asked me here? Because I stopped three weeks ago. Cold turkey." *Kate will Master it.* How am I supposed to lose that label when it's ingrained?

My chin raises. "And I haven't given in." *A feat considering how much I've wanted to.* The curiosity kills me. Could I bring Ethan back, just one more time?

"I asked you to come here because this is a place you used to love. This section is just where I happen to be right now." Nick replaces the book on the shelf.

"Oh." I blush. "Sorry."

"It's okay. Go. Explore." He smiles encouragingly.

So I do. I go to the second floor, where they still have a children's reading nook and possibly the same yellow and red bean bag chairs. *I loved curling up in one of those with a stack of books. My mom perused the shelves downstairs and I stayed here, in the red chair, and let myself go away in my imagination.*

Nobody is here on this Thursday night, so I sit on a bean bag. The filling shifts, making noise. This seat used to envelope me like a cocoon. Petite as I am, the red bean bag chair can't hold me the same way anymore. I reach for the closest book on the shelf. It's binding is shabby, and the corners of the cover flip back. White lines have worn into the picture. But I know this book. It's about a girl who does odd jobs to earn money for summer camp, but things keep going wrong for her. I open it and read, remembering the words like I'd read them just yesterday. As if I were a young girl again, the story sweeps me away.

"You ended up in the children's section?" Nick says from the top of the stairs. He comes toward me. "I would have pegged you for a romance kind of girl." Nick sits cross-legged beside my bean bag.

"This is where I sat when I was little. And it still smells the same. Musty paper. And something else." I turn my nose up to the air. "Burnt coffee? Whatever it is, I like it."

Nick stands. "Ready to go?" He points at the book in my hand. "Are you getting that?"

I put the book on the shelf. "No, that was a book I read when I was young. Next time I'll spend my time in a more mature section."

"There will be a next time?" His grin is lopsided. He looks proud of himself.

"There will definitely be a next time."

We go downstairs, and I wait near the exit while Nick buys his book. My phone rings, and when I see who it is, I step outside.

"Evie, hi. How are you?" I sit on a nearby bench, wrap my arms around myself, and use a lifted shoulder to hold the phone to my ear.

"Kate! I'm so happy you answered." Evie's voice makes me think of her face. When I see her face, I think of her standing in her house. When I picture her house, I think of Ethan.

"I haven't talked to you in a long time. I was trying to give you space. Do you need more or have you had enough?" Her voice is serious, but it has a joking edge to it.

"I'm happy you called."

"Good. And I'm well, thanks for asking. How are you?"

Nick sits down next to me and sets the bookstore bag between us.

"I'm hanging in there," I say into the phone but I'm looking at Nick. He zips up his sweatshirt.

"Can you talk right now? Or are you busy?"

"I was in a bookstore but I'm finished. I can talk."

Nick gives me a thumbs up. He crosses one leg over his knee, grabs a book out of the bag, and opens it.

"I want to talk to you about Nick."

I clear my throat and eye my companion. He's flipping pages. Not looking at me.

"What about him?"

"We see him often. And he talks about you a lot. He told me Ethan asked him to take care of you. How do you feel about their agreement?"

"Okay, I suppose. It's not all that surprising, when you think about it."

Evie laughs. "Right? It really isn't. I'm going to say something a little crazy, so just bear with me here."

"Okay," I draw out the word.

"If something were to develop between you and Nick... It would be okay with me. More than okay. He's a fantastic person."

My gaze flies to Nick, afraid he's somehow heard Evie.

"Oh. Um. Thanks?" I'm too surprised to come up with anything better.

"It's just that, well, you're young. And Ethan would want you to find happiness again. And then there's Nick, a person Ethan loved. And there's you, a person Ethan loved. It kind of makes sense, you know?"

First Harper, now Ethan's mother. And neither of them know about the night I kissed him. *I* don't want to know about the night I kissed him.

"I see where you're coming from." I switch my phone to my other ear, further from Nick. Just in case.

"So you have my blessing. I mean, he hasn't said anything specifically. But he talks about you constantly. I just thought..." She trails off.

"Evie, it's fine. Don't worry." I picture her shifting her feet, worried she's said too much.

"Also, I called because Thanksgiving is next Thursday. I invited Zane and his parents, but his mom said they have family visiting. Just want to make sure you're coming."

"Yes, of course. It's at your house this year, right? Last

year it was at my mom's, so that makes this year your turn."
Dread fills me. I don't want to go to Ethan's house.

"Technically it's my turn." Evie clears her throat. "But
we're having it at your mom's again." Her voice sounds far
away, like she's lost in her thoughts. I get the feeling there's
more to the story than she's letting on.

"Sounds great." I'm quick to be positive. "What can I
bring?"

"Your apple pie, of course."

"I'll be there, pie in hand."

"Dinner is at four, like always. I'll let you get back to
what you were doing. "

We hang up and I put my phone in my purse. Nick sets
his book down.

"Evie?" He asks.

I nod. "How'd you know?"

"Good guess. How's she doing?"

"You probably have a better idea of how she's doing than
I do. She said you see them often."

"Not in the last week." He says it with regret, as though a
week is too long.

Guilt washes over me.

Not in the last five months.

"Have you said anything to Evie about...?" How can I
even say this? The words feel funny in my throat.

Nick's eye's narrow. "About what?"

"She said she wanted to give us her blessing. In case..."
My face is on fire. My hands travel through my hair, and I
look up at the night sky. It's so much easier to talk to the
muted inky black. "In case you and I were to develop a relationship." My face screws up on the last word.

Nick doesn't say anything. I sneak a peek with one eye.

He's...smiling? And shaking his head.

"Evie's something, isn't she?" He laughs once after he says it.

He doesn't seem bothered by her words. I guess I don't need to be either. "Ethan used to call her a force. She called to remind me about Thanksgiving next Thursday."

Nick nods. "She left me a voicemail this afternoon. It's at your mom's house, right?"

"Yes. I'm bringing apple pie."

"Lucky me, I've been instructed to just bring myself." He gets up and offers me a hand. "Want to grab dinner? Let someone else cook for you tonight."

"Are you giving me a Thursday off?" I follow him to the parking lot.

"Just this once. Last week's steak and veggie tostadas were amazing. And don't even get me started on your spaghetti." He kisses his fingertips and sends the kiss out to the sky. "For my next lesson, I want to learn how to make chimichangas. I didn't even know that word existed until I moved out here and saw it on the menu at a Mexican restaurant."

I laugh at his enthusiasm. "Deal."

Nick turns around and walks backwards. "Deal." He grins and continues to walk backward the rest of the way to his car.

"Show-off," I mutter. But I'm laughing.

I'm laughing.

***

APPLE PIE IS MY SPECIALTY. I used to do the lattice top, but then I replaced it with a cinnamon crumble and became the most popular guest at Thanksgiving dinner. My initial thought when I wake on Thanksgiving morning is that I'm alone in the apartment, and that knowledge brings relief. Harper stayed at her mom's house last night with her sisters.

I'm assembling my ingredients, Macy's Day Parade blaring from the living room, when I get a text message.

Can I get a baking lesson this morning?

I smile at Nick's question and type my response.

It is a Thursday... If you come now you'll get here while the coffee is still hot.

I watch the three little dots move for a few seconds before his message pops up.

On my way.

A baking lesson... This should be interesting. I'm a bit of a control freak when it comes to making apple pie.

I look down at myself, and consider changing. My cornucopia pajama pants have been my Thanksgiving sleep-wear for so many years they're frayed at the bottom. I twist my leg to get a better look at just how many white threads are sticking out. *A lot.* But I'm not changing. I like these pants. I will, however, brush my teeth.

Nick arrives with donuts. I pluck one from the bag.

"Seriously?" I say around a mouthful of maple long john with turkey shaped candies on top. "Like we aren't going to eat enough unhealthy food today."

He waves off my complaint and takes another bite of his donut, the cream filling oozing out. With one finger he catches it and licks it off. "Turkey is healthy. Green beans are healthy."

I take another bite. "Not when my mom covers them in cream of mushroom soup, cheddar cheese, and fried onions."

His eyes widen. "Really?"

"Um hmm."

He stuffs the rest of the donut in his mouth. "Don't care." He grins, the donut showing.

I wrinkle my nose. "You're super gross right now."

He finishes chewing and looks at me pointedly. "Says the girl with a candy turkey stuck to her cheek."

I run my hands over my cheeks, but Nick shakes his head and reaches over, brushing his fingers across my forehead.

"I lied. It was on your forehead. I just wanted to watch you try to get it off your cheeks." He laughs. I narrow my eyes at him.

The parade announcer's voice booms into the kitchen with his excitement over the next float. It's a good reminder that we need to get started.

I take the bag of green apples from the fridge and set them on the counter with the corer and peeler. I take one apple out of the bag and demonstrate how to use the tools.

"The apples will be your job. I'll handle the dough." I go back to the fridge for the butter I cut into cubes last night.

"Why don't I get the dough?"

"Because it's the hardest part. It requires very precise measurements. Baking is different than cooking. You can't just toss in a little of this and that."

He eyes the cubes of butter I've set on the counter. I go to the pantry for the other ingredients, and come away with the flour, salt, sugar, and cinnamon.

Eying Nick pointedly, I say "And don't even think of suggesting I skip the recipe this morning."

He gasps melodramatically. "Skip the recipe? In a baking situation?" He laughs at himself. "Don't worry, Kate. I know your limit."

I give him a look and unload my haul. We work side by side on the counter with the half wall, so we can watch the parade. I don't know if it's the holiday or the sugar high, but for the first time since June the pain in my chest feels a little less sharp.

***

I PULL into my mom's driveway at the same time Evie walks out of her front door. She rushes across the street, a big smile on her face. I hurry from my car, meeting her halfway.

"I'm so happy to see you." Her eyes hold relief. "I was worried you would cancel."

I pull back. "And rob you of the chance to eat apple pie with cinnamon streusel topping? Never. Where's James?" We're standing close enough that I can see the dark circles she has tried to hide with concealer.

She laughs at my pie comment and, with a dismissive shrug, blames James' absence on a cold. I get the feeling I'm missing something. Does it have anything to do with why Thanksgiving dinner was moved to my mom's house? Vaguely I remember Mom mentioning something's going on with Evie. *When was that?* I can't recall the exact date. It was sometime during my dark days.

The sound of a car's engine diverts my attention. We hurry to my mom's driveway to get out of the way of the car coming toward us. When it gets closer I see it's Nick. He pulls into the empty space beside my car and climbs out.

"Are we celebrating Thanksgiving outside today?" He grins and hugs Evie, waving at me when she lets him go.

Evie snorts. "This might be warm for a Connecticut boy, but we Phoenicians consider this cold." She rubs her hands on her arms. "Let's go inside. Your mom probably needs help."

I grab the apple pie from the front seat, Nick takes it from me, and we follow Evie inside.

My mother greets us with a big, happy smile. She's wearing an apron and her hair is a mess. Evie heads straight for the kitchen after stopping to hug my mom. In a few seconds I hear her banging something around. *We'd better get in there.*

"Kate, I can already smell that pie." My mom bends at the waist and sniffs the air next to Nick. "Just wait until you try the topping on that pie, Nick. Amazing."

"Oh, I know." He grins at me, a playful look of guilt on his face. "I snuck a pinch of it this morning when Kate was watching the parade."

My mom's jaw drops open. She glances at me and then back to Nick. "Oh, really?" She squeaks. She turns and motions for us to follow her to the kitchen. "So, Nick, you were over at Kate's this morning?" She practically shouts the words *over at Kate's this morning*. Evie turns from her post at the sink, a potato in one hand and a peeler in the other. Her eyes look interested. *Very* interested.

Nick sets the pie down on the only remaining counter space. "This morning I had my first official baking lesson." He glances at me. "Maybe next time Kate will let me touch the dough."

"Keep dreamin'." I pull the little container of streusel topping out of my purse and set it next to the pie. Nick eyes it hungrily. I give him a warning look. "Don't even think about it. That's not extra. It has to go on the pie last and bake for a few minutes."

"Fine," Nick mutters. He walks to the kitchen sink and washes his hands in the other basin. Next to him Evie's potato peels fly through the air. One lands on his shoulder.

He plucks it off and offers to help her. My mom hands him a second peeler and he gets to work.

I stand back, struck by the sight of Evie and Nick standing at the sink with each other. They looks so... comfortable. At home with one another.

The way I feel when I'm with him. He's so open and honest, always ready to be there for me. I think back to last weekend and his hand on my heart. *Your wounds don't scare me.* I lean back on the counter, my head tilting to the side as I listen to their conversation.

Evie's words from the other night float through my head. *Find happiness...blessing...with Nick.*

The most stubborn part of my heart finds this idea repugnant. But I'd be lying if I said there wasn't a piece of me that feels drawn to him.

28

NICK

"Thank you," I take the coffee from the girl and offer a polite smile. A dash of hurt and embarrassment creeps into her eyes, but she's quick to push it aside.

"Let me know if you need anything else," she says, her tone different than it was five minutes ago when I stepped up to the counter to order.

A flirtatious head tilt told me she found me attractive, and when she bent forward so her shirt fell open more, I knew she meant business.

There's nothing wrong with her. She's pretty. I'm just not interested.

She opens the door into the coffeeshop and walks back in, leaving me alone out here on the patio.

Phoenix isn't so bad now that it's not blazing hot. It's cold in the mornings and progresses to mildly warm as the day continues. It has everything I could ever think to want in terms of food and entertainment. I live close to school, close to my job, and close to Evie and James.

And, of course, Phoenix has Kate.

As much as I don't want to admit it, the lines of my mission are no longer clear-cut.

When did that happen? I think back to June when I first met her, and every day since then, and I can't see an exact point when the lines began to blur. Was it so gradual I didn't notice?

And now that my feelings for Kate have grown to a size that even I can no longer ignore, what is there to do about that?

She's Ethan girl. Not mine. I was sent here to bring her back to life, not fall in love with her. This isn't some cheesy movie. This is real life. And in real life, there are people who won't want us together.

But there are some who will. Evie, for starters. The only person who really matters when it comes down to it. James matters too, but he's not participating in life much these days. If he's not in his woodshed, he's... well, I don't know where.

These thoughts have been running through my mind on repeat, caught on a hamster wheel. It's only been a week since Thanksgiving. The day Evie and Mrs. Masters made it clear they were rooting for me and Kate to get together.

But I don't think either of them know what Kate has been up to these past five months. She was very good at hiding it, but I recognized the signs.

To be fair, I think she's overcome the excessive drinking. Her eyes are brighter, her complexion glows.

Her old self is creeping out. Or maybe it's the new version of her. The person she was forced to become.

The person I'm finding it hard to keep at arms' length.

***

I'VE BEEN INVITED over to Chad's house for dinner tonight.

On my way over, I stop and pick up nice flowers for his wife. His two boys are five and seven, so I grab a couple toy trucks for them.

Chad's house is small, and very close to the houses on either side of him, and the neighborhood is clean and well-kept.

He opens the front door before I can knock. Smiling, he welcomes me in and says, "The boys told me you were here. They've been waiting at the window." Chad looks over to the open room right off the front door, and my eyes follow.

A set of small toes sticks out from behind a chair, and a giggle floats up into the air, followed by a stern *shhh*.

"Oh no, Jamie and Wes aren't here today?" I direct my words toward the toes. "Bummer. I was really hoping to give them the toys I brought. I guess I'll have to play with them myself."

The toes disappear from sight, and a second later two dark-haired heads pop up from behind the chair.

"We're here," they cry, rushing out.

"Oh, good." I palm my chest in mock relief.

"Boys," Chad says, his tone gently reminding them of something.

Both boys stop in front of me and hold out their hands. "It's nice to meet you Mr. Nick."

Man, these kids are cute. One's missing a front tooth and the other has a streak of blue marker on his cheek.

"Here." I hand the trucks to their new owners.

Both boys let out whoops of excitement and tell me thank you, then they're racing from the room like rockets.

"They have tracks in their room. I bet money that's where they're headed."

Chad leads me through the small hallway and into

kitchen. His wife stands at the stove, her back to us, stirring something that smells incredible.

"Babe, meet Nick." His wife turns around, wooden spoon in hand and a smile ready.

Chad looks at me. "Nick meet—"

"Babe, I know. I heard you say her name." I hold out the flowers.

Chad and his wife laugh. She walks closer, hand extended. "Kristan, actually."

I shake her hand and she takes the flowers from me. Grabbing a vase from under the sink, she sticks them in and turns on the faucet, then goes back to the stove. Chad turns off the water when the vase is half-full.

"Thank you for the flowers," Kristan says over her shoulder. "I hope you like pozole."

"I have no idea what that is," I answer honestly. "But I'm here for it."

"Nick's a bit of a foodie," Chad explains to Kristan. "He gets cooking lessons from a mystery woman every Thursday night."

I sigh and shake my head. In a moment of weakness, I told Chad about Kate's lessons, and he hasn't let it go.

"Is that right?" Kristan asks, moving the pot off the burner. She looks at me, her expression expectant, but I don't have much to add.

"Aw, you're keeping it close to the vest. That means you really like her." She grins and pulls bread from the oven.

"Do you need help with anything?" I ask, hoping this topic will fizzle out.

"Of course not. You're a guest." She spins to look at Chad. "You, however, can set the table."

He salutes her and pulls out a drawer, gathering silverware.

Dinner is enjoyable, and the boys are even more fun. They are rambunctious but respectful. The kind of kids I hope to have one day.

There was a time when kids weren't something I even saw in my future. But now I'm feeling like maybe I can have the things I believed were reserved for other people.

Kate's face pops into my mind, and at the same time my phone rings.

Normally I wouldn't let a phone call interrupt dinner, but it's Harper, and that immediately makes me think it's about Kate.

Smiling apologetically, I get up from the table and excuse myself to the back yard.

"Harper, what's up?"

"Oh, you know. A little of this and a little of that."

I frown. This doesn't sound worth my time.

"Kate okay?" Kate's the only connection between me and Harper, so if the call isn't about her, I'm not interested.

Harper blows out an irritated breath. "Yes, she's fine. I'm not calling about her. I wanted to see if you had anything going on tomorrow night. I planned a big event to celebrate the merging of Kate's company with Trent's, and I wanted to know if you'd like to go with me."

Capturing my bottom lip between two fingers, I squeeze and think about her offer.

I don't care to spend any unnecessary time around Harper, but Kate on the other hand...

"Sure, what time?"

It's not nice of me to attend a party with Harper when I don't care for her, but my conscience is eased by the fact she doesn't care about anybody but herself. She might not care even if she knew why I agreed to go.

Harper gives me the details and I end the call by telling her I'm having dinner at a coworkers house and need to go.

She says goodbye with a flirtatious tone, and I get the feeling I'm falling on a sword. But I'm quickly learning that I'll do just about anything for Kate, including accompany Harper to an event.

All my missions in the Army were life or death. But this mission?

It may be my most dangerous one of all.

29

KATE

"Do I need to dress you tonight?" Harper's standing in my bedroom, hands on her hips. She looks into my bathroom mirror and watches my curling iron release a section of hair.

It's the night of my work party. All day I've toyed with the idea of suddenly coming down with an illness. If I had better attendance at work in the past six months I might develop a sudden case of food poisoning, but the fact is that I don't have a stellar attendance record right now, and I can't afford to miss out on this event.

I wind my last length of hair around the hot wand and avoid Harper's gaze. "I didn't go shopping." Maybe it's because I think it's just a silly party, or maybe it's because I'm trying to keep myself from making a big deal about being Trent's new colleague. Either way, I was planning on wearing a cocktail dress I already own.

"Of course you didn't." Harper spins and walks away.

She's been a royal pain in the ass all day. I was granted a few hours reprieve when she went to the event site to oversee set-up, but then she was back, full of energy and annoying remarks. My patience is starting to wear thin.

"Here." Harper sails back into my room. I set down the curling iron and walk to where she stands next to my bed. "Don't spill a drink on it or I'll kill you." She carefully lays a plastic bag on my comforter and removes the dress.

It's knee-length with a deep scooped neckline. "I love that shade of purple." I run my hand across the fabric. It's smooth and cool.

"It's aubergine," she snaps.

Breathe... She's just stressed. This party is a really big deal for her.

"Thanks for letting me borrow it."

She points a stiff finger at me. "No stains."

"I heard you the first time," I murmur.

"And use this clutch. I have another one that looks just like it, so we'll be twins." She tosses the shiny silver purse on my bed. "I'm going to get dressed. Nick will be here any minute."

What?

I open my mouth to ask, but she's already gone. *She did that on purpose.*

I follow her. Just like she wants me to. Just like she knows I will.

I stop at the entrance to her bedroom. "Why will Nick be here any minute?"

Harper steps carefully into her dress. She pulls it up and admires herself in the floor-to-ceiling mirror on her wall. *I'm pretty sure only blondes look that incredible in aquamarine.*

"Can you zip me?"

She gathers her hair and holds it out to the side. Her gaze is down, expectant.

Dutifully I grab the metal and yank. The sound of the zipper mimics my irritation. Short and loud.

"Why will Nick be here any minute?" My voice is strained by the effort I'm expending to stay calm. She's up to something.

She looks at me through the mirror. On her face is a carefully placed look of innocence and surprise.

"Oh, he didn't tell you? That's weird, I thought you were close."

I breath deep. "Tell me what?"

"Nick asked if he could attend the event with me."

My heartbeats pick up. *It's not a big deal,* I tell myself. *Nick's single. Harper's single. This was bound to happen.* And yet, I hate it.

Nick's kind, funny, and caring. He's truthful, almost to a fault. He's insightful, and empathetic. He's an all-around good person. He gave me a coloring book to heal my broken soul, for God's sake.

And Harper... She's not going to start boiling kittens anytime soon, but she's not the girl for Nick.

But he asked her out. Sort of. Why didn't he mention any of this to me on Thanksgiving? We were all there, minus James, stuffing our faces with too much food, and Nick didn't tell me he was coming to my company party. Or that he's interested in my roommate after all.

My smile is forced. It makes my cheeks puff up and my eyes squint. "Good for you. I know you've been hoping he would be interested in you."

Harper turns around. "Oh, Kate, don't be upset. Liking Nick just isn't in your best interest."

I balk. "What are you talking about?"

"It would just be weird, you know, with the whole Ethan connection."

I keep my mouth shut and let my irritated sigh exit my nose. "Please stop speaking in riddles."

"Oh, you're still doing the denying thing. Sorry, I thought your attraction to Nick was out in the open." She bares her teeth, making a face that says '*whoops*' for her. "Don't worry, I'm going to take him off your hands. Help you avoid a situation that wouldn't be any good for you." She pats my shoulder.

I'm so frustrated and irritated with her that I want to pull my hair out, strand by strand.

I return to my room to get dressed, and refuse to think about the two of them going on a date tonight. To *my* work party.

The *aubergine* dress slips over my head. My hand glides over the soft fabric. In the mirror is a girl who looks so different than the girl who, a little over five months ago, lay in her bed dying of a broken heart. *I've come so far.*

I grab Harper's silver purse off my bed and go find her. "Have fun with Nick tonight." I stick my head into her room. "I'll see you both there."

"Wait, let me see you." Harper walks from her bathroom, threading an earring through her earlobe. I stand up straight.

"You're perfect. Good thing you lost that wine weight. A dress like this would show any imperfection."

Was that a dig? Or a compliment? I can't tell.

"Right... Thanks. See you at the party." I hurry from the apartment. I don't want to be here when Nick arrives to pick up Harper.

My sigh of relief fills my car as the needle on the speedometer ticks higher and higher.

***

I DIDN'T KNOW Royal Palms was at the base of Camelback. But there it is, and there is the sign for the resort. I follow the directions spouting from my phone until I reach the narrow driveway and turn in. My car bumps over the stones as I stare up at the mountain towering over the resort. The setting sun has swathed the peaks in pink. Shadows lie on the sides facing east. My car rolls to a stop in front of the valet. He takes my keys and points me in the direction of the event room.

I step through two big, Spanish-style wooden doors and into the party. Sarah spots me right away and comes over.

"Isn't this place beautiful?" She points at the wooden beams on the ceiling, then to the intricate tile beneath our feet.

I glance where her finger tells me to, but just for a second. My gaze is stuck on what's beyond the other set of doors leading out to the large patio and pool. Camelback sits right in my view. Pain and yearning skitter across my chest.

"Come on, let's go say hello to Lynn." Sarah yanks my arm, taking me away from the open doors.

Lynn stands at the end of the bar, sipping a glass of wine. We make small talk, but it's hard to focus. I keep thinking of the last time I was on Camelback. I reach down and run a hand over my healed ankle.

Someone else joins us and wants Lynn's attention, and I use it as my cue to walk away with Sarah. She wasn't really participating in the conversation with Lynn anyway, even though it was her idea to go say hi. She added a 'hmm' and 'how interesting', but for the most part her attention was fixed on who was entering the party. It's clear she sees this merger with Maxim as her big opportunity to find the man of her dreams.

A server with a tray full of bright pink martini's stops us and asks if we would like one. Sarah takes two and pushes one into my hand. "Drink this. I need you to be happier."

"I'm happy," I grumble. I look down at the martini. At least it's not wine. A martini, I can resist. I'll hold it and pretend.

"Well, you should be. You look amazing." She motions with her drink. "That guy over there thinks so too."

I follow her gaze. When I see who it is, I snap my eyes back to Sarah.

"Please tell me he isn't looking anymore."

"He's not *looking at* you so much as he is *walking to* you."

I want to run and hide.

Trent stops in front of us with a plate of food in his hand and an insincere smile plastered across his face.

"Kate. Long time no see. Or talk." His voice sounds friendly, but I know what's beneath the smooth tone. He's conniving. He's manipulative. And he still hates me.

"Careful, Trent. One might think you've missed me."

Trent chuckles. "You look good, Kate. Finally crawl out of the bottle?"

My sharp intake of breath leaves the top of my lungs with an ache.

Trent twirls one of his long, ugly fingers in the air. "Word gets around."

Who would there be to talk about me? I don't go places. I don't see people. Just Nick. And Harper.

Oh my God. Harper.

I've come to expect her attitude, her intolerance for my grief, her snarky comments. But this?

"Nice to see you again, Trent. My friend and I were just

headed to the ladies' room. Excuse us." I grab Sarah's hand and march away, leading us through groups of chatting people. I don't even know if I'm going in the direction of the restroom. I just know I'm headed toward the front of this large, wide open event room. *I could leave now, before Harper and Nick arrive.* The idea is tantalizing. Lynn has already seen me. There are enough people here that she wouldn't miss my absence. I'm still walking in that direction when the massive wooden front doors open, and in walks Harper. And Nick.

My sudden stop makes Sarah bump into me. Bright pink liquid sloshes over the full glass and onto my dress.

I'm struck by how good they look together. The tall blonde with curves in the right places, the dark haired man with piercing blue eyes. *Her dress matches his eyes. Sort of.*

Harper grins when she sees us, and she looks genuinely happy. This is where she shines. She has Nick on her arm, there haven't been any problems with the event, and everyone is having a great time. Of course she's happy.

I can't even begin to fake a smile when Nick and Harper reach us.

"Sorry we're late. We had a drink before we left." Harper winds her arm through Nick's and looks up at him. The satisfaction on her face is so blatant, I almost feel embarrassed for her. Since when does Harper try this hard for any guy? *It's usually the other way around.*

She leans in and curves her shoulders toward me. "Have you seen Trent yet?"

My nose wrinkles as I recall his obnoxious words. "Yes."

"How did that go?"

"He said something very interesting, actually. Something that only one person could have told him."

Harper's careful not to have a reaction. I see her eyebrows start to rise, but she pushes them back down.

"Well, you know Trent. He's all about starting shit."

"Who the hell is Trent?" Nick's voice is hard.

"This guy that hates Kate." Sarah pipes up from beside me. "And Kate hates him too." She sticks out her hand. "I'm Sarah Maxwell, by the way. I work with Kate."

"Nick Hunter." He turns to me as he shakes Sarah's hand. "Trent's here?"

"His company is merging with my company."

Nick's lips form an angry line. Memories from Halloween flow through my mind. Michael against the wall, Nick's arm at his throat. The wild, untamed look in Nick's eyes. We don't need a repeat performance.

My hand rests on Nick's forearm. The one that Harper doesn't have her arm wound protectively around.

"Trent is all talk. I've been handling him for a long time."

Nick's gaze is intense. "How do you know him?"

I swallow hard. "He was Ethan's college roommate."

"Ethan never mentioned him. He must not be that important."

"He's not." I mean it in every way possible. *He's not worth your temper, Nick.*

Nick nods and relaxes his stance. "Okay, cool. Everything's fine then."

I relax too, and the DJ switches to a fast song.

"I love this song. Let's go, the dance floor is set up outside." Harper pushes her clutch to my chest and pulls Nick across the room and out to where I saw the patio and the pool. And Camelback.

A server stops next to me, and I set my full martini on his tray.

This is going to be a long night.

***

I'M SITTING ALONE at an outside table. The sky is dark, but the bright bulbs strung from the trees lining the outdoor event area give off an incandescent glow. The pool shines a watery blue. I keep waiting for someone to fall in it when they walk by. Sarah was swept away by a guy, and from the thumbs up she gave me behind his back, she's having a good time with him. Harper hasn't let Nick leave her side. I'm pretending not to notice his frequent glances.

I don't like watching them together. I don't want him to get hurt. He's emotional and sensitive, two things she has a distaste for.

My phone vibrates inside my clutch, and the whole table shimmies. I grab the phone and open it to the home screen.

You've got to be kidding me!!!!

What? Trent's texting me? Wait, this isn't my phone. It's Harper's. Trent's texting Harper?

I scroll down until I reach the beginning of their text messages.

Trent: Hi Harper, it's Trent. Hope you don't mind I'm reaching out, Kate gave me your number a long time ago and I've been meaning to use it. Heard you're planning a big party for us.

Harper: Hey Trent. The word is true, I'm putting together a fantastic event to celebrate your company merging with Kate's. Bet you were happy to hear the news.

Trent: I'm happy because it means I'm getting promoted. Lowest performers are getting canned. And I'm not one of them.

Harper: Congrats on the promo.

Trent: Thanks. How are things with you? Kate still a big bore?

Harper: Things are weird. Kate's finally crawling out of her hole. She's been medicating with the bottle, if you know what I mean.

Trent: No way? Kate Masters?? Perfection personified?

Harper: Yep. But now she has someone to help her move on from Ethan.

Trent: Poor bastard. Who?

Harper: Do you remember Nick Hunter, the guy Ethan was friends with from the army? Remember him from the funeral?

Trent: Yes...

Harper: I think there might be something starting with them. Kate's beginning to act like Kate again, but not until he started coming around. I tried to stop it, but I'm not sure it worked.

Trent: WHAT?

Harper: I feel the same way.

Trent: Classic Kate. She's finds a way to screw Ethan over, even when he's not alive.

Harper: Before you go apeshit, keep in mind I'm not positive they're into each other. I just have a feeling.

Trent: When are you going to figure out what the deal is?

Harper: I'm working on that. Kate denies she likes him, but she lights up when he's around. And he goes out of his way to care for her. I'm telling you, it's coming.

Trent: And here I thought I was just reaching out to you to say hello.

Harper: More than you bargained for, huh?

I stop reading.

I'm done.

I'm so done with her.

Slowly I slide the phone back into the purse. My eyes find Harper on the dance floor. She faces Nick, her arms on his shoulders, and shakes her ass. Nick's eyes meet mine, and he holds my gaze. He looks like he has so much to say. *What if Harper's right? What if Evie's right?*

No.

Ethan.

My Ethan.

It doesn't matter that Nick is a great person who slowly, day by day, coloring book by cooking lesson, walked with me through the darkest part of my life.

He's not Ethan, and that's all that matters.

I break our gaze.

"Well, well, well, look who we have here." The voice comes from behind me. A lock of my hair lifts from my shoulder.

I don't turn my head.

"Trent, we've already seen each other tonight. But then again, I'm a big bore, so you probably don't remember."

He leans down until his face rests on my shoulder. The scent of whiskey is so strong it burns my nostrils.

"What would Ethan think of you?" His whisper is soft but cuts through me, a sword piercing my heart. "You've become a drunk and a slut. So much for the perfect Kate Masters Ethan was stupidly in love with for so many years."

Don't engage. He's drunk. His face gets heavier the longer it's on my shoulder.

"Kate, are you okay?"

Nick's at the other side of the table, knuckles white as they grip the chair he stands behind. *Always so ready to defend me.* Harper runs up behind Nick. She has the concerned 'v' in the middle of her brows, but I know it's not concern for me. Harper only cares about Harper. I've learned that the hard way.

I lean away from him and stand, forcing Trent to stand

too. My shoulder throbs a little from his heavy head. I take one step away from the table.

"I'm fine." I assure Nick before his temper boils over. "Harper, Trent is going to need an Uber."

Nick walks around the table. His arm grazes mine as he extends it. "We haven't met. I'm Nick Hunter." His tone is even, but I know how much he's holding back.

Trent stares at Nick's open hand and sneers. "We haven't met *officially*, but I know who you are. Ethan told me about you, and he always said good things about his new friend. Of course, he didn't know you were a girlfriend thief."

I spin to face Trent, my hands up. "Go home before this becomes a scene. You wouldn't want that, especially with that big promotion coming your way."

"I don't think so, *Katie girl*."

My hand flies to my heart. *It's been so long since I've heard that.* Why did he have to use my nickname? *Because he knew what it would do to me.*

I don't want to show Trent it worked, but I can't control the way my lips tremble.

"Oh, so you aren't a totally unfeeling bitch. Just a drunken slut." Trent's words ooze out of his mouth like a poisonous sludge. I'd be more upset if he hadn't slurred twice while he was spewing his vitriol.

"Don't talk to her like that." Nick's voice is low and threatening.

"She doesn't need you to defend her, Sergeant Hunter." Trent curls a lip at me. "Let me tell you about Kate. She's heartless. She led Ethan on for years. She made him think he could have her when he never really could. Feint, run, feint, run. That's her game. Ethan was a nice guy, and all she did was hurt him."

He pauses to wipe his chin.

"Then she decides she's had a change of heart. Suddenly, she loves Ethan." Trent's gaze returns to me. "If only he were alive to see what a liar you are." Trent spits his venomous words at me. "Admit it, Kate. You never loved Ethan. It was all just one of your games." He stares at me, arrogant, confident I'm guilty of every transgression he listed.

I'm far beyond angry. My arms are on fire, my pulse races. I can't recall a time I've ever felt such fury. Every cell in my body zings, hurtling through me like a pinball machine.

I lunge at Trent. My palms hit his chest with a dull smack, and I push with all the strength I have.

Trent stumbles back, until the back of a chair catches him. I follow, quickstepping until there are only six inches between us.

"I loved Ethan," I scream in his face.

I feel wild.

Untamed.

Feral.

My arm rears back. My fist lands on the left side of his face. It hurts my hand, but I hardly notice the pain. He makes an incoherent noise and sags back against the chair, one arm draped across the top. His other hand comes up to his cheek.

I want to do that again. I raise my hand, but before I can swing, two strong arms grab me around my waist and pull me away.

Nick drags me the few feet back to our table. He holds me securely to the side of his body as he leans over to grab my purse.

My adrenaline flows. My ears feel hot.

Harper's at Trent's side, her arm around him, her hand

cradling his hand on his cheek. She's looking left, yelling to someone to get ice.

We have to pass Trent and Harper to leave. Nick pulls me toward them, his arm tightening around my midsection. In a few seconds we're beside them and my feet are tripping underneath me in Nick's haste. Trent has his victim's face on. I glare at him.

"You're a pathetic little boy," my voice is low. "Grow up."

My words are barely out before we've passed them. Nick pulls me into the event room and through the dining area. Everyone stares, frozen in the midst of whatever they were doing. The music thumps but seems out of place in a room of statues.

Nick won't let me go, not even when we get outside. It's not until my car pulls up and the valet opens the passenger door that Nick unwinds his arm from my waist. And even then he positions himself between me and the doors to the event room. I head to the driver's side, but Nick shakes his head.

Fine.

I climb in the passenger seat and buckle my seatbelt. I slump, the fight slowly ebbing from my body.

Nick climbs in the driver seat. He puts my car in drive and steers it over the winding stone driveway. I turn back, trying to catch a glimpse of Camelback, but it's a dark, moonless sky and clouds have moved in. I turn back around as Nick comes to a slow stop at the end of the little road taking us away from the resort. He glances at me, then back out to the cars rushing by.

"You really lost your temper." He says it casually, as though he's commenting on the weather. A smile pulls at the corner of his mouth. *Is he amused?*

"So much for keeping my temper a secret," I murmur,

studying his profile as he waits for a chance to join traffic. *His hair is the exact same color as mine. Why is this the first time I'm noticing this?*

I watch his head turn left and right as he leans forward to see past the trees that line the street. *That white shirt brings out the olive tone of his skin.* I can see why Harper's attracted to him. *But I'm not.*

Nick eases my car out of the resort, leaving behind my roommate who I thought was my friend and the other person who certainly never was.

"Are you going to tell me what happened back there?" Nick throws me a questioning glance. A light rain starts, sending thin haphazard streaks of water down the windshield. I reach over and turn on the wipers.

Trent's drunken, belligerent face resurfaces in my mind. "I don't care what Trent says about me. He can call me a liar and a slut and whatever else he wants. I know that stuff's not true. But he can't say anything about Ethan. I won't tolerate it."

"Kate, correct me if I'm wrong, but it didn't sound like he said anything *bad* about Ethan." The smile that pulled at his lips is gone now.

"It was what he said about me and Ethan, as a pair. I just can't stand the thought that what I had with Ethan could be dragged through the mud." My hands curl into tight fists on my lap as Trent's words roll through my mind. I squeeze my eyes shut and will myself to calm down.

My heart rate slows, and I open my eyes. "You sounded pretty angry back there, too."

"I was when I heard him talking about you like that. But you seemed so calm. You said you knew how to handle him. Then suddenly..." Nick laughs and ruffles my hair. "You're a tiger."

"Hardly." I flick my right hand a few times. It's starting to hurt.

"Was that your first fight?" Nick glances at me as I massage my wrist.

"Are you trying to determine if you can go out in public with me again?"

"Not quite. You saw me with Michael. I was afraid I'd scared you away."

The headlights of oncoming traffic illuminate Nick's eyes. A quick glimmer of fear goes through them.

"Michael deserved that." I've already told him this, but it seems he needs reassurance.

He leans his arm on the center console and throws me another brief glance. "So did Trent."

I bite my lower lip. I wonder if there will be repercussions for giving him what he deserved?

I think about what it felt like when my fist made contact with Trent's face and remember Nick's question. "That was my first fight, by the way." *Do those words really belong to me?* The further the clock moves from that moment, the harder it is to comprehend. I *hit* someone. And I wanted to do it *again.*

"How many fights have you been in?" I ask. If not for what I saw in my bedroom on Halloween, I would have a hard time believing he was capable of such things.

Nick grimaces. "More than my share."

"How many?" I press.

"I was a troubled teenager."

The rain stops, and the wipers make a screeching protest on the windshield. I reach over and turn them off. "Did you win any of those fights?"

Nick shoots me a withering look. "Some. It hurts to get hit in the face." He pauses, then snickers. "Just ask Trent."

I drop my face into cupped hands and drum my fingers against my forehead. The adrenaline has faded, making way for disbelief. "I hit someone. Me. Kate Masters. Master of Everything." I shake my head at the impossibility of it. *Improbable, but apparently not impossible.*

Nick taps the brake for a red light and turns to me, his lips pursed. "Did you just say *'Master of Everything'*?"

"It's a high school nickname."

Nick laughs so hard he lays a hand across his stomach.

"What's so funny?"

The light turns greens. I jab my finger at it because he's too busy looking at me and laughing to notice.

"That's a terrible nickname."

"Rude."

"It is. What a ridiculous expectation to have for yourself. And for everyone else to have for you. Who the hell gave you that name?"

I cross my arms. "My dad."

Nick smacks his forehead. "Sorry."

"I earned the nickname. I was on the yearbook committee and student council, and I ran track. I took advanced classes and got A's and was the valedictorian."

"The opposite of me." A dark look comes onto his face.

"I think it's safe to say neither of us are the people we used to be."

Nick nods slowly. He stays quiet, and it makes me sad. It's the first time I've seen him withdraw.

He pulls up in front of my building and cuts the engine. He climbs out and walks around to my side, holding out my keys.

"Give me a call the next time you want to hit something."

I blink twice, surprised. "I would never hit you."

Nick gives me a wide-eyed look. "I don't want you to hit

me either. I meant to call me so I can take you to find a punching bag."

A little bubble of laughter wells up. *Happiness.* I picture the bubble as a color, maybe rose gold. A warm hue.

Nick waves. "See you soon."

He's leaving?

"How are you getting home?" I ask.

"My car is here." He points at it. "We drove Harper's car."

"Do you want to go for a walk?" I don't want him to go yet. He has this warmth about him I like to be around, even when he's saying whatever comes to his mind.

He pauses, smiling. "Lead the way."

"Can you give me a minute to change my shoes?" I lift a leg out to the side and point to the silver strappy heels on my feet.

"Yes, but you have to keep the dress on. That way I won't look too fancy for you in your sweats."

I gasp and swat at his arm. He ducks out of my reach.

"Oh no, here comes the fist of fury."

"You better watch out." I flex my non-existent bicep. "I'm strong."

"I thought you said you didn't want to hit me."

I'm laughing again as I make my way up the stairs to my apartment. *Another rose gold bubble.*

It isn't until I'm lacing up my tennis shoes that I hear what I just said about myself.

I'm strong.

But I'm not.

I'm not.

Am I?

30

KATE

Nick walks with a flashlight. When he first pulled it out of his car I asked if he was also planning on using his head lamp. I earned a dirty look for that joke.

He keeps the beam of light trained in front of us, and I'm having a hard time resisting the urge to tease him. I learned my lesson after I laughed when I saw him pull it from his glove compartment.

"Preparedness," he said in that commanding tone of voice he gets sometimes.

The flashlight is nice to have, not that I'll admit it. The arc of light swings across the pavement as Nick uses one hand to undo a top button on his shirt.

A familiar resinous smell hangs thick in the air. I breathe deeply, letting the unique scent fill my lungs.

So does Nick.

"What's that smell?"

"Creosote. It smells best after a rain."

"That's not like jumping cactus, right?"

I snort. "What an East Coaster."

Nick playfully narrows his eyes at me. The beam of light trails into the street when he looks at me.

"Don't take your eyes off the sidewalk. We need that flashlight trained on the path." I push my lips together, but some laughter escapes anyway.

"Ha ha." He stops and points to a set of swings at the park across the street. "Want to make a bet?"

I eye the swings. "What is it?"

"I bet I can beat you to the swings."

"This dress isn't really—"

"Go!" Nick yells, taking off.

He's fast, but I'm fast too. The fabric of my dress rubs against my thighs, higher and higher. There's no way I'm stopping to adjust it. I don't like to lose.

He smacks the metal bar of the swings when he reaches it. I'm only a few seconds behind.

"Unfair." I yank down the bottom of my dress and gulp the fragranced air. *It's been a long time since I've been out of breath. Obviously.*

"You need to be on your toes. Think like a winner." Nick grins, bouncing from foot to foot. He doesn't look even slightly winded.

"Yes, Sergeant." I give my best salute.

He grabs the chains of a swing and pushes it toward me. The rubber seat dips when I sit. His hand goes to the small of my back and he gives me a gentle push.

"Remember when you were a kid and you went as high as you could and then jumped off?" He sounds wistful.

"No way. I wasn't a jumper."

He pushes me again, higher this time. "No surprise there."

"I'm not a risk taker. I'm sure you've figured that out by now."

"Yet you live with someone who is the exact opposite of you. That's kind of a risk."

Harper... For a short period of time, I forgot about her and Trent's messages. *What am I going to do about that?*

"Do you like her?" I wince at my bluntness. I didn't mean for it to come out like that. Thank God he's behind me, so I don't have to see his face right now.

"Do I like *Harper*?" He sounds incredulous, and not in a good way. "Uh, no."

Relief streaks through me.

With a push on my back he propels me higher.

"Why did you go to the party with her?"

"To be there for you. In case you needed me."

Not the answer I was expecting.

"Why would I need you?" I ask, annoyed. *I don't need a babysitter.*

He has pushed me so high that my voice sounds far away as I come back to him and move away again.

"Jump!" he yells when I'm at the peak of the arc.

"No," I yell back.

I come to the bottom, and he pushes me up again.

"Jump, Kate!"

I come back down and straighten my legs, digging my feet into the sand. It slows me down enough that I dig my heels in at the lowest point and stop myself completely.

I look back at Nick. He shakes his head, but his eyes twinkle. "You're incredibly stubborn."

"And you push limits. Why did you think I would need you at this party?"

"I knew there would be drinking. I wanted to make sure you stayed strong. Like an accountability partner."

"I'm not in recovery," I tell him, exasperated.

He raises his eyebrows. "Aren't you?"

"I don't attend AA meetings."

"You're in your own special brand of recovery. So am I. It's called, *Life Broke Your Heart*."

Death broke my heart. Not life.

"Why didn't you ask to come to the party with me? Why Harper?"

He clears his throat. "You would have told me no if you knew why."

He's right.

His hand falls against the small of my back and he pushes me again.

"What is Trent's problem with you?"

So many flippant answers run through my head. *Trent's a dumb ass. Trent's jealous Ethan always chose me over him. Trent has the emotional maturity of a toddler. Trent sucks at life.* I could go on.

The swinging slows while the question hangs between us. Eventually I come to a stop. Nick sits on the swing next to me.

Of course he wants to know the backstory. I would too.

"Trent thinks I *enjoyed* leading Ethan on. Ethan made it clear he loved me, but he also made it clear he was willing to accept only friendship from me." It's so easy for me to recall the dashed hope on Ethan's face. "I should have stopped being his friend when I knew how he felt. All those years he spent waiting for me while I dated other guys." My shoulders slump. "I can only imagine the kind of pain I put him through. It was so wrong of me. I was very, very selfish. How could I have been so willing to hurt him? My best friend?" I shake my head slowly as the words hang in the air.

Nick reaches over to brush my hair behind my ear. "I didn't mean to upset you."

My tears free fall. "I can't escape the fact that I hurt

Ethan while he was alive. It's just something I have to live with."

"Seems unfair." His eyebrows pull together.

"What does?" I take a deep breath to stop the sobs.

Nick shrugs. "The double standard."

"What double standard?" My head flinches back an inch.

"Ethan dated other people while he waited for you to change your mind. You shouldn't be punished for doing the same."

Nick's defense of me is sweet, but unnecessary. Ethan didn't date.

"Ethan's date to senior prom doesn't fall into the same category as the few relationships I've had."

Nick shakes his head. "No, no, I'm not referring to that kind of stuff. I'm talking about Emelie."

A rush of air sucks into my lungs. My heart races. My stomach feels heavy.

"Who?" I whisper.

Nick doesn't answer fast enough, and I'm up from my swing and standing in front of him. His face moves from confusion to understanding to guilt.

"Who is Emelie?" Black wisps of the dislike I already feel for this girl curl around her name as it moves over my lips.

Nick's hands extend, like he's pleading Ethan's case. "She's a girl Ethan dated while we were in Germany. It was between deployments." Nick's face scrunches up. His fingers grip his head and he groans loudly. "Dammit, why did I assume you knew about her?"

Because Ethan and I didn't keep secrets. Because we told each other everything. Because nothing existed between us but pure, honest love... Except I can't say those things. Not anymore.

Did he love her? How long did he date her? Did he sleep with her? *Ethan's hands on someone else...* Bile rises. Anger travels through my veins, white-hot and pulsing.

Since Ethan died I've been sleeping on tear soaked pillows. My pain and suffering for my best friend, my *soul mate*, had only just begun to lessen. Nick brought the sun back into my life, but it was nowhere near illuminating my entire sky.

I'd cast Ethan as the perfect white knight and me as the black-robed villain, willing to hurt him because I couldn't stand the thought of letting him go.

But Ethan lied to me.

How many times had I talked to him on the phone? Through email? How many lies had he told? How many stories were edited for my ears? He spent seven months in Germany with his weekends free. Weekends he said he spent with Nick. *And Emelie.*

Salty tears sting my eyes. *My Ethan.* My selfless, amazing, beautiful Ethan. He'd been perfect in my eyes, far closer than I could ever get. Never once did I doubt his loyalty, his dogged determination to make me his.

Emotions flow through me, ephemeral but strong. Hurt, betrayal, anger, agony, embarrassment, disappointment. How could Ethan lie to me? He was flawless, the consummate man. Apparently his patience, which I'd viewed as enduring and immeasurable, was limited.

"Kate?" Nick's voice is soft, tentative. It brings me back from all the thoughts banging around in my head. He reaches for me. I'm just out of his reach, and I don't close the distance.

"I want to go home," I tell him.

We start for my apartment. Our unevenly matched footfalls are the only sound.

But not in my head. Not in my heart.

The inside of me is a tornado, an earthquake, a wildfire. My emotions thrash, my foundation shakes, and the heat of my temper rages on.

Fervently I wish for a time, just twenty minutes ago, when I didn't know all this.

We arrive at my apartment, and Nick pulls me into him briefly, one small hug, and lets me go. He points to my apartment, and I turn and walk up. At the landing I look back and see he's still standing there, arms crossed. He gives me a wave and I go inside.

***

LAST NIGHT'S events fill my mind the instant my eyes open. No birds chirping, no leisurely stretch. Just immediate dark thoughts of my roommate who's gossiping about me, the person I hit in the face at a work event, and Emelie.

I can't do anything about Emelie or Trent. But Harper is a different story. I'm sick of being her punching bag.

I get out of bed and change. My limbs feel strong, solid, full of power. I'm pissed off.

Harper's not in her room or anywhere in the rest of my apartment. She'll have to come home sometime. While I wait for her, I organize the pantry. All of Harper's food gets pushed to the right. *That'll make it easy for her to pack.*

After that's done I move on to the fridge. The garbage fills up with outdated food.

Finally I hear her key in the lock. I hop up on the counter. She'll have to see me when she walks past the kitchen.

And she does.

Her hand flies to her chest. "Jesus, Kate. You scared me."

"Long night?" I raise my eyebrows. The rest of my face doesn't change.

"The night was great after I did damage control from your drunken scene." She glares at me pointedly. "What were you thinking?"

Yesterday I would have lowered my head and felt embarrassed. *Not anymore. No more people pleaser.*

"I wasn't drunk," I say through gritted teeth.

Harper's eyes widen. "You hit Trent while you were completely sober?" She brings a hand to her forehead, pushing back her hair. "He said he wouldn't press charges because you were drunk."

"Well, then, I was drunk."

Harper narrows her eyes. "What did you do for the rest of the night? *After* you caused a scene?"

"We need to talk about—"

"You left with my date. Thanks for that." Her upper lip snarls on the last word.

I wave aside her words. "I'm not interested in talking about that right now. I saw—"

"Why are you friends with Nick?"

"He was Ethan's friend. He was grandfathered in. Now stop interrupting me. I saw—"

Her hands go to her hips. "Do you think Ethan would appreciate it becoming more than friends?"

I sigh. "This again? Nobody said that was happening."

"I'm just saying." She holds her hands up like she's some kind of innocent. *That could not be further from the truth.* "Kate, you're missing what's right before your eyes. You've been a zombie for months and—"

"You'd be a zombie too, if you lost the love of your life."

Harper rolls her eyes. "Here we go again."

"What the hell is wrong with you?" I hop off the counter. My feet stay rooted to my landing spot.

"You are what's wrong with me." She jabs a fingernail in the space between us. "You've been moping around here for months, drinking like a fish and sleeping more than a dead person. Where did my roommate go?"

"Your roommate has been in hell. Her own personal hell."

"You're taking too long to come back from it."

I'm not even angry anymore. I'm astounded. "It's ludicrous you think you have a right to an opinion about my grief process."

"If I have to live with you, I get an opinion."

I take a long, slow breath. Fluid fills my ears when my teeth clench. "You're not the only one wondering where her roommate went. You were never sensitive or very caring. But you could at least understand, and tolerate, basic human emotions. Since Ethan died, you've acted like my tears are made of stomach acid. Why are you so terrified of my grief?"

"Because it's been going on and on for months." She gestures with two hands on either side of her head. "We get it, Ethan died. It was terrible. Poor Kate. Now it's time for you to pick up and move on. I want my normal roommate back."

I will never be normal again. There will never be a moment, not for the rest of my life, where I won't remember what I lost. At the core, that is our problem. Harper believes I should go back to normal because she's never cared enough about a person to be devastated by their loss.

"As soon as times got tough, you turned on me. I needed a friend, not a judge." I lean forward, maintaining eye contact. "You aren't my friend. You've made that abundantly clear. And you're no longer my roommate. I want you out of my apartment."

Her mouth forms an astonished O. Her tongue moves like she wants to speak, but she can't form a sentence.

I wish I had a camera. Someone has finally stunned the sharp-tongued, quick-witted Harper into silence. And it's me, her demure sidekick, whom she pushed too far.

I walk to my room and shut the door, leaving Harper and her stunned face behind.

31

KATE

I DON'T KNOW WHAT HARPER'S DOING IN THE REST OF MY apartment, but she's being loud.

When I told her to move out I didn't think she'd start immediately. Within an hour of shutting my bedroom door I heard cardboard boxes folding, the screech of tape rolling out of a dispenser, drawers and cabinets closing with just a little too much force. I'm trying to concentrate on the words in a book I've already read, but the sounds of the front door opening and closing, over and over, make it difficult.

The part of me that likes to please people and live a life free of bumps wants to go out there and smooth things over. The other part of me knows this needs to happen, even if it's ugly and makes her upset with me.

When Sarah texts to ask me to get dinner tonight, I can't accept fast enough. Whatever takes me away from this place, I'll do.

Now there's a new sound beyond my door... Voices.

I go to the door and listen to the muffled conversation. Harper's, and then a male voice. *Why is Nick here?*

My hands cup the ear I have pressed against the door.

"Harper, what are you doing?" He sounds mystified.

"Baking a freaking cake." I hear a thud. "What does it look like I'm doing?"

"Okay, I'll try a different question. Why are you moving out?" Nick's voice sounds irritated.

"Your girlfriend kicked me out." Her tone is challenging.

"Why?"

"Because I pushed her too hard. Because she likes you better than me right now. Because you let her be a baby and hang on to Ethan's memory like a life preserver." Another thud, the sound of a box sliding across the floor. "By the way, thanks for leaving me alone last night. *Again.* The second Kate did her *damsel in distress hits a dude* routine, you were rushing in to save her."

"Do you hear yourself?"

"Last time I checked, I'm not deaf."

"You might as well be. I thought Kate was your friend. Try putting yourself in her shoes. How would you handle the situation she's in?"

"With more dignity than Kate. She has been moping around for months, pining for a man who isn't alive anymore. I care enough about her to kick her in the ass and get her back into life."

"That's not at all what she needs." Nick's voice rises.

"Excuse me, newcomer, are you telling me that *you* know what she needs? You've known Kate for five seconds. All of a sudden you're her new best friend? You know her better than I do? Everyone was feeling so sad for poor Kate. How devastating, Kate must be beside herself. Poor Kate, poor Kate. I simply suggested it was time she get ahold of herself and re-enter the world."

"You sound jealous."

Harper makes a noise, almost like a choke. "And just what do I have to be jealous of?"

"The attention Kate was getting. You just said it yourself. Everyone was feeling bad for Kate, so you decided the only way to get their attention off Kate was to have her move on."

I hear another box move across the floor, then two more.

"What you said just now is so absurd that I'm not even going to respond to it. Just know this. I saw Kate when she came home from your apartment. She looked happy, or at least not totally devastated, for the first time since Ethan died. She won't admit it, but it's you who made her feel that way. If you care about her at all, don't try to be anything more than a friend to her."

It falls quiet, the only sound a jingling of keys, then a clink. "Tell Kate I left my key," Harper says. "It's my only copy."

The door closes hard. Discussion over.

She's gone? Just like that? If I'd known she was really leaving, I would have at least said goodbye. Nearly four years of memories, but only the last five months were bad. I'm mad and disappointed in her, but I'm sad too.

A light knock on my door startles me. I jump back and open it.

"What are the chances you heard that entire exchange?" Nick's smile is bemused.

I blush, embarrassed to admit I was listening in. "High," I concede.

His head falls back as he laughs soundlessly.

"So, you finally sent the Wicked Witch of the West packing?"

"Nick!"

My disapproval is out of habit. Actually, it's not a bad name for her. "I take it you weren't Harper's biggest fan."

"I didn't like how she talked to you."

"She's always been self-centered, and I never cared. But ever since Ethan died, she began failing miserably in the friend category."

I lead the way out of my room and walk into Harper's open bedroom door. The heaviest of all her furniture is still here. I pull open a dresser drawer. Empty. I open two more. Empty and empty. *I didn't think she'd move out in a matter of hours.* "I wonder when she'll get the rest of her things. And where she went." One of her sisters? Her mother's? I look at Nick. "Why are you here, by the way? I don't think it was to field Harper's wrath."

His eyes crinkle at the edges as they gaze intently upon my face. "I thought you might want to talk."

"What about? Harper? Trent?" My fingers dig circles into my temples as the most painful name of all teeters on the tip of my tongue. "Emelie?" Her name feels like a dirty word.

I want to hide the Emelie revelation under a rock and pretend she doesn't exist. I can't handle it. I feel like I'm going to break. This is all too much.

Nick's expression is pained. "Please don't let what I told you last night make you feel differently about Ethan. He loved you with every cell in his body. He thought you were absolutely perfect."

My hands drop from my head. "I'm so far from it."

"You're definitely not perfect. You are beyond Type A. You have zero fun. It's like you're waiting for someone to hand you a roadmap so you can follow it. You have no idea what to do next."

"You really know how to make a girl feel good about herself." I leave Harper's room and sit on the couch. My body sinks into the cushions, and my head tilts back.

Nick leans over me, his hands gripping the back edge of

the couch. Just like the night in his apartment, his face is too close.

When I look into his blue eyes, I see flecks of gray. He has a faint scar on his jaw, next to his ear. It's shaped a lot like the one on my forehead.

Nick's expression is so earnest I stop noticing details about his face and listen to his words.

"You're funny. At least, I think so. And when you smile, which is rare, your eyes crinkle on the edges. You can cook like a professional chef. Last night I learned you're a fast runner, even in a dress. And you're intelligent." His mouth twists into an ironic smile. "You're not perfect. But you're a whole lot of other great things."

As usual, I blush.

"Oh, yeah. And you blush pretty much on command. It helps me read you."

"What am I thinking right now?" I flip over on the couch and stand on my knees so I'm facing him, the couch cushions supporting my front body.

"You're wondering why I'm saying all these things."

"True."

"I'm saying them because you need to hear them. You need someone to believe in you. Someone who doesn't expect you to be the Master of Everything." He rolls his eyes. "Can you please just be Kate?"

I bite my lip, my uncertainty spilling out. "I don't know who Kate is anymore."

"That's okay. You don't have to know. Just be."

My lip trembles. I can't help it. He's being so kind.

Nick leans over further and pulls me into him. His chin rests on the crown of my head.

"You can cry if you need to."

"I don't know if I need to. I don't know if I should."

"That's okay too."

I push off his chest and get off the couch, standing so we're face to face. "I'm so confused. There are things happening inside me, and I don't want them to happen, but I feel like I can't stop them." My hands cross over my heart. "I'm feeling again, Nick. I'm cooking and I'm smiling and last night you made me laugh and I pictured my laughter as bubbles of happiness. Five months ago I wanted to *die*. And now I'm smiling? How is this possible?"

He watches me. No answer. *I don't need one.*

"And I'm pretty sure you've single-handedly saved me from myself. And Harper's been annoyingly insistent about you being more than a friend. Which obviously is ridiculous because this is just a friendship. We're grieving partners. I mean, come on."

Nick is silent, still. His eyes don't leave mine.

"Is that how you feel?" He regards me with that even, steady gaze of his. It's the same gaze that tells me it's okay to cry, to grieve, to let the sadness out.

"Isn't that how you feel?" My tone is as unsteady as my heartbeats.

He stares at me for a long moment, then nods.

Thank God. Because if he didn't...

I'm not going there.

"You can add crazy to my list of cons."

"I'll make sure to do that." He pulls his keys from his pocket. "I have to get going. I'll see you later. If you want to talk about...you know, Emelie... Just call me." He walks to the front door.

"Goodbye," I say to his retreating back.

I want to text him and ask why he left in such a hurry, but I'm terrified of the answer.

***

"So, you just kicked her out?" Sarah asks.

I nod. We've been playing twenty questions since we sat down at the restaurant. It's a Mediterranean place, not my pick. The hummus is delicious though. Sarah uses the straw to stir her iced tea. "That totally doesn't sound like you."

"She's been the opposite of a friend for a long time. Since Ethan died, pretty much. I mean, she was there for me right after he died. She made me shower and she tried to get me to eat. But it was like she gave me a week to grieve and then expected me to move on. And the longer I took, the more disgusted she became with my feelings." I pause to take a bite of my salad. "It was so weird. She's never been much of a touchy-feely person, but this was heartless on a whole new level." As I say it I feel the sting of Harper's behavior, but it's not totally unwelcome. It's keeping me from falling apart over Emelie.

"I'm sorry." Sarah squeezes my arm. "First you lost Ethan, and now Harper. You still have me."

"And Nick," I add.

"That's my next question. Who is Nick to you? I thought he was just Harper's date but then he jumped in and dragged you away."

How have I not told her about Nick? I've been friends with him for months. What is wrong with me? *You were a zombie. Just like Harper said.*

"Nick was in the Army with Ethan. They were basically inseparable. He was discharged and moved here the week Ethan was killed, and we met at Ethan's funeral. He's been amazing and kind and totally unafraid of my brokenness."

"So you've been helping each other get through the

passing of your mutual best friend? If life were like a movie, you would fall in love with Nick now."

I groan. "You're such a romantic."

"When do great guys just fall into your lap? Never. Trust me."

"I can agree that the idea of falling in love with him sounds very romantic and movie-like. But there's one huge problem."

"And that would be?"

"I'm still in love with Ethan." *I think, anyway.* I'm also furious with him.

"It's been"—Sarah counts on her fingers—"five-ish months since Ethan was tragically taken away from you."

"In three days it will be six months."

"How do you stay in love with someone you can't see, hear, or touch anymore? I'm honestly asking you this question. No judging." Sarah looks genuinely curious.

"If I close my eyes and focus hard enough, I can hear his voice. It's getting harder to remember the scent of his skin, but I can still smell his cologne. And touch... It's going to sound crazy, but Ethan's touch is burned onto me. All I have to do is close my eyes, and I swear I can feel his fingertips running across my cheek." My fingers brush one side of my face, and I find my skin is wet from a trail of tears I didn't know I was crying.

My face reddens. I feel bare. Too bare. I said too much to a person that's hardly close enough. She'll think I'm insane for insisting I can still *feel* Ethan.

Sarah covers my hand with her own. Instead of running, she's reaching. "I don't even know what to say. I'm sorry you have to go through this. I wish there were something more I could do for you."

"It'll just take time, I suppose. Some unknown magic

number of days and then I'll realize I've moved on." My fingers rub my eyes. "But what can I ever move on to? I'm so beyond broken. No one will want to compete with a ghost."

"Maybe Ethan won't always be your ghost." She taps a finger on her chin. "It changes things for you though."

"What do you mean?"

"Well, when you do move on, the man will have to be beyond special. You can't be with a person who isn't understanding of what you've been through. He'll have to be secure enough to share you with Ethan, in a way."

I laugh once, a disbelieving sound. "Who would be willing to share a woman with another man, alive or not?"

Sarah's eyes grow wide, innocent. She shrugs and looks down at her menu. "I think you know the answer to that question."

I know exactly who she's talking about. And she's wrong.

"Somewhere there are rules against that kind of relationship."

"Life, fate, the universe, they all broke the rules on you." Her voice gets louder and her words are spoken with strength, like there's an injustice she needs to defend. "You need to start breaking some rules." *She's defending me. To me.*

I want to hug her. I want to shout and jump because I've just realized that she is my *friend*. Not my coworker who I happen to get along with. Sarah's the person I wanted Harper to be. She's the person I needed this whole time, and she was right here all along.

32

NICK

CAN A MOMENT EXIST FOR LONGER THAN THE TIME IT'S GIVEN?

Because the moment in Kate's apartment when she asked me the status of our friendship has been living on inside my head since I gave my answer.

Her face fell a fraction after I confirmed what we are to each other, and I wanted to take my lie back and tell her just how much I'm feeling for her. I wanted to tell her that I'm no longer here out of duty.

I'm here by choice.

But I couldn't do it. I couldn't make myself say the words. They were stuck in my throat, the way I think they're hiding behind Kate's patched heart.

What we're feeling is so outrageous, so beyond the scope of typical, and the realization of it is paralyzing.

So we both ran from it. We let the words hide inside of us, terrified to come out and rock the boat.

I left Kate's apartment without a plan or a place to go. I needed to be away from our denial.

I've been driving around for an hour, trying to figure out what to do about our situation.

My mission was to help Kate through her grief. I was supposed to put her back on her feet and make her into a functioning part of society again. That would mean she would eventually meet someone else.

When I was putting down roots here, I wasn't thinking about anything beyond settling in somewhere following my time in the service.

I didn't think about what it would mean when Kate was back on her feet. I didn't think about what seeing Kate whole again would entail. But now I know it means eventually seeing her happy with someone else.

Someone who's not me.

And all because I'm afraid of how it looks on the outside for the two of us to be together.

In my whole life I've never been afraid to piss people off. Why am I starting now?

***

I'VE COME to the one and only place I can think to go.

It's a place I've managed to stay away from, but I think it's finally time.

The cemetery is dusty and dirty, little clouds of earth swirling up around my shoes and settling on my shoes.

I'm facing a problem only my best friend can help me solve. It seems weird, coming here to ask for help from someone who can't hear me and probably wouldn't want to help me with this problem even if he could hear me. But I'm stuck. I don't know what else to do, or who else to talk to.

This thing with Kate goes so far beyond what I'm capable of handling alone.

It doesn't take too long to locate Ethan's headstone. They

are buried in the order they died, and in the last six months many more rows have been added to the space.

So many other loved ones, grieving their departed. I read the dates on the small, rectangular headstones as I walk to Ethan's. Nobody else has a date of birth as recent as Ethan's. Everyone who died since him and was buried in the Veteran's cemetery were old. The way it's *supposed* to be.

When I get to Ethan's, I squat down and pull a water bottle and handful of paper towels out of the back pocket of my jeans.

I pour the contents of the bottle over the flat concrete and metal headstone, then follow that up with a thorough wipe-down. When I'm finished, the towels are covered in dust and the metal shines in the overhead sun.

Then, from my front pocket, I retrieve a single-serve bottle of the whiskey Ethan liked. Twisting off the top, I take a small sip and pour the rest out in the sandy dirt beside his headstone.

Then I sit back in the dirt and sigh, tossing the bottle aside.

"Part of me wonders if you knew what I was going to be getting myself into when I agreed to come here." I shake my head at Ethan's full name. *Ethan James Shepherd.*

"Did you know how difficult she would be? Did you know she would lose herself so completely? It's impressive, really. I don't know how many people possess her ability to love so deeply. The downside is that she hurts more when something goes wrong. I've never thought it was a worthy trade-off, but after meeting Kate, I see I was wrong."

My hand rubs the length of my forehead as I face the truth. "I think Kate might be someone I could love like that." I cringe, even though I'm the only person around. This is hard to hear, and even more difficult to admit out loud.

"I think she might feel the same way. I get these flashes from her. Little cracks in her veneer. She lets me hold her. And hold her tightly, too. She has never shied away from my touch. And lately, she's been responding to it, instead of simply *allowing* it. We had this moment earlier today, this little flicker, where we almost broke through the barriers we've set up around what we're supposed to be to each other.

We didn't go there, but I know we both wanted to. I *know* it. She didn't say the words she wanted to say because she's held back by the thing that always holds her back. Her grief over you is so consuming that she can't see around it. I've done my best to help her, but it's clear there are some parts of it she has to conquer on her own. And me? The words stayed stuck in my throat because I needed to talk to you first." I smile wryly. "Even if it is a one-sided conversation."

I sit back a little, wrapping my forearms around the outsides of my bent knees. "What do you think, brother? Should I go for it with Kate?"

I laugh a little and glance around. I'm still alone out here. My gaze settles back down at Ethan's name. Suddenly a conversation I had with him pops into my head.

I was seated on my bed in the barracks, and Ethan was on the ground. We'd just finished watching a movie, and the only thing we cared about was what to do next.

"What did you think about the dad in that movie?" Ethan asked, taking me by surprise.

I shrugged. "He did a shit job planning for his family in the event of his death. They lost everything when he died. It was a decent movie, though." Kind of sad, not our usual pick, but beggars can't be choosers.

Ethan's expression grew serious. "I think we should make plans."

"For the wives and kids we don't have?"

"For the people we love. Our lives are at risk every second we spend out here. We've been lucky so far, but..."

I shook my head. "Find some wood to knock on."

Nothing in this place is made of real wood, so Ethan pretended to knock on his head.

"Anyway," he said, serious again. "I mean it. Who would you want me to take care of if you were killed out here?"

I didn't hesitate. "My mom."

"That's what I thought you'd say."

"Do you want me to take care of Kate?"

He nodded. "She'll need help. She's," Ethan paused, running his hand over his head. "She'll get stuck. It's hard to explain. She feels emotion the way a capsized boat takes on water."

He looked down at the ground, and I swear I saw something glisten in his eyes.

"Do you want to stop talking about this?" I offered, getting off the bed and settling beside him on the ground.

Instead of accepting, he shook his head. "If I die, I want Kate to be with someone just like me. Because I'm right for her, and that means whoever he is will be almost as right for her as I am." He smacked me on the back and looked my way, his face a mix of emotions. "Me and you, we're a lot alike."

I chuckled. "You mean you want to stop talking about this too?"

"Yeah, I do. It's depressing."

We got off the ground and Ethan offered a hand. We shook, cementing our agreement.

And that was the end of it. We didn't talk about it again. I hoped to hell I'd never need to call upon the agreement we made that afternoon, but hope is a fickle bitch.

But now, sitting here in the sunshine and staring at Ethan's headstone, I see so clearly what I missed that afternoon in the barracks.

Ethan wasn't only asking me to take care of Kate. He was giving me his blessing. He was hand-picking a man he deemed worthy of the girl he spent his life loving.

He couldn't have known Kate and I would fall for each other, but he wanted to make our path clear, if that's what were to happen.

I can't speak for Kate, but I know how I feel, and I'm finished keeping the truth about how I feel to myself.

I stand up, brush the dirt from my jeans, and salute my best friend. My comrade-in-arms. My brother.

33

KATE

It's Monday morning. Not until I opened my eyes this morning did I realize there may be repercussions for causing a scene on Saturday night. Best case scenario, I walk into work and Lynn doesn't say anything. Worst case scenario... *I don't want to think about that.*

I'll shove the worst case scenario into a locked trunk, right beside the Emelie bombshell.

I've dropped my bag in my cube and returned with coffee when an email from Lynn pops up.

Please come see me when you arrive.

Lynn looks shocked when I step into her office door.

"That was fast." She crosses and uncrosses her arms, looking everywhere but at me.

"I was sitting at my desk when you sent the email."

"Oh. Hmm. Okay." Lynn shuffles papers on her desk, knocks one off, bends down to pick it up.

Her hand flicks out, the movement jerky. "Please sit."

I've never seen Lynn nervous. Dread parks itself in my core.

Lynn closes her office door while I sit. *A closed-door meeting. This is bad. This is really, really, bad.*

She settles herself in her chair, fidgets with the bracelets on her wrist as she clears her throat multiple times.

"Lynn, are you okay?" My voice wobbles.

She doesn't answer, but she does finally meet my eyes.

"Kate, this company doesn't one-hundred-percent belong to me anymore, which you already know. The decisions are no longer made by me alone. For months you've had trouble with being late and, for a while, showing up at all. I documented this, but gave you a lot of leniency because of what you were going through. But then Saturday night happened." She stops, taking a deep breath. "Following that incident, it has been decided you're no longer right for Maxim/Simone."

What?

Me? Fired? Not right for a company?

WHAT?

My head feels dizzy. I take a deep breath.

"Lynn, look, I know I've had a hard time. But isn't there some kind of warning you can give me? Saturday night was highly uncharacteristic of me. Trent Blackmore and I have an unpleasant personal history, but it's something I can put aside and be professional."

Lynn's face is apologetic. "I wasn't there when it happened. But other people were, and when they checked your file...well... I'm sorry. Security is waiting at your desk to walk you out."

"I need security?" My stunned mind can't comprehend this.

"After the altercation Saturday night, they think it best."

"Lynn, that is really ridiculous. That was the first time in my life that I've hit someone. And to be perfectly honest, Trent deserved it."

Lynn looks at me with such sadness I feel bad for her. *She doesn't want to do this.*

With a deep breath I stand. My gaze sweeps Lynn's office, a place I've been so many times since I started at Simone when I was twenty-two. The words embossed on her displayed diplomas are burned into my memory.

I hold out my hand. "Thank you for allowing me the opportunity to sharpen my skills and exercise my talents at Simone PR." My eyes burn, but I hold back the tears.

Lynn's lips pull to one side when she grabs my hand. "I remember when you were a fresh-faced college graduate who had to learn to craft press releases that weren't elaborate and long winded. You're a fantastic writer. Don't let this, or anything else, stop you from pursuing your dream." She releases my hand and drops into her chair.

I walk out, limbs wooden. I need to get out of here before the shock of being fired wears off and I start to cry.

Just like Lynn said, the security guards are at my desk. I nod to them. It only takes two minutes for me to pack my belongings. A couple pictures, some energy bars, the pen my mom gave me on my first day at Simone. The coffee I made before Lynn called me in sits next to my computer, full to the brim. I leave the small box I spent so much time in and I don't look back.

My eyes are focused straight ahead as I walk, the security guards just a couple inches behind me on either side. The only change in my gaze is when I pass Sarah's cube.

She's standing at the opening, eyes crinkled in concern, face shocked.

"I'll call you," I say quietly as I pass her.

We get to the elevator, and I keep my eyes on the doors. I

don't want to see anybody. I don't want to know who can see me.

The doors open, and an expletive flies from my lips before I even know it's there.

Trent steps off. His face is smug. "Sorry about your luck." He pats my shoulder and begins to walk. My heart hammers. He's a few feet away when he turns back to me. "You know, Kate, you should see someone about that temper of yours. And for all the drinking." He clucks his tongue and tries to look pained. "Poor Kate."

"Say what you want to say, Trent. Soon enough everyone will see the bruising on your face is just like your heart. Dark and ugly."

I lift my chin and step onto the elevator.

I don't turn around until I know the doors have closed. One of the security guards presses the button for the ground floor and I stare disbelievingly at the seam the closed doors have created.

Jobless. That's me.

Best friendless. That's me.

Ethan-less. That's me.

The elevator doors open and the guards walk me to the exit. One holds open the door and I step out into the sunshine. I murmur my thanks and meet his eyes. The corners of his mouth turn down in a sympathetic frown. He steps back into the building and the door closes. The new Maxim/Simone insignia on the glass stares back at me. I want to be strong. Square my shoulders and march to my car, let anyone watching from the many windows above see that my chin is up. The shock and my obliterated pride keep me from doing that.

I keep my eyes on my car as I walk to it. Tears fall, but I don't wipe them until I'm safely in my car. Once the tears are gone from my eyes I drive out of my space, pausing at the edge of the parking lot exit. I look out to the street. Which direction should I go? I don't want to go home and face an empty apartment. An apartment that should be empty all day, because its resident is supposed to be at work.

I was counting on work to keep me from dealing with Emelie. Now she's back, looming large in my head. I imagine her, blond hair and blue eyes. She's wearing a dirndl and carrying a stein of beer in each hand. Right now it's the only image I can come up with for a German woman.

Yesterday Nick stopped by to see if I was ready to talk about Emelie, but he's not the person I should be talking to about her. I can't yell at him for Ethan's lies. But there *is* someplace I can go.

I wait until there's a break in the two-way traffic, then I pull out. I point my car north and drive. As much as I want to, I don't look in the rearview mirror at the building I'm leaving behind.

***

THERE'S a vague familiarity about this place. I recognize the sandy pebbled land, the wispy excuses for trees, the concrete and stone ramadas. But I don't feel like I *know* them. My memories of that day are hazy, fuzzy on the perimeter. All the people, gathered here to say goodbye to Ethan.

Why am I here now? To say hello to him?

No. To yell at him.

I stop at the directory and find his grave number. Slowly I drive through the small winding roads, following signs with numbers. A few other cars dot the landscape here and there, but not where I'm headed. I drive for another minute until I find the number I'm looking for. I pull off into the gravel and park, gazing out at row upon row of headstones. I'm alone out here.

I climb from my car, my legs awkward and reluctant, like my brain and heart disagree about this visit. *Get away from here. This will make it final.* My brain wants to protect my heart. My headstrong and passionate heart will hear none of it.

I walk along the rows until I find the right one. My steps are hesitant and very quiet. Something a newbie would do. Maybe now I can get up the nerve to visit my father.

Ethan James Shepherd. My gasp is sharp, painful. There it is.

It's just... There.

His name. His memory.

I sink down into the dirt. My fingers bump along the letters carved into the bronze plate. His name, the dates of his birth and death, and different abbreviations. *BSM.* Bronze Star Medal. *PH.* Purple Heart. Over and over I trace three letters in particular. *KIA.* Killed In Action.

"Hi," I say softly. I thought I would feel stupid, but I don't. "I don't know how to start. Or what to say. I spent the whole drive telling myself I wasn't allowed to turn around." My hand stays lying across his first name. When I do that, it feels like maybe he's not as far away from me as I think.

"I miss you. A lot. I don't know what you can see, or if you can hear. Maybe you already know all about the last six months. Maybe you know what happened this morning. I don't know."

I rub my eyes. "In case you don't already know what's happened, let me just tell you things are messy right now. I know about her. Emelie." I make a face when I say her name.

"You could have told me, you know? You didn't have to lie."

The tears start. "You left me here in this world without you. I'm struggling to become a whole person again. I don't have you, I don't have Harper, I don't have a job. It's like somebody erased my life and set the paper on fire. All I am is ash."

"In your stead you sent Nick. Who else better to bring me back to life? Did you know I would need him like I have? Did you know he would save me from Michael, from a dark mountain, and from myself? Maybe *I* am the dark mountain." My shoulders shake with a mirthless laugh. "Yes, yes, I'm getting my creative chops back. Did you hear me call my grief a dark mountain?"

I sit back, gather dirt in my hand and watch it fall through my fingers like a sieve. Only the largest fragments remain.

"Where am I supposed to go from here? I'm dangerously close to healing. I can feel myself on the precipice. And after it happens? What will my life be like? Eventually I'll be the person who used to love Ethan Shepherd." Every fiber of my being turns away from that thought, horrified. My love for Ethan, stated in past tense... *It feels so wrong.*

"Kate? I thought that was you."

My shoulders jump, startled by the real voice behind me.

James looms over me, the sun behind his head. He folds his legs into a seat beside me.

"You got dressed up to sit in the dirt?" He sways as he asks. His acrid breath wafts over to me.

I lean away. "Are you okay?"

"Never better," he says flatly. He reaches a hand beside him and brings up a six-pack of beer. I shake my head when he offers one to me.

"James, it seems you've already reached your limit. Are you sure you should be drinking those?" My voice is tentative, the equivalent of a tip-toe.

He cracks open a can and gulps. "Yep, I'm sure I should be drinking these," he says after he brings the can back down. "That's my son right there. I picked out his name." He points at the headstone. "Evie wanted to name him after her dad. Can you believe that?"

"Crazy," I murmur. It's what he needs to hear.

James drains the first can and starts on the second.

"My fault." He nods his head quickly, agreeing with himself. "He went into the Army to make me happy. This is my fault." He pours a little of his beer into the sand beside Ethan's name.

"It's not your fault. You didn't know this was going to happen."

"I put him in danger. That's the long and short of it. I put my own kid in danger. Don't bother denying it." He drains the second beer.

I climb to standing. Sand has made its way into my shoes and squishes between my toes. "I'm going to call Evie."

He reaches out to me. "Please don't. Not yet. Call her when I'm done. For now I just want to sit here quietly and stare at my son's name. It's what I came out here to do. Will you sit with me?" His voice has a pleading, desperate edge.

I sink back down. I know what he's doing. How many months did I do it myself? Drank until oblivion, just to remember. Some people drink to numb the pain, but not me. Like James, I wanted the pain to be as raw and real as possible. That was how I kept Ethan.

What changed me?

Nick.

I let him in, and my substitute Ethan went out.

I sit silently beside James. He drinks beer after beer, and I don't stop him. He was drunk when he showed up. What's the harm in letting him do what he came here to do?

He finishes the final one, and I help him stand. We walk, his heavy arm draped across my shoulders, his feet crossing over each other every few steps. It's a lot for my body to handle.

"Why'd you come here?" His words are thick, soaked in alcohol and too big for his mouth.

"The same reason as you, I suppose. To talk to Ethan." My car is only twenty feet away. James's weight is getting to be too much. I'll get him to my car and call Evie.

He stops walking suddenly. Somehow I know what's coming. I've made it two steps away as he bends over and vomits all over his feet.

***

"I'M SORRY. I'm so sorry," Evie says again. It's her fifth apology in as many minutes.

"It's okay. Honestly. I'm just glad I was there." I look at James, passed out in my backseat. He's too big for the space, but he managed somehow. *We managed.* There was a lot of me shoving his limbs into place and him mumbling incoherently.

"I won't think about what could've happened if you hadn't been there. At least he had a cab drive him to the cemetery." Evie rubs her temples. "Now you know our dirty little secret. This is my James since Ethan died. Either drunk or passed out." Tears form in her eyes. "I don't know what to do."

I feel bad for him. I feel bad for her.

"He's sick, Evie. He needs help."

She nods, lips pursed.

"Nick might be able to help you. Not professionally, just personally. His mom was an alcoholic. He..." I pause, unsure, but decide to keep going. She needs to know she isn't alone in this. "He helped me. I spent the first few months coping like this." I nod my head at James's prostrate form.

Evie's eyes widen. "You?"

"Yeah. Me. Kate Masters. Medicating with alcohol. I know how unbelievable it sounds."

"Does your mother know?"

"Not that I know of."

"And Nick helped you?" She eyes her husband.

"Um hmm."

She walks to the open car door and picks up a slack foot. "Too bad Nick's not here to help us lug this guy inside. Where are his shoes, by the way?"

"In my trunk. He threw up on them."

She looks up at the sky and exhales loudly. "It's like he's in college again."

I laugh, picking up James's other foot. "Come on, let's get our game plan together."

We discuss how we should extract him from the car and just how angry Evie should be. Among all our planning, hanging behind every proposed strategy, is a palpable disbelief. How did we ever get to this point?

34

KATE

THE WEIGHT OF WHAT HAPPENED HAS FINALLY HIT ME.

I was fired from a job I loved.

It wasn't until I walked out of the Shepherds' house, leaving Evie alone with her still passed out husband, that the realization sunk in. What will I do when I wake up tomorrow? What will this mean for my future?

I lean against my car and look across the street.

For once I don't look at my childhood home and see my dad. I see the spectacular color blooming from pots that line the walkway. I notice the ivy growing along the facade. I see the green, lush lawn with its recently mowed newness. *My mom takes care of all of this by herself.*

Movement from behind the wooden side gate catches my eye. I cross the street and peek through the wide slats. My mom's bent over her garden, muttering to herself. Nostalgia hits me hard.

"Mom," I call out. I sound distressed. I'm an adult now, with adult-sized injuries, but in my heart I'm a sad little girl who needs her mom. Life has knocked me off my bike and tossed me onto hot asphalt.

She hurries to unlock the gate. The fence swings open, and I rush into her arms.

"What's wrong?" She strokes my hair. "Are you okay?"

"Ethan." It's the only word that makes it past my waterfall of tears.

"Oh, sweetheart. I know." She holds the back of my head with one cupped hand. "I know," she croons.

"How am I supposed to survive without him?" More tears slip down my cheeks.

My mom sniffles. "You don't have a choice. You have to find a way to make it through. That's all I can say."

"How long will it hurt?"

"Quite a while. Maybe forever. When you love someone the way you loved Ethan, or the way I loved your father, they never leave you. Slowly the pain fades, but in your case I don't think it will ever fully leave." She takes my face in her hands and looks into my eyes. "You lost your love, your best friend, and your future. That's going to leave a scar."

She lets me go but grabs my hand and leads me to the love seat on the back porch.

"Sit," she orders.

I listen, folding my legs underneath myself. She disappears and reappears a moment later with tissues.

"Thanks." I noisily blow my nose.

She sinks down beside me. "Honey, what happened to make all this come out?"

"So much. And all of it since Saturday night."

"Start with Saturday night then."

"I punched Trent. And Ethan was dating someone in Europe and lied to me about it. I kicked Harper out. And this morning I was fired."

My mother does her best to fix a calm expression. "I see."

I pour out my heart. I tell her everything. The way Harper's been treating me, my dependence on alcohol, the dreams, my friendship with Nick, the disastrous work party, Ethan's German girlfriend, and my disgraceful exit from Simone.

"Ethan wasn't a liar. He wasn't. But he lied to me. How many lies did he have to tell to keep Emelie a secret? Or omissions? How many of his stories were changed to keep me from finding out?" I shake my head slowly. "I just don't understand. My Ethan, my perfect, perfect Ethan. He lied to me." Even as I say the words, I can hardly believe them.

My mother's quiet, the tip of her tongue touching her upper lip. It's her thinking look.

"Have you considered perhaps Ethan had a reason for not telling you about Emelie?"

"What reason would that be? We told each other everything. Or I thought we did."

"He didn't want you to think he'd given up on you. Because he hadn't. And can you really blame the guy for seeing someone else? Sweetheart, he waited for you for ten years. He was loyal, but he wasn't a monk."

"Are you saying I need to re-set my expectations?"

My mom looks unsure. "Ehh... Sort of. The tricky part is that you can't have expectations anymore. Ethan's gone. He's not here to live up to them or fall short. And he can't defend himself either."

She's right. I'm going to have to let it go.

"As for everything else you said... I'm glad you stood up to Harper. She's not a bad person, but she's not your friend either. You don't have to tolerate a person who only likes you when it suits them. I'm not going to lecture you about abusing alcohol, because I think you've figured out that you don't need to do that anymore. I'm very sorry you lost your job. I know what it means to you to do good work and be a good employee. Good workmanship is something your father passed on to you." She tilts her head to the side. "Maybe too much of it."

I laugh without mirth. "Can you have too much good workmanship?"

"When it makes you lose sight of your dreams, absolutely."

"I dream of being a good employee and making worthwhile contributions."

She gives me a pointed look. "You used to dream of being a writer."

"That was a long time ago, Mom."

"So?" Her eyes challenge me.

"So, I was a child with childish aspirations."

"Well, here's what I think. And I know you didn't ask me. Tomorrow you will wake up and have more time on your hands than you know what to do with. You have money in the trust your dad set up before he died. I'll authorize you to have some of it, and you can spend your days writing. After the past six months, I think you have more than enough material."

"You want me to write a story about Ethan?" My mind weighs the possibility. *But...that's...probably a good idea.*

Mom nods. "Ethan, Harper, Nick, the whole ugly mess."

I roll my head on my shoulders. "Mom, I don't know. It's been so long since I've been creative in any capacity that doesn't directly suit a boss, a professor, or an admissions counselor."

"Will you try it? For me?"

It's not like I have anything else to do. I picture myself waking up and sitting down to my computer with a cup of hot coffee, my hair in a top knot with a pencil stabbed through it. *Cliché. Lose the pencil.* A flicker of excitement runs through me.

"I'll do it." *I'm breaking a major rule. Leaving time between jobs.*

"That's my girl." She ruffles my hair. "Now let's talk about Nick."

"What about him?"

"I think he has feelings for you."

My hair whips me in the face with the force of my head shake. "Not even, Mom."

"You just told me all about what he did for you the night you hit Trent. And, *hello*, the coloring book? That alone should tell you how much he cares about you."

"He's looking out for me. Like Ethan asked him to."

She points a finger at me. "Keep telling yourself that. Just don't expect him to wait around for ten years."

"I'm sure some lucky woman will snatch him up in no time." My face puckers like I've eaten something sour. *It's those words. Those words were sour in my mouth.* Of course I don't want someone to take away my closest friend. Not when I have so few.

"You'll have to move on sometime, Kate. And this thing with Emelie might finally be what you need to move forward."

I sit back in my seat. "Please explain."

"You say Ethan was perfect. But he wasn't. He was great, don't get me wrong. He was as close to perfect for you as you could get. But he wasn't without his flaws. Maybe that's why you're having an immensely difficult time letting him go."

"Ethan was my life, Mom. That's why I can't let go. He was my everything. He was my future. He's in almost every memory I have. He is *everywhere*." My shoulders and head slump from the weight of my words. "Who am I without Ethan?"

She puts a finger under my chin and lifts my head. "You are my wonderful, stubborn, hardworking daughter. You're a protective, watchful sister to a bizarre little brother. You are a good, loyal friend. And you'll grow to be more than that, too. You have to figure out how to be happy and fulfilled without Ethan. And you can't do that until you start to move on."

Her words bounce through my head, resonating loudly each time they land. Before Ethan died I had other titles I wanted to obtain in life. And then on that terrible day when my life was shattered, I saw those titles fly out the window with my future. Do I still want those things?

An image pops unbidden into my mind. A large cardboard box, packed full of pain. The words *For Kate* scrawled on the side in black marker.

Right now that box is sitting on my closet floor, tucked behind a row of dresses. Safely out of sight.

It's time.

"Mom, thank you. Everything you just said...well, it's having its intended effect." I stand, using two hands to pull my mom up. I squeeze her tight. "I knew you would make it all better."

"Sometimes a girl just needs her mom." She pulls back to smile at me.

"I'm sorry I shut you out. It sounds silly now, but I was terrified of talking to you. I knew you'd say things I needed to hear and I'd start to feel better. And if I felt better, I'd lose Ethan."

"Honey, I knew what you were doing. I've been there."

"I think I forgot that. My head was a scary, messed up place."

"I had you and your brother to live for. I couldn't give in to my desire to go off the deep end. But I can empathize."

I hug her again. "You're the best. Thanks for not going off the deep end."

She laughs. "I love you."

"I love you too. Walk me out?"

She falls into step beside me. When we get to the gate I turn to her.

"Do you remember that box of Ethan's things Evie gave to me? I think it's time to go through it." A heavy feeling settles onto my chest. *Dread.* "Wish me luck."

"It'll be hard. But you'll be okay."

My foot pushes against the gate and it opens. "Thanks, Mom. For everything. I'll see you soon. I promise."

I cross the street to the Shepherds' driveway, careful not to look at the house. I don't want to know if James is awake. I don't want to know just how angry Evie really is with him. I back out and drive, keeping my focus inward. My mother's words brought me to this point. But only I can make it all happen.

***

THE KITCHEN IS SPARKLING. The ceiling fans are free of dust. I've organized my junk drawer. I can't put it off any longer.

With a deep breath and squared shoulders, I leave the safety of the living room and go to my closet, plucking a box of tissues from my dresser on my way.

Pieces of soft fabric slide aside, and there it is. *For Kate.*

I laugh once, a short, disbelieving sound. This box should come with a warning label. *Caution: Extreme Pain Ahead.* With a deep breath I open the box.

On top is Ethan's hat, the one with the signature of his favorite baseball player under the brim. Gently I pull it out and put it on. It tips and lays haphazardly on my head.

My eyes shut, and I reach in again, turning the box into a grab bag.

I feel the cool smoothness of glass and pick it up, opening my eyes to see my prize. *The cologne he wore in college.* Two sprays and the air fills with twenty-year-old Ethan. My inhale is deep and long.

In ten minutes' time I'm surrounded by artifacts. Ethan's books, a shirt he wore frequently, the picture of me he drew for his ninth grade art project. Letters sent from my middle school self, complaining of terrible boredom while my best friend was gone at a two-week summer camp. When we were twelve the separation felt like an eternity. Little did we know that when we grew up, the Army would teach us what real separation felt like. And then, of course, the final separation. *Death.*

The taste of salt covers my lips, and my shirt is wet. My tears have found their final resting place on my chest, on my lap, and in my mouth.

The box is almost empty. Two trophies, an envelope, and a clay mold Ethan and I made of our hands are the only things left inside.

I reach for the envelope and find it's sealed. My hands shake when I turn it over and read the front.

KATE. Penned by a hand that wrote my name hundreds of times. My trembling fingers rip the envelope in my haste.

Katie girl,

I'm writing this letter, and I hope to hell you never read it. When I'm done with my time in the Army, I'm going to rip up this letter and burn it. But if you are reading this, it means I didn't make it. Shit. I want to make it. I want to be with you, forever. I want to be your husband. I want to build a life and a family with you. I want to hold you tight and let my body show you how made for each other we are. But if you're reading this, then none of that will happen for us. The babies I know belong to us will never be. The t-ball games I'm supposed to coach will never happen. The tears I'm supposed to wipe from your face while our daughter gets married, will be wiped by someone else.

Writing these words is making me feel sick. We just spent my leave together, and it was incredible. Finally your stubborn streak calmed down enough for you to admit that you love me too. It took you long enough. A decade. I knew I would never give up on you.

If you're reading this, we only shared a short time together. And I want you to know it was the best time I've ever had. Not that all those times since we met when we were five weren't great, but being able to grab you and kiss you made it that much better. I spent years wanting to reach out and touch your face when you were laughing. Now I can, and I can't imagine anything better.

This sucks. I have to say some hard stuff that I don't want to say. Okay. Here it is. Ultimately, I want you to be happy. That's really all I've ever wanted, though I will admit I wanted that happiness to be with me. But if I'm not around, then I still want you to be happy. And that means you'll have to find it with someone else. I won't lie to you, I'm not crazy about that idea. But if I'm not here to take care of you and love you, then I want you to find someone else who will. If you deem him worthy, then you have my blessing. Just promise me you won't settle. That's all I ask of you.

How am I supposed to wrap this up? I feel like I could talk to you forever. These are my last words to you, and I wish I had something profound to say. I don't. I can only think to say something you already know. I LOVE YOU.

Your Ethan

. . .

I press the letter against my chest and sob. Great, big, ugly sobs that bend me over and wrack my body. My chest thumps and my shoulders heave.

I'm crying for Ethan. For his life that was cut short. For our future that was cruelly snatched away. For the kisses that will never happen and the love I can no longer give to him. I cry for the little girl and boy who thought they would be best friends forever.

"Ethan," I say over and over, louder and louder.

I grab his shirt from the floor beside me, spray it with his cologne, and pull it over my head.

I lie on the floor, prone and wailing, a heaping mass of sorrow. I think I fall in and out of sleep, but I'm not sure.

Eventually my tears subside. I sit up. Somehow, some way, I feel better. Clearer. Refreshed. New.

Carefully I re-pack Ethan's box. The last item is his shirt. I pull it over my head, smell it one more time, and place it on top.

The letter goes back into the ripped envelope and into my nightstand. I sit on my bed, knees pulled up to my chin, and picture the little white rectangle in the drawer.

Ethan wants me to be happy.

I walk back to my closet, push the box back into its spot, and go start the shower.

The water washes away salt from my dried tears. I watch as it spins and swirls down the drain and envision all my fear and anguish going right down with it.

I raise my face to the spray and relish the feeling of peace quietly growing inside me.

35

KATE

My parched soul needed Ethan's letter. Without it, I'm not sure how long it would have taken me to get to this point.

On day two after being fired I purged my apartment. I emptied every cabinet and drawer, every box and closet. I came face to face with everything I own and every memory of Ethan those belongings drew forth. Instead of cringing when the inevitable hurt shook me, I embraced the memories and the requisite pain that went along with them.

Loose pictures of me and Ethan were gathered and placed in one album. The infamous yellow lingerie went into my new Ethan box. Other things went into the box too. Like the necklace he gave me on our last birthday. *Me & You.*

The contents of my apartment may be clean and organized, but the decorations are sparse. After I took down everything that belonged to Harper and put it in her room, I saw a lot of white walls and bare surfaces.

So now, on the third day since I was fired, I'm shopping. The woman at the home store is very happy to help and too willing to share her opinion.

"You don't know your aesthetic?" She regards me like I'm a lunatic.

"Nope," I say, looking around the store. I answer all her questions about colors and pieces of furniture I already own.

She leads me around, talking endlessly about design and color palette and the flow of a room. When I point to a painting, she tells me it won't match the color of the existing couch. I look at the vibrant swirls of red, the big yellow sun in the corner, and I feel wistful. *I like that one.*

We keep going, and before long I have everything I need to replace Harper's decor.

The saleswoman rings me up and recites the total. I pause, credit card in mid-air, and look back at the painting. "I'll take the painting, too," I tell her. *Rule breaker.*

She shakes her head. "But it won't—"

My upright palm stops her mid-sentence. "I'll take the painting, too. Thank you."

I walk out of the store, three big bags in one hand and the painting in the other, and I'm smiling.

***

DAY four since I was fired. I receive a text message from Harper. She'll be here at ten to get the rest of her things.

She arrives dressed in a pencil skirt and high heels. Two men wearing matching T-shirts and pushing a dolly come in behind her. She points them to her old room after glancing around the living room.

"Where's my stuff?"

"Hello to you, too. I put your things in your room." There's so much I want to say, so many words filling my mouth, but I don't know how to start. *We lived together for almost four years. How did it come to this?*

We stand, separated by a distance that seems greater than two feet, while the movers work on Harper's room.

"I'm sorry about what you found on my phone." Her voice is even.

My shocked eyes sweep to her, but her watchful gaze stays on the movers.

I look ahead. "I appreciate that. I'm sorry this is how things are ending between us."

"Things didn't have to be like this." Frustration tinges her voice. "You didn't have to stop being you."

Yes, I did. If I hadn't stopped being Master of Everything, I would never have come to this point, standing on the brink of reclaiming the person the old me had locked away. And whoever the new me is going to be.

"You'll never understand, Harper. My mistake was in expecting you to be someone you're not. For that, I'm sorry."

She doesn't respond. I wait for one full minute, then I grab my purse.

"I have somewhere to be. Don't worry about locking up, I won't be long."

I start for the door, stopping to let the guy carrying the nightstand go in front of me.

"Kate?" Harper's tone is unsure. Somewhere in my name there's regret trying to break through the barrier she's built.

I turn back and meet her eyes. Emotions fight a war on her face.

"What is it?" *Will this be the moment she accepts her own feelings instead of being repulsed by them?*

Her face shuts down as if a switch was hit. She points to the wall behind me. "That painting doesn't match the—"

"I know." I smile. "Bye, Harper."

***

"WHAT DO YOU THINK?" The large, bald man finishes wiping the remainder of ink from the inside of my wrist. To take my attention away from the pain I've been thinking of Harper, of whether she'll still be at my apartment when I return. And what I would say to her if she is. But now that he's finished, my thoughts of her fly out of my head instantly.

My gaze moves from the garden gnome on the counter. It's been my focal point for the past thirty minutes. I look down at the image of the small bird, its wings spread wide as it rises.

"I love it," I breathe, the feeling of freedom and recovery overwhelming my heart.

He sits back in his chair and looks at me. "It fits you."

"Thank you." My eyes drop back to the mythical bird taking flight on my wrist.

He covers my tattoo and gives me care instructions. I keep glancing at the white bandage on my wrist as I hold the steering wheel on the drive home. My stomach flutters with excitement. *Rule breaker.*

My phone rings.

Nick Hunter.

As much as it pains me, I let it go. It's his fourth call.

Right now, I'm focused on me. On becoming Kate.

Covering my heart are long, ragged scars, pink in their newness. I'm bare and I've been broken. I'm a blank slate, washed clean by pain. And I want to get to know the new me.

When I get home I send Nick a text.

I'm doing great. Really. I'll be in touch soon. I have a

chimichanga cooking lesson with your name on it.

Then I pull out my laptop, peek at the Phoenix on the inside of my wrist, and get to work.

***

FOR TWO WEEKS, I write.

Every memory of me and Ethan.

My dad's death.

Master of Everything.

Falling in love with my best friend.

The death of my best friend.

Losing myself.

Finding myself.

I write, and I write, and I write. Pages and pages of memories and feelings and painful recounts. Poured into one messy outline. But it's there. It's a start.

When I'm finished, I call Nick.

Recalling my times with him, my fingers flying over the computer keys, allowed me to *see* him.

He didn't need cooking lessons. He wanted me to focus on something besides my brokenness.

He didn't need me to go to the used bookstore with him. He wanted me to rediscover a lost part of myself.

He didn't need to color with me. He wanted me to let go and enjoy something just for the sake of enjoying it.

His phone rings and rings. Finally, his voicemail picks up.

I push away from the desk and put on my jacket. For two weeks I've been eating like a mouse, distracted by the words tumbling out of me. And if I'm going to thrive, not just survive, I need real food.

36

NICK

Nick, Hi. It's Kate. I mean, obviously. You saw the missed call. Of course you know it's me. I, uh... it's been a while. I wanted to say hi. Maybe you can come over for dinner soon? I... I miss you. Call me back.

I can't help the grin sliding across my face, even as I hoist the Christmas tree over my shoulder and walk it out to my car. The palpable nervousness in her voice was adorable, especially because I know what it means.

Kate's been MIA for two weeks. She sent me that one text telling me she was okay, but that was before she disappeared. As much as I hated it, I left her alone. After the tenuous moments we shared the last few times we'd been together, I knew it meant Kate was doing hard work deep down in her soul.

I know from experience that soul work is best done alone, where there are no judgments and no cares. It's painful, exquisite, and difficult.

A night of looking deep inside is what landed me in the recruiter's office four years ago.

The choice to join the Army wasn't easy, and there were

times I wondered if I'd made the wrong decision. But then I met Ethan, and I saw a bright spot in the day-to-day difficulty of being a soldier.

I could compare losing him to being stabbed in the heart. In fact, I could compare the experience of losing him to various instances of physical suffering, but the best way to describe it is simple.

It was the worst pain I've ever felt in my life.

But within the pain lay a purpose.

My path to Kate.

After my third time listening to her voicemail, I slip my phone in my pocket and grab my keys. Kate's been holed up in her apartment for eighteen days. I know this because I've driven by her place and checked it out. Her car was parked in its spot. When I went by at night, the lights in her apartment were on.

But I know from talking to Evie that she hasn't heard from Kate, and neither has Kate's mom.

My guess is that, now that Kate's learned to stand on her own two feet again, she has been taking in her surroundings and figuring out how to move forward.

And she's ended her solitude with a phone call to me. And an invitation to come over for dinner soon.

But soon doesn't work for me. *Soon* is an indefinite word, and I'm a definitive guy. And when it comes to matters of the heart, patience isn't my strong suit.

Which is how I ended up with a Christmas tree strapped to the top of my car.

I'm betting if Kate hasn't been out of her apartment in two and a half weeks, then she hasn't decorated for Christmas either.

My thumbs tap the steering wheel in my excitement as I pull into Kate's complex.

Oh no.

Her car is gone. She has finally ventured out.

I glance up at her place through my windshield.

AIO.

Adapt. Improvise. Overcome.

New plan. Haul the tree up the stairs, snip the ties so the tree looks big and full, and tie a note to it. I'm sure there's a receipt I can write on somewhere in this car.

I get the tree up the stairs, and use my pocket knife to cut the ties. Before I head back downstairs to scrounge in my car for something to write on, I lean against the wall and catch my breath. It's not climbing stairs carrying a Christmas tree that has exerted me. It's doing all that while being *excited.*

Maybe I'll hang around for a bit, in case Kate's not too long. I want to see her face when she sees the tree. First she'll probably have that little 'v' form in between her eyebrows. She'll walk forward slowly, because I've learned Kate doesn't race toward something unknown. She'll look at me with those beautiful eyes as understanding dawns, and then her smile will be soft and round. Then—

Footsteps. On the stairs. It could be anybody, but maybe it's her.

My heart pushes against my chest. I see her face first, then the rest of her appears as she ascends and leaves the last stair behind.

It happens just like I imagined it would. The 'v'. The slow walk forward. The understanding, and then the smile.

My chest feels warm, and my throat is tight.

God help me, I'm sunk.

37

KATE

HOME FROM THE GROCERY STORE, I PARK MY CAR IN MY SPOT and see Nick's car two spaces away. My insides flutter. *What is he doing here?*

Two grocery bags in each hand, I step onto the curb and stop, peering at my feet.

What is all over the ground?

Short, stiff green things.

Pine needles?

I follow their trail up the stairs.

A Christmas tree leans against the wall next to my door. And next to the tree, leaning against the wall, is Nick.

He pushes himself upright as I walk to him. He's smiling. I'm smiling.

"A Christmas tree?" I ask, excitement growing in my stomach.

He runs a hand over the needles, and the scent of pine fills the air. "Do you know it's almost Christmas?"

"I just realized it when I went grocery shopping. The music on the radio and the decorations at the store clued me in." I set down the bags and touch the tree. The needles are soft.

"What have you been doing?" Nick reaches out, his hand resting against my upper arm. His eyes are soft when he looks at me. The warmth on his face reminds me of his tender, kind treatment of a fragmented girl.

"I've been writing." I unlock the door and push it open. Nick picks up my groceries and nods me in. I go in first and lead him to the kitchen.

"You've been redecorating, too." He looks out past the half-wall to the rest of the apartment. "I love the painting. It's...vital."

"Alive." I say the word I think of when I look at it.

He looks at me, eyes penetrating. "Exactly."

The intensity of his gaze makes my stomach feel funny. I start unloading groceries.

"I'll be back in a minute." Nick walks out.

When the door opens again, the Christmas tree enters first. Nick has one arm wrapped around the center of the tree. He holds a tree stand in his other hand.

He stops and looks at me. His eyes dance, excited. "Where do you want me to put this?"

"Um." I hurry ahead of him to the living room and look around. I pull my new table aside and point. "There."

We work together, me holding the stand and Nick lowering it in, tightening, adjusting, until it sits centered in the stand.

We step back to look at our work.

"It's perfect." I'm grinning. My apartment smells like Christmas. "You're like a real live St. Nick."

Nick throws his head back and laughs. I like watching his obvious happiness.

I get the two boxes of lights and ornaments from the

bottom of my linen closet, and we decorate. He laughs at the photo ornament of me and my brother when we were six and eight.

The box on the ground is empty, its contents hung on the newest addition to my home. "That's it. We're done."

"Not yet." Nick strides to the kitchen and comes back with a bag, handing it to me.

I pull a box from the bag. Inside the box, nestled in tissue paper, is a porcelain bird. I take the ornament from the box, and it dangles in the air between us.

"A Phoenix," I say, amazed, watching the colorful rendition of the bird sway.

Nick touches a wing with a fingertip. "Do you know about the legend?"

I pull up my sleeve and offer my left wrist. "This is one of the things I've been doing."

He grabs my hand and studies the tattoo. "Rising from the ashes." His eyes lift to find mine. "That's what you've been doing."

I blush. *That part of me hasn't changed.* I find a good spot, front and center, for my new ornament and secure it to a branch. I step back to admire the tree. The lights twinkle and bounce off the Phoenix.

"Thank you, Nick. For...everything." I grab his hand and squeeze.

He walks backward to the couch, pulling me with him. We sit down, facing each other. I lean an elbow against the back of the couch. My head rests on a curled fist.

"Can you tell me more about what you've been doing since I last talked to you eighteen days ago?" Nick gives me a challenging look. "Yes, I was counting. No, I'm not embarrassed."

I laugh.

Nick grins. "Start talking, Masters."

I take a deep breath and let it out. "This is going to sound insane, but it all starts with Trent. In a crazy, dumb way, I almost want to thank him. He unknowingly delivered me a proverbial kick in the ass. If I didn't see his texts to Harper, I wouldn't have been so mad. And if I wasn't so mad I might not have punched him. And then you wouldn't have carried me out and gone on a walk with me and told me about Emelie."

Nick's face falls. "I feel awful about that. I shouldn't have assumed you knew about her."

"I'm happy you told me. Really. Because it made me pause long enough to think about Ethan in a different way. It made me realize that he wasn't the perfect person I made him out to be. And that's not a bad thing."

"And Trent gets the credit for all this?"

I shake my head quickly. "Just for being the catalyst."

Nick nods. "What else?"

"The Monday morning following the party I was fired from Simone and—"

"Wait, what?" His eyes widen.

"I was fired." I say, my voice calm. I've come to terms with it, and now I'm even grateful for it.

"On what grounds?" His eyebrows draw together, indignant arches on his forehead. *My defender.*

"I was late or called in sick more times than my boss ever should've allowed. The incident at the party got the attention of new higher ups from the merger. They did some digging, found Lynn's documentation of my tardiness over the six-month time period, and drew a conclusion."

His eyebrows return to their normal place. "Why don't you sound upset about it?"

"I was at first. But after I told my mom, she helped me see this as an opportunity."

"To do what?"

"I used to write stories. A lot of them. And I stopped when I got older because there were other things to do." *Other things to master.* "My mom suggested I write a book about me and Ethan. So I started."

Nick grins. "That's awesome. When can I read it?"

"Not for a long time. It's a very rough outline right now. Hardly even that. It's more of a collection of memories."

"Did it hurt? When you recalled everything?"

"Yes. But it was also invigorating. I was in control of the story. And the outcome. For six months I've been out of control. Things were happening *to me* instead of me making things happen. At least that's how it felt."

"I'm proud of you." His face is earnest. He winds the fingers on his right hand through the ones on my left. *So warm.*

"I'm proud of me too."

I look down to our intertwined fingers. Whether I knew it or not, this hand was holding mine as I crawled, stumbled, and walked through the most painful experience in my life.

Nick.

I look up to his eyes. Such softness there, when they crinkle like they are right now. Eyes that have seen me at my worst and cried with me. *Shared grief is half the sorrow.*

My throat feels dry. I gulp.

His fingers untangle from mine. Then he trails a soft, lingering touch across the top of my hand. He flips my hand over, and I watch as his fingers brush across the Phoenix on my wrist and across my palm, down to my fingertips.

Electricity zings across my skin. My heart beats faster. His fingers make the same route a second time. A third time.

The rules. I can't break them all.

My head flinches back and I find myself looking into concerned eyes. *I want to let this happen, Nick. I do. But... Ethan.*

My hand starts to recoil, but Nick grabs it, holding it in his strong grasp.

"You're feeling what I'm feeling. Yes or no?" His intense gaze locks me in place.

"Yes," I whisper.

"You're terrified, yes or no?"

"Yes."

"You think this is wrong, yes or no?"

"Ethan," I croak.

Nick keeps his grip on my hand and motions between us with his free one. "This isn't wrong."

"How do you know that?"

"Because Ethan was my best friend too. If he couldn't be with you, then he would want to help you find someone to be with. I felt terrible when I realized I was attracted to you. I thought I was a horrible friend. I told him I would take care of you, so I tried to put my feelings aside. But it didn't work. Every time I got a reluctant smile from you, no matter how small, it felt like a personal victory. I wanted to help you fight, and I needed your help too, even though I didn't realize it. You needing me gave me a place to put my grief.

I watched you grow stronger, and each time felt like a celebration in my chest. When I realized it was my heart, I knew I had to get myself figured out. So I went to Ethan's headstone. I sat beside his name and talked to the wind. And then I remembered a conversation we had. It seemed so inconsequential at the time. He said, *If I die, I want Kate to be with someone just like me. Because I'm right for her, and that means whoever he is will be almost as right for her as I am.* Then

he patted my back and said, '*Me and you, we're a lot alike.*'
That day at his headstone I finally understood why he said
that to me. He was giving us his blessing ahead of time. Just
in case."

I hear Nick's words, but I almost can't believe them.

Me.

And.

You.

I gasp.

"Kate, Ethan may have asked me to look after you, but
the rest of it is me." He lifts my hand and lays it against his
chest. "My feelings for you are my own. No one put them
there besides you and those eyes that sparkle when you're
being silly. I like when your temper flares, because I understand what that's like. I like watching you close your eyes
and make motions in the air with your fingers when you're
trying to recall a recipe. And when you kicked Trent's ass
while you were wearing that purple dress, well... It was hot."

I can't help that I'm staring, trying to absorb what he's
saying.

"You hate me now and want to kick me out, yes or no?"
He flinches away from me, like he's readying himself for a
painful answer.

Do I? Do I want to refuse my feelings? For ten years I
denied my feelings for Ethan. *That was a mistake.*

Sarah's words come back to me. *Life, fate, the universe,
they all broke the rules on you. When you do move on, the man
will have to be beyond special.*

I look at Nick's face, waiting patiently for my answer. I
have so much more to learn about him, but I know for
certain I don't want to be without him.

"I don't want to kick you out." I smile shyly.

Without a doubt, I know Nick is the man who is beyond

special. The one and only person who won't feel threatened by my tears when I cry them for another man. He won't fear that I have loved another so deeply, because he loved that person too.

Nick Hunter. Of course.

He leans in, forehead and nose pressed to mine. His gulp is audible. The tip of his nose slides off mine, caresses my cheek as it moves across and comes to a stop at my temple. I hear his nervous breath. His head moves back and forth, his lips grazing the far side of my cheek.

His hand rests at the base of my throat, runs lightly along the length of delicate skin until he's cradling the back of my neck. His lips drag back across my cheek to the corner of my mouth and he stays there, drawing it out.

Finally his lips meet mine, and *oh my God. This* is our real first kiss.

The seconds tick by as we sit, unmoving, our lips and our hearts in disbelief. *This is really happening.*

I move first. I press into him, pushing his lips with my own. And he responds.

It's sweet, it's soft, it's everything it should be.

He pulls back and stares at me. My breath comes in quiet pants.

"You were kissing me just now, yes or no?" he asks playfully.

I blush anyway. "Yes, Nick. I was kissing you."

One of his fingers runs along my cheekbone. "I like when you blush."

"Good. I do it a lot."

He smiles, then leans forward and kisses me again.

My heart feels full and light as I settle into his arms. There is no pain in this space. Only contentment. And it's made sweeter because I know what it feels like to suffer.

On the day Ethan went away, the lights went out on my world. In the dark I stumbled, fell, and struggled to get back up. Scraped and bruised, heart in pieces, I slowly climbed to my feet. One by one, the lights came back on, their luminescence changed. Now I stand in the soft glow of these new lights, the scars on my soul illuminated. I see the beauty in the injured flesh, because I know what it means.

I made it through the darkness.

SIX MONTHS LATER

KATE

I'm lost in my own closet, staring unseeingly at my clothes.

One year.

It's been 365 days since my life stopped and fate forced me to my knees, put me through the greatest trial of my life, and made me stronger.

And here I am.

Six months past the moment I learned to let Ethan go. I know it's acceptable to be sad, it's okay to cry whenever I want and for however long I want. I have someone who welcomes my tears and sometimes lets his own tears pool with mine.

I'm standing in my closet, crying, and not for the first time today. And it won't be the last.

A little peek of red catches my eye, the fabric barely visible from its hiding spot behind my only heavy coat. The soft fabric glides from the plastic hanger. I hold the dress to my face, the memory of wearing it pressing into me. Once again, the red dress catches my tears.

That day, just one short year ago, was the worst of my existence. How can so much heartbreak fit into such a short period of time? How have I gone 365 days without talking to my best friend, my Ethan? In what cruel twist of fate could it be that right now, I'm getting ready to go to the one-year memorial of the day he was killed?

Evie called last night, reminding me of the time for today's gathering, as though I could ever forget. Today is a big day, not just because of the date. James is thirty days sober, a feat that will be challenged by a visit to Ethan's grave. He'll need all of us today. His wife, my mom, me, Nick and Zane. We'll all need each other.

Two strong arms encircle me from behind. I lean back into Nick, grateful to unload a little of my weight. A tear that doesn't belong to me hits my bare shoulder and slides down my arm.

"Do you remember this?" The dress dangles in my outstretched arm.

Nick moves one arm from its grasp around me, reaching out to take the dress. He holds it out in front of us, quietly studying it.

"Should I?" He sounds wary.

"It's what I wore to Ethan's funeral."

"Ahhh." I feel his head nod. "I remember now."

I step out of his embrace and hang the dress back up where I found it.

A different sundress goes over my head, and I step into my shoes.

I turn to Nick, placing my hand in the open hand he's holding out for me.

"Ready or not..." A sad smile pulls up one side of his mouth.

There are times when I swear I can sense Ethan, smell

the sweet scent of his skin, feel the silkiness of his hair. A tall man with black hair is Ethan, just for a split second. My rational, practical brain knows all this is impossible, but my heart is always the first responder.

The pain in my heart has decreased, but I know it will never go away completely. And I don't mind that. It is an exquisite reminder that I have loved beyond measure.

And I will again.

I'm not holding back with Nick. Time is infinitely precious. I won't waste it by being afraid. Ethan fought so I can be free. Free to love and free from fear. I won't forget that.

***

NICK

Today is not a pleasant day, but it's a day that won't disappear just because we don't want it to exist.

Kate woke up crying. Maybe she was dreaming about Ethan. Maybe she was dreaming about his death. She'll tell me when she's ready.

But I was there for her. My arms were open and ready. She rolled into me, and we stayed under the covers until we absolutely had to get up.

As much as Kate needs me, I need her in equal measure. If I didn't have her, I wouldn't have allowed my grief to surface. It would have stayed buried, churning down below, and who knows what it would have turned me into. Kate's sadness and grief allowed my own a chance to temper and cool.

We've been together six months. At first it was hard. The

new-relationship passion, excitement, and jitters led to inevitable feelings of guilt.

We talked about it all, even when it was uncomfortable or embarrassing. That's the thing about meeting at a low point in life. Pretenses are gone, and the truth is easier to speak.

Once we admitted the guilt we felt, we were able to move past it. Neither of us wanted to miss out on the new-relationship excitement.

And we didn't. And we're still not missing out on anything.

I love Kate with a passion that consumes my heart, my mind, my whole body. She's my first thought every morning and my last thought at night.

And, because we moved in together two weeks ago, I can reach over and pull her close whenever I want to. Which is always.

We're going to Connecticut in a few days. Kate will meet my mom. And I'm going to ask for my grandmother's wedding ring.

I don't know when I'll ask Kate to marry me. It might be a big, elaborate plan. It might be when we're sitting on the couch. It could be next week or next month.

All I know is that the woman I love and want to spend the rest of my life with is in love with me too.

Our path to each other wasn't pretty, but it's ours and we'll make the most of it.

The End

ALSO BY JENNIFER MILLIKIN

The Time Series

Our Finest Hour - Optioned for TV/Film!

Magic Minutes

The Lifetime of A Second

Hayden Family Series

The Patriot

The Maverick

The Outlaw

The Calamity

Standalone

Better Than Most - preorder, releases October 5th, 2023

The Least Amount Of Awful

Return To You

One Good Thing

Beyond The Pale

Good On Paper

Full of Fire

ACKNOWLEDGMENTS

First and foremost, my husband. This story is as much a part of you as it is me. Thank you for giving me the freedom to mold our story until it fit the characters I created. You are my love. Nothing will ever come close to the bond we share.

Jonnie Prewitt. Your support of this novel means everything to me. Your grace and peace astounds me.

My best friend, Kristan. Quite possibly my biggest and loudest cheerleader. Thank you for putting up with my annoying self-doubt. It would be okay if you wanted to hit me. Or pinch me. Maybe just a little? And thanks for pointing out those two mistakes I missed. How embarrassing!

To all my beta readers, specifically Melissa, Crystal, and Bridgett. You ladies rock.

Leia Stone, USA Today best-selling author of a million amazing books and indie author supporter extraordinaire. Thank you for being in my corner.

To Robin Patchen, my editor. Thank you for not taking it easy on me. Sorry about the dehydration headache you got from reading the manuscript. If it was proper I would insert the teeth baring emoji here.

And last, but so very, very not least, Tyler Prewitt. A hero. A warrior. And my best friend. You gave all, and in doing so you gave me everything. You will never, ever be far from our thoughts.

ABOUT THE AUTHOR

Jennifer Millikin is a bestselling author of contemporary romance and women's fiction. She is the two-time recipient of the Readers Favorite Gold Star Award, and readers have called her work "emotionally riveting" and "unputdownable". Following a viral TikTok video with over fourteen million views, Jennifer's third novel *Our Finest Hour* has been optioned for TV/Film. She lives in the Arizona desert with her husband, children, and Liberty, her Labrador retriever. With thirteen novels published so far, she plans to continue her passion for storytelling.

Visit jennifermillikinwrites.com to sign up for her newsletter and receive a free novella.

Made in the USA
Las Vegas, NV
06 May 2023

71667683R00208